Attack On Nui Ba Den

A VIET NAM WAR NOVEL

1SG DAVID L ALLIN, USA, RET.

Table of Contents

FOREWORD

The battle described in this novel was real. Sometimes aptly referred to as the Nui Ba Den Massacre, it was a short but bloody encounter between the Viet Cong and American forces isolated on the peak of an extinct volcano in Tay Ninh Province, near the Cambodia border. As an infantryman serving near the mountain a year after the battle, I heard rumors about the firefight, but nothing very specific. Recently, however, I came across a website created by Ed Tatarnic, whose cousin was one of the men killed on the mountain that night. Ed did an incredible job of researching the battle, acquiring official after-action reports from the National Archives and contacting survivors for their stories. Ed graciously forwarded many of those documents to me, to which I added other documents and accounts, some only recently declassified.

For those of us who served in Tay Ninh Province, a land otherwise flat as Kansas, Nui Ba Den, the Black Virgin, always hovered on the horizon, a dark foreboding beacon that provided a landmark for navigation, but also reminded us of the precariousness of our situation. We knew that while the U. S. Army controlled the summit, the Viet Cong and North Vietnamese Army controlled the rest of the mountain. Sometimes, at night, we could see the flares and tracer rounds at the peak that marked another firefight up there, one we were glad to not be a part of. It was an ominous reminder that American and South Vietnamese forces faced a truly uphill battle to control the country.

All of the characters in this novel are fictional, but the course of the battle and the major events described are as accurate as they can be based on the sometimes contradictory accounts in the historical record. The tremendous number of American casualties and the inadequate response to the attack were, in my opinion, a failure of leadership, and not a reflection on the competence or bravery of the men on the mountain. The long periods of enemy inactivity had lulled the men on the peak—and the leaders at Division level in Tay Ninh—into a false sense of security, and as a result

1

defensive measures and training were totally inappropriate for such a vital but isolated facility.

This book is written from the point of view of an Army Security Agency linguist. The Army Security Agency—ASA—was a military wing of the National Security Agency, charged with gathering signals intelligence by intercepting enemy transmissions. The ASA's part in the Nui Ba Den battle was kept secret for many years, and it is almost certain that their presence on the mountain is what sparked the battle. It is no coincidence that the VC attacked only one week after the ASA's intercept site became operational. The assault had the effect the VC undoubtedly intended: immediately afterwards the ASA withdrew from the site permanently.

The garrison on Nui Ba Den was an ad hoc assemblage of men and units, the nature of which certainly contributed to the lack of a coherent defense. Administratively it was a provisional company of the 125th Signal Battalion, but it was comprised of radio operators and technicians from various units, a platoon-sized force of infantrymen, a contingent of Special Forces advisors and their Vietnamese counterparts, the ASA detachment, and a few support personnel. Many of these men reported operationally to their parent units, and only administratively to the local commander, leading to a lack of cohesiveness that undoubtedly contributed to the disaster.

Again, all the characters in this book are fictional, but the battle was real, and the events of that night must have been terrifying for all concerned. It was a little-known firefight with much larger implications than were recognized at the time. There were many mistakes made in the weeks and months prior to the attack, and confusion reigned when it began, but there were also many examples of heroism that night, most of which went unheralded.

PROLOGUE

The flight of helicopters swooped across the area northwest of Saigon like a small swarm of angry wasps, arrowing toward the distant conical mountain known as Nui Ba Den, The Black Virgin. The extinct volcano, rising above the flat terrain of Tay Ninh Province like a fifth grade science project placed in the middle of a football field, was the highest ground for scores of miles in any direction, and that gave it strategic significance. Military radios of that era primarily broadcast on the VHF—Very High Frequency—band, and the range of their signals was mostly limited by "line of sight." The radio signals could be attenuated or even blocked by trees, buildings, and even the curvature of the earth, because if the sending radio and the receiving radio couldn't theoretically "see" each other, the signal might not get through. That limited the range of the radios to less than 10 miles in most circumstances. Elevated 3000 feet above the plains of Tay Ninh, however, Nui Ba Den's peak could be seen up to fifty miles away in any direction, providing a unique location for a radio relay station that could ensure good communications all across Tay Ninh Province and War Zone C, all the way to the Cambodian border.

The helicopters all bore markings for the Army of the Republic of Viet Nam—ARVN—but the pilots and crew were Americans, as were about one-third of the passengers. It was late 1964, and the recent Tonkin Gulf Resolution had significantly altered and expanded the American involvement in Viet Nam. Up until then most of the American military men in South Viet Nam were advisors with the Military Assistance Command Vietnam—MACV—and the combat advisors were primarily Green Berets of the Special Forces. With the impending arrival of regular Army and Marine units ordered to Viet Nam by President Johnson, it was imperative that vital locations like Nui Ba Den be seized to support the expanded war effort. Thus this mixed force of Green Berets and ARVN soldiers were on their way to occupy the mountaintop. They

3

had to do it by helicopter, because the steep wooded slopes of Nui Ba Den were unmarred by any sort of road to the top. Over the last thirty years the summit had been held in succession by the Japanese, the French, the Viet Minh, and the Viet Cong, and was now was destined to be occupied by the Americans. The Black Virgin was going to be assaulted one more time.

As they neared the mountain, the Hueys—officially Bell UH-1 Iroquois utility helicopters—gained altitude, roaring up to the peak and circling around it from a safe distance, reconnoitering for any enemy activity or defenses. The summit consisted of two peaks, one slightly lower than the other, connected by a wide saddle. It was barren and rocky, often swept by high winds and driving rain, and appeared to be a very inhospitable place. There were a couple make-shift huts on the higher peak, and the ruins of other small buildings scattered among the boulders, remnants of previous occupations, but there was a relatively flat area on the lower peak. As the choppers circled, the men aboard could see two men pop out of one of the huts to stare at the deadly air parade. One of them ducked back inside for a moment and returned with an AK-47. He brandished it at the choppers, and then took aim. The other man tried to stop him from firing, but the armed man shoved him aside and fired a burst at one of the choppers. It was a terrible mistake. Each of the choppers had M-60 machine guns mounted on swivels in the side doors, and all six immediately opened fire. A rain of bullets sparked off the rocks, kicked up puffs of dirt between the rocks, punched holes through the huts, and punctured the bodies of the two Viet Cong. The small men in black pajamas danced like they were having seizures before collapsing in heaps. The gunfire continued, blasting away at the huts and any other structures that might hide the enemy, until finally the commander of the mission called for a cease fire. Still circling, the men in the helicopters observed closely the summit of the mountain, and the flanks as well, to ensure that there was no longer any resistance.

When no further ground activity was noted, the commander ordered the first chopper to go in and deposit its human cargo. Wheeling out of the circle, a helicopter swooped down toward the lower peak and quickly landed on the open area while the Green Berets and South Vietnamese soldiers on board leaped off and spread out into a hasty perimeter. As soon as the last man was out, the chopper roared back up into the air and rejoined the rotating formation overhead. The Green Beret sergeant on the ground ordered the men to expand the perimeter and search the surrounding rocks. When nothing was found, he signaled an okay to the choppers, and one by one the others brought in their passengers. While the soldiers spread out and secured the entire mountaintop, the last chopper unloaded crates of tents and supplies, then rejoined the others circling above. After receiving reports from his sergeants, the Special Forces commander got on the radio, thanked the chopper pilots, and gave them permission to return to base.

The Americans, and the South Vietnamese, now controlled the summit of Nui Ba Den. They would hold it for the next eight years, erecting many buildings and bunkers to secure it, and setting up antennas for their radio relay mission. All the construction materials and supplies had to be brought in by helicopters, because no road existed, and none could be built as long as the Viet Cong controlled the rest of the mountain, which they did the entire time. It was a lonely outpost, despised by the men who served there, but it played a vital role in the expanding war. Strangely, the Viet Cong largely left the Americans on the summit alone, not bothering to try to push them off, except for one very terrifying night in 1968. And that was a massacre.

ONE

His stomach lurched when the aircraft hit a thermal updraft, and he tightened his already death-like grip on the aluminum frame of the sling seat in which he was precariously perched. Through the porthole window across the cabin he caught a fleeting glimpse of the mountain as the helicopter swung by it on its final approach. Specialist Fifth Class William Mathis was returning to Dui Ba Den after a six month absence, this time arriving in one of the large twin-rotor Chinook cargo helicopters. Twisting around he tried to look out the small round window behind him, but about all he could see was sky, scattered clouds, and an endless plain of green and brown far below. The chopper swerved again, and suddenly the mountain swam into view, looking as ominous as ever.

The steep slopes were covered with dark forest and brush that cloaked the mountain in green, with only occasional outcroppings of grey rock. Only the very summit was bare, a jumbled mass of boulders interspersed with rudimentary wooden buildings and canvas tents that looked even less inviting than Mathis knew it to be. He had visited the small base camp last June, as part of the EARDROP hearability test conducted by the National Security Agency to determine if it was a suitable location for a radio intercept site. Mathis was part of the Army Security Agency, a military arm of the NSA devoted to tactical signal intelligence activities, and he had been sent to Nui Ba Den to evaluate the quantity and quality of Viet Cong and North Vietnamese Army radio communications that could be picked up from the peak. That brief excursion had been beset with constant rain and high winds, but nonetheless they had found the signal environment to be rich and varied, offering a gold mine of intelligence on enemy movements and activities in this area near the Cambodian border, and even across the border. Now, in early January of 1968, Mathis was on his way back.

Mathis had been trained as a Vietnamese linguist, specializing in listening to enemy military radio communications and doing traffic analysis, using bits and pieces of overheard comms to develop a map of the enemy order of battle and predict their future movements and actions. On his initial foray to the mountain he had been amazed at the number of radios they could quickly identify, and the clarity of the transmissions. The test had been extremely successful, despite its brevity, and Mathis had assumed he would be sent back very shortly to begin full operations. Of course, he failed to allow for bureaucratic inertia and logistical problems, and had spent six months in Japan transcribing weeks-old audiotapes recorded at other intercept sites, including ship-borne and air-borne intercept platforms. Now, however, NSA and the Army had finally gotten their act in gear, and he was on his way to Nui Ba Den to be a point man for setting up the intercept site.

"Are we there yet, Daddy?" Booker asked loudly, to be heard over the noise of the engine and blades. Warrant Officer Cody Booker was also ASA, a signal maintenance technician assigned with Mathis to set up the intercept site. While he technically outranked Mathis, as a warrant officer he had no real command authority, and had made it clear to anyone that asked that he wanted no command authority. He was the technician, and nothing more. He set up and fixed the radio and recording equipment, but wanting nothing to do with actually running the operation. That attitude left Mathis as the de facto NCOIC, a role he was not really prepared for. He had never been in charge of anything, and had no confidence in his ability to effective direct operations now. Mathis looked over at Booker, sitting on his left, and nodded. Booker was a small man, short and wiry, and his curly brown hair was already streaked with gray. His uniform was crumpled and stained, his boots were only laced halfway up, and he wore a sky blue scarf around his neck. He grinned at Mathis and pumped his fist in the air. Mathis had no idea what Booker meant by that, but had learned not to ask, either.

The chopper jerked again and Mathis could feel it slowing to a hover; suddenly it bounced as it landed. The helicopter crew chief immediately lowered the rear ramp and signaled to Mathis and Booker to get out, while several soldiers from outside ducked and rushed in to start unloading the cargo the chopper also carried.

7

Mathis grabbed his duffel bag, briefcase, and M-16 and pushed his way through the incoming crowd until he was outside, being roasted by the exhaust from the jet turbines that powered the chopper. He scrambled away from the chopper and stopped at the edge of the helipad, a large square of concrete at the east end of the base camp. The north, east and south sides of the pad had only a narrow band of rocky soil beyond the concrete before the ground dropped away steeply. The ground to the west rose slowly up toward the main peak across a wide saddle, where there was a cluster of crude wooden and canvas buildings. At the top of the peak was a stone and mortar building called the Pagoda, topped with a number of aerials and antennas. The shape of the stone building did vaguely resemble some of the Buddhist shrines Mathis had seen, which presumably led to the building's nick-name. It was the biggest and sturdiest building on the summit, for it housed all the delicate and expensive radio relay equipment. Booker joined him in surveying their surroundings.

There was a mechanical scream as the Chinook's engines spooled up, and Mathis turned to see it lift off, leaving behind a pile of crates and boxes surrounded by the men that had unloaded them. All the soldiers, Mathis noted, were wearing only their jungle fatigues, with no helmets, pistol belts, or weapons, and several without shirts. As the clatter of the chopper faded away, Booker said, "Well, this must be the place. Where's the welcoming committee?"

"I don't even know if they're aware we're coming," Mathis admitted. "That's the orderly room over there." He nodded toward a narrow building halfway to the Pagoda on the left, with an American flag flying from a short flagpole.

"Better go check in," Booker said. "I want a room with a king-size bed and color TV."

"Yeah, right," Mathis scoffed, hefting the duffel bag over his shoulder and heading up the hill, fumbling with his rifle and briefcase.

"Doesn't hurt to ask," Booker said, following behind.

The orderly room was a long wooden building with a metal roof, raised on short stilts due to the uneven ground beneath. Mathis and Booker stepped up into the building through a screen door to find an open area cluttered by two desks, a table, and several metal chairs; plywood walls on either side separated the building into three rooms. There were two metal file cabinets on the back wall, and along the left wall was a wooden mail-sorting table with a stack of cubbyholes, some holding letters or notes. There was only one person in the room, the company clerk, who sat behind one of the desks typing something in triplicate. The clerk had a chubby round face and extremely blond hair. He glanced up when they entered, but kept typing for a moment before ripping the pages out of the typewriter and separating the carbon paper from the white sheets with a flourish. Laying the white pages and the carbon sheets into two neat stacks on the desk, he smiled at them and said, "Welcome to Nui Ba Den, gentlemen, as close to Heaven as you can get here in Nam."

Booker chuckled. Mathis dropped his duffle on the floor and said, "I'm Specialist Mathis, and this is Warrant Officer Booker. We're here to set up the new radio research site."

"Oh, yeah," the clerk said with a hint of slyness. His name tape said "Kerrigan," and the patches on his sleeves showed he was a Spec 6. "The secret guys. We heard you were coming."

"So what do we need to do to in-process?" Mathis asked. Beside him Booker was gazing around the room with bored curiosity.

"You got orders?" Kerrigan asked, holding out his hand.

Mathis laid his rifle on his duffle bag and set his briefcase on the edge of the clerk's desk so he could open it. Inside he found the mimeographed sheet and handed it over to Kerrigan. Booker pulled a poorly-folded sheet of paper from his shirt pocket, smoothed it out, and passed it across as well. Kerrigan studied the forms for a minute, and then set them aside.

"I'll take care of the paperwork," Kerrigan told them cheerfully. "Mr. Booker, you'll be staying in the officer's hooch, just up the hill, with the CO and the XO. Deluxe accommodations complete with a cot and a blanket. I'll take you there as soon as I finish with Specialist Mathis here."

Mathis turned when he heard the screen door slam as another person entered the orderly room from outside. It was a thin Spec 4 with brown hair mostly covered by a boonie hat. He ignored the new arrivals and headed over to the mail table, searching for the box with his name on it.

"Kasperek," Kerrigan called to the man, "you got any empty bunks in your hooch?"

Having not found anything in his box, Kasperek turned and glanced over at the two new arrivals. "Yeah," he said judiciously, "Thompson's bunk is empty right now. But he's coming back, isn't he?"

"Don't think so," Kerrigan answered. "Word is, he's getting emergency leave back to the States. His mom's real sick, or something."

"Too bad about his mom," Kasperek said, "but good for him."

"Yeah," Kerrigan agreed. "So can you take Mathis here and get him set up in Thompson's old bunk? Maybe take him to Supply to get bedding and stuff, show him around the camp?"

Mathis thought about telling Kerrigan he had been here before, but decided it would only complicate things. There had been a different company clerk when Mathis had visited seven months ago. Besides, the first time he was here it had rained constantly, and he had never had a chance to really explore the small encampment.

"Sure," Kasperek said, nodding at Mathis. "I'll get your duffle." He handed Mathis the M-16 and picked up the long tubular canvas bag, pausing while Mathis closed and latched his briefcase. Mathis then followed Kasperek outside and down between two rows of buildings. The first building on the left was well made with a metal roof, and the noise and smells coming from inside clearly identified it as the mess hall. "That's the mess hall," Kasperek said unnecessarily. The other buildings were less substantial, mostly wooden platforms with canvas walls and roofs. Some had the sides raised sloppily to reveal the rows of cots inside, some of them

10

wooden folding cots, others metal-framed beds with thin mattresses. Wooden foot-lockers were scattered about, and helmets and rifles hung from support posts.

"This is our billet," Kasperek announced as they approached the third building on the left. Like the others, its wooden floor was perched on short wooden beams and concrete blocks to make it level, since the ground was an uneven mix of dirt and stone. The entrance was at the narrow end, between the hooches, and Mathis followed Kasperek around the corner of the second building and up the short flight of stairs into the third. It was not as neat and tidy as Army barracks Mathis had been in before; in fact, it was a mess. The rows of cots along either side were uneven and jumbled, with one cot even turned perpendicular to the rest, and a couple cots had what looked like shower curtains hung around them. Foot lockers, ammo crates, boots, and shower shoes littered the floor, which did not appear to have been swept in weeks. Uniforms, helmets, M-16s, M-79 grenade launchers, and civilian bathrobes all hung from nails or hooks on the posts supporting the roof and the cross beams above. Kasperek led him to the far end of the barracks, where the next to last bunk on the left was empty. It was one of the wooden folding cots, with one of the end cross-pieces missing.

Kasperek dumped Mathis' duffle bag on the cot. "That's my bunk," he said, pointing to the one on the other side, a metal-framed bed with a mattress neatly wrapped in an Army blanket. Kasperek's area was notably neater and cleaner than others in the hut, and Mathis's estimation of Kasperek went up a notch. "Here's your foot locker," Kasperek told him, pointing to the dark green wooden box at the end of the cot. "Shit!" Kasperek blurted, seeing the new padlock on the locker for the first time. "Let me find out who glommed onto that and get him to empty it. Son of a bitch."

"Thanks," Mathis said, taking off his helmet and laying it and his M-16 on the bunk. "Meanwhile, is there somewhere I can secure my briefcase? It's got important papers in it."

Kasperek eyed the briefcase for a moment, as if judging its size. "I think I can't fit in my foot locker, at least for now." Reaching into his pants pocket for a key, he stepped over to the locker at the end of his bed and squatted down to unlock the padlock and open the lid. The box was stuffed with clothes and personal items, all neatly folded and packed. At one end was a colorfully printed cardboard box for some kind of electronic device. Kasperek lifted out several ironed uniform shirts and placed them on his bed, then took Mathis' briefcase and pushed it into the vacant space. With a little pressure on the lid he managed to close it and relock the padlock. "Let's go to Supply," he said, standing back up.

"What about my weapon?" Mathis asked.

"Leave it," Kasperek advised. "No one's going to mess with it. Why would they?" It was a rhetorical question. Everyone on the mountain top had their own weapon, so why take someone else's? There was nowhere to go with it.

* * *

After escorting him to Supply for bedding and helping him get his sleeping area squared away, Kasperek offered to give Mathis a brief tour of the camp. Although he had been there last June, he had not had much time back then to explore, and he also assumed things might have changed since then. Last year the site had been owned by the Special Forces, but in November the 25th Infantry Division had taken control and created D Company (Provisional) of the 125th Signal Battalion as the administrative and operational authority on the mountain. Mathis was hoping the facilities might have become a little less austere since June.

"That's the club," Kasperek said, waving his hand at the hooch across the pathway as they came out of the billet hooch. He led Mathis further down the path, pointing out the shower tent on the left and the water purification shed on the right, until they stopped at what looked like a giant bomb crater half-filled with water. "This is the reservoir." Beyond the far edge of the hole the ground sloped away out of sight, and Mathis could see the vast plain that surrounded the mountain, mostly forest in that direction, with scattered fields and rice paddies closer in.

"Looks like a really big bomb did this," Mathis commented.

Kasperek shrugged. "I think some engineers built it. Probably used explosives to blast it out of the rock."

To their left was a larger hooch, well-fortified with sandbags. "Green Berets," Kasperek explained. "Along with the sidgees."

"Sidgees?" Mathis asked, having never heard the term before.

"CIDG. Civilian Irregular Defense Group. South Vietnamese mercenaries, basically. The green beanies and the sidgees do radio relay for the SF and ARVNs, and also provide security for the camp."

"Huh," Mathis grunted, absorbing this information.

"Behind their hooch is the mortar pit. Not that anyone here knows how to operate the mortars. Come on." Kasperek led Mathis around the showers and billets, following a pathway that led through the rocks up toward the Pagoda. Pointing to his left and right, he identified the officers' quarters, operations building, ammo bunker, and generator shed. Along the way they passed other soldiers, to whom Kasperek would nod in greeting. None wore helmets or web gear, none carried weapons, and few wore their uniforms correctly. At first Mathis had been pleased by the laxness he had observed here, having always chafed a little at the Army's many rules and restrictions, but a kernel of concern was growing in the back of his mind. They were, after all, surrounded by the enemy, and the soldiers he had seen did not appear to be concerned about or prepared for any enemy activity.

At the highest point on the summit was the Pagoda, a stone-and-mortar building with an odd-shaped roof crowned by a maze of antennas, some mounted on metal pylons. The building did have a vaguely oriental shape to it, and very few small windows. "This is the Pagoda," Kasperek told Mathis as they approached, still unaware of Mathis' previous visit. "They say it was built to look like this so the VC won't attack it, because it looks like a religious shrine or something."

"Huh?" Mathis said doubtfully. "The VC are communists, and therefore atheists. Why would they care about religion?"

Kasperek shrugged. "Beats me. But that's what people tell me."

"Yeah, well, the Army never lies," Mathis replied sardonically. Kasperek nodded. Then a thought occurred to Mathis. "Maybe this was a shrine built by the Vietnamese from before the war, and we just took it over."

Kasperek shrugged. "Could be," he said doubtfully, "but I'm pretty sure we built it."

"Whatever," Mathis said. They circled around the building to the west side and climbed up on some rocks at the shoulder of the peak. There was a small wooden bunker just below them, and beyond that the mountainside dropped away sharply, the rocky slope giving way to small bushes and weeds, and farther down were stunted trees. Just in front of the bunker, stretching to the left and right, was a single strand of coiled concertina wire. Mathis took all that in peripherally, because his attention was on the spectacular view from this vantage point.

Stretching to the horizon in any direction was the plain far below, a checkerboard of rice paddies and forest, a few roads, and the city of Tay Ninh. There were only a few scattered clouds, one of which was blocking the afternoon sun, and it was all kind of hazy, due to the high humidity, but amazing nonetheless. The bright blue sky overhead, the various shades of green and brown below, the moving shadows of the clouds, and the sheer vastness of the scene, overwhelmed Mathis with their beauty.

"I can see for miles and miles," Mathis sang softly.

Kasperek grinned at him. "The Who! My favorite song by them."

Mathis smiled. "Mine, too."

"Did you see them on the Smothers Brothers show?"

Mathis shook his head. "What?"

"It was so cool. I was on leave and saw it. They did "My Generation," and at the end they smashed all their instruments, and Keith Moon's drum set blew up. Then Tommy Smothers came out with his acoustic guitar, and Pete Townshend grabbed it and smashed it, too. So Tommy says, "Hey, Dickie, bring your bass out here.""

"Oh, man," Mathis said with real regret, "I wish I could have seen that."

"Yeah, you should have." They just stood there quietly for a minute, taking in the view and thinking about the Who. Mathis was starting to feel a real kinship with Kasperek, despite having met het him only a short time ago. "I need to get that album," Kasperek said wistfully.

"Well, when you get home," Mathis suggested. He doubted there were any record players up here.

"I'll have my folks get one and send it to me. I've got an eight-track player in my foot locker."

"An eight-track?" Mathis asked in amazement. "Up here?" All the eight-track cartridge players he had seen had been in cars or in big stereo systems. The format was new, but it was growing rapidly.

"It's a battery-powered portable," Kasperek explained. "It's mono, and not very loud, but it's better than listening to 'Polka Party' on AFVN."

"Cool. I'd like to see it."

"No sweat. I'll show you after dinner. Speaking of which, maybe we ought to head toward the mess hall. That's one good thing about being up here, and maybe the only good thing. The food's not bad. They send up good supplies, and our cook is pretty good. Best food I've had in the Army, although that isn't saying much."

"I guess they've got to give you something for being up here," Mathis mused as they turned around and headed back down the slope.

"More money would be nice," Kasperek suggested.

"Yeah, like that'll happen."

* * *

After going through the line with their trays, Mathis and Kasperek found spaces at one of the many picnic-type tables and took their seats on the bench. Kasperek introduced Mathis to some of the other guys who sat at their table or walked by, and Mathis smiled and nodded, knowing full well he would forget their names immediately. As long as they wore their uniforms, however, he could always read their name tapes. What was more of a problem were the usual questions about what unit he was with and what his MOS—Military Occupational Specialty—was. No one recognized the Army Security Agency patch on his shoulder, an eagle's talon gripping lightning bolts, and his MOS was equally unknown. So he gave the safe answers he had been instructed to use: he was a communications security specialist for the 509th Radio Research Group, sent to help ensure that Army and ARVN radio procedures were being properly followed. While that was, in truth, one of the ASA's tasks, it was only a minor part of their overall mission. Their major task was intercepting, recording, transcribing, translating, and analyzing enemy radio traffic in an effort to predict where and how the enemy would next attack. That effort, however, was so highly classified that Mathis could not reveal it to anyone outside of the ASA, regardless of their rank.

The mess hall was crowded and noisy, and with almost everyone wearing the same jungle fatigues, to Mathis it was simply another conglomeration of soldiers. A couple Vietnamese men in white shirts, black slacks, and stained white aprons scurried about cleaning tables and refilling the tray and silverware racks. In one corner, apparently separating themselves from the others, a couple tables held a mixed group of Americans wearing green berets and Vietnamese wearing tiger-stripe camouflage fatigues. Mathis gulped down his food, out of force of habit, but did notice that it was unusually good for an Army mess hall. When he and Kasperek were finished, they stood up and carried their trays over to the garbage cans to dump what was left and hand the trays to a couple more of the Vietnamese KPs through a window. As Mathis turned to head out the door, he heard his name called out.

"Hey, Bill," a familiar voice said. Mathis turned around to see Daniel McDaniel, a Green Beret staff sergeant he had met while attending language school. McDaniel was tall and stocky, built like a football lineman, with blond hair and intelligent blue eyes.

16

"Hey, Dan," Mathis replied with a smile, holding out his hand to shake.

"Just get here?" McDaniel asked. Mathis noticed as Kasperek moved up beside him.

"Yep, today. Dan, this is John Kasperek. Maybe you already know him."

"Seen you around," McDaniel said to Kasperek. "Nice to meet you. You with ASA, too?"

"Naw," Kasperek said, "I'm with 125th. Tactical Wire specialist"

McDaniel nodded and turned back to Mathis. "Haven't seen you since DLI. How you been?" Then he asked the same question in Vietnamese, and Mathis winced. He frowned at McDaniel and gave his head an almost imperceptible shake to warn him off. McDaniel looked puzzled for a moment, and then raised his eyebrows as he understood. "That's Vietnamese for 'how are you'," he explained innocently to Mathis, but obviously for Kasperek's sake. Mathis glanced over at Kasperek, and could see from his expression that he now had a lot of questions.

"Good, good," Mathis told McDaniel, and then tried to change the subject. "So what do you do here?"

"Ah, we do some radio relay for the ARVNs and provide security here at the base camp. The usual Army bullshit." Although he spoke in a nonchalant tone of voice, Mathis could see the apology in his eyes. "You?"

"We're doing a commsec survey," Mathis lied, knowing McDaniel would know it was a lie for Kasperek's benefit. "Gonna set up a secure radio relay station." McDaniel knew Mathis had been taught Vietnamese, and probably had an inkling of what he really did, but was trying to help Mathis keep that secret.

"Okay. So I'll see you around for a while, then?"

"Oh, yeah, I'll be here a few months, anyway. Unless the Army changes its mind, and that hardly ever happens."

"Yeah, right," McDaniel agreed with a chuckle. "Well, hey, I got to get back to the team hooch. I'll talk to you more later." With a brief wave the Green Beret walked off smartly, and Mathis and Kasperek strolled away from the mess hall in the direction of their billet.

"What's DLI?" Kasperek asked curiously.

"Uh," Mathis said and then stopped walking. Kasperek stopped, too, and raised his eyebrows as Mathis looked around to see if anyone was near. He leaned in close to Kasperek and lowered his voice. "It's the Defense Language Institute. That's where I met McDaniel. We were in the same Vietnamese class. But no one here is supposed to know I speak Vietnamese. So can you keep that secret?"

Kasperek shrugged. "Sure, I guess. But why?"

"Because we don't want the ARVNs to know we're monitoring their communications," Mathis temporized. "It'd probably piss them off."

"Don't trust them, huh?" Kasperek suggested with a knowing look.

"I wouldn't say that," Mathis replied with a look that indicated that mistrust was exactly the reason.

"Okay, I get it," Kasperek grinned.

"So what albums have you got?" Mathis asked, resuming their walk to the billet.

* * *

"It's gonna be tight," Booker remarked as they studied the small room. They were in a corner room of the Pagoda, one originally intended as a supervisor's office, which had now been repurposed as the ASA Secure Compartmented Intelligence Facility, or SCIF. Of course, they didn't call it that here, in front of the other soldiers on Nui Ba Den, since that would give away its real mission. Instead they referred to it as the radio research room, hoping that would be innocuous enough to deflect any real interest. Mathis looked around and sighed. It was indeed pretty small for what they hoped to accomplish. The building itself was moderately secure, being built of rock and mortar, with thick walls and a ceiling made with heavy wooden beams and corrugated steel overlaid with sandbags. Even the interior walls of the room were made of stone, making it ideal for a SCIF. Mathis wondered if perhaps the officer in charge of the design had planned to occupy that office and wanted it to be fully protected.

"Those windows have got to go," Mathis said judiciously, eyeing the openings in the two outer walls. The two windows were a little larger than the others in the building, probably so the original occupant would have a good view.

"Gotta have ventilation," Booker responded. "All those radios gonna generate a lot of heat. Maybe we can wall up most of one window, just leave a slit up at the top, and frame in an exhaust fan high up in the other to pull air out of the room. Not totally secure, but what are you gonna do?"

"Need a better door, too," Mathis noted, examining the door frame. The room had a simple thin wooden door, designed for a little privacy only.

"Yep." The wiry warrant officer kept studying the layout, his brow furrowed as he placed the equipment in his imagination.

Mathis pulled a tape measure out of his pants pocket and began measuring the door and window frames, jotting down the numbers in a small notebook. Booker stepped around the room, spreading his arms wide at various locations and half-sitting like he was at a desk or table, all the while muttering to himself.

"Have they got engineers lined up for this?" Mathis asked.

"Fuck if I know," Booker said with disinterest. "They better. I don't do doors and windows, just electronics."

Mathis knew that it would end up being his responsibility to get the SCIF built, despite the fact that Booker was senior and technically in charge of the construction. Booker was an electronics guy, and had no desire to do anything else. Resigned to his fate, Mathis decided he would ensure the room was done right, and let

19

Booker take the credit. He took more measurements, including the length and width of the room, and drew a small diagram.

"Is this going to work for you fellows?" a deep voice asked from the doorway. Mathis turned to see a tall, muscular black man with captain's bars on his collar smiling at them. The name tape said ASHBROOK, so Mathis knew this was the company commander of D Company and, for that matter, base commander, a man he had not yet met.

Booker, who had stayed in the officers' quarters last night, looked up and said, "Hey, cap'n. It's kinda small, but I guess we can make do."

"And, uh," Ashbrook squinted to read Mathis's nametape, "Specialist Mathis, you're assisting Mr. Booker?"

"Yes, sir," Mathis said.

"Good. Good. And you'll be doing radio research in here, then?" Ashbrook's tone was tentative, and he was obviously hoping for more information, but had probably been told not to ask.

"That's right, sir," Mathis told him, without elaborating.

"Okay. Outstanding. Well, I've got to get back to work. If you all need anything, just let me know. I'll be over in the Ops building."

"Thank you, sir," Mathis told him with a simulated smile of gratitude.

"Right," Booker echoed. Ashbrook nodded and left.

"What do you think they told him we were doing here?" Mathis whispered to Booker.

"Beats the shit out of me. But last night he kept talking about submarines, for some reason."

"Submarines?"

Booker shrugged. Mathis shook his head and went back to his diagram.

TWO

"What's this symbol?" Mathis asked, holding up the sheet of paper and pointing to the scrawl with one finger.

Kasperek leaned over and studied it for a second. "Co-ax. Coaxial. It's a type of cable."

Mathis grunted and went back to his typing. They were in the orderly room, late in the evening, while Mathis typed up a supply list Mr. Booker had compiled. Kasperek had CQ runner duty that night, and Mathis had volunteered to be the actual Charge of Quarters so he could use the only working typewriter on the Rock. Of course, that meant they would both be there all night, staying awake in case someone from Tay Ninh called, but for Mathis, at least, there was little else to do. He had already sent out diagrams and measurements of the modifications needed to convert the room in the Pagoda into a SCIF, and now all they could do was wait for the engineers to arrive and do the actual construction. Kasperek sat in an office chair with it leaned back against a post.

The orderly room didn't have a lot going for it. In addition to the clerk's desk at which Mathis was sitting, there were a couple filing cabinets, the mail sorting table and boxes, another desk piled with boxes, a six-foot table that was bare except for a couple pencils, and a small stand by the wall with a field telephone and a switchboard. Each of the sockets on the old-fashioned switchboard had a number label, and tacked to the wall above it was typewritten key showing which socket went to which of the other phones scattered around the camp. A couple of the entries had been crossed out and new locations noted in pencil. The other locations were mostly other buildings, such as the Ops building, the mess hall, officers' quarters, and the Pagoda. Mathis had noted that only two of the perimeter bunkers had phones, which made him wonder how the guard bunkers would report any suspicious activity.

Kasperek's eight-track was playing the Moody Blues, *Days of Future Passed*, the volume just loud enough to be heard over the steady drum of rain on the metal roof. There was an annoying click as the machine changed tracks in the middle of a song, and Mathis looked up from the typewriter to roll his eyes at the interruption. Kasperek shrugged. They had previously discussed this flaw in the eight track format, and were resigned to it, but both agreed a better way would need to be found.

Splashing footsteps outside announced the arrival of someone who came in through the open door wearing a dripping poncho, the hood covering most of his head. The figure stopped in the middle of the room and pushed the hood back, revealing himself to be Staff Sergeant McDaniel, without his green beret. "Hey, Bill, John," he greeted them with a smile. "What are you guys doing here?"

"CQ," Mathis answered. "I needed to use the typewriter. What do you need?"

"Just checking mail," McDaniel answered. "Is that yours?" he asked, nodding toward the eight-track.

"John's," Mathis told him.

"Far out! Is that the Moody Blues?"

"Yep," Kasperek answered. *"Days of Future Passed."*

McDaniel pulled the wet poncho over his head and hung it from a peg by the door, leaned the M-16 he was carrying against the wall, and then squatted down to examine the little yellow plastic eight track player. "Did you get this at the PX?" he asked.

"No, my folks sent it to me. The PX never has anything good."

"Don't I know it." McDaniel stood up and walked over to the mail sorter, poking his fingers into one of the cubby holes. "Still nothin'," he grumbled. "Nobody loves me."

"I could write you a note," Mathis jokingly offered.

"Could you put some perfume on it and sign it with x's and o's?" McDaniel grinned at him.

"Hey, whatever floats your boat." They all chuckled.

McDaniel pulled over another office chair and straddled it backwards, crossing his arms on the back. "So how do you like it here on the Rock so far?" he asked Mathis.

"Sucks," Mathis said in a matter-of-fact tone. "Big hairy donkey dicks."

"You got that right." McDaniel turned his head toward Kasperek. "How long you been up here, John?"

"Three months," Kasperek answered wearily. "Three long, boring months. I haven't had this much fun since my dog died."

"Bet that," McDaniel agreed. The three men fell silent for a minute, listening to the end of the song, "Tuesday Afternoon," a spoken piece with hidden meanings.

As a new song began, McDaniel asked Mathis, "Where's your weapon, Bill?"

"Back at the billet," Mathis answered. From the look of disgust and disappointment he saw on McDaniel's face, Mathis knew that was the wrong answer.

"You are supposed to have it with you at all times, soldier," McDaniel intoned. "Now go get it."

"Yes, Sergeant!" Mathis replied, coming to attention in his chair while feigning a look of earnestness.

McDaniel grinned at him. "You don't have to call me Sergeant, at least here among friends. The sidgees call me Two-dan."

Mathis and Kasperek both chuckled. "Two-dan? Because you're Daniel McDaniel?"

"Yeah, it's easier for them to pronounce. Now go get your weapon."

"Seriously?" Mathis asked, leaning over to look out the door at the rain that continued to fall.

"Do you know how to field-strip and clean an M-16?" McDaniel asked pointedly.

"Not really," Mathis admitted. "I was trained on the M-14 in basic, and haven't touched an M-16 until I got here."

"Don't you think you ought to know how to use it, just in case?" McDaniel gave him a parental look, and Mathis knew he was stuck. He nodded. "So go get it, and I'll show you. I'll even let you use my poncho. I'll stay here and be HMFIC while you're gone."

"HMFIC?" Kasperek repeated as a question.

"Head motherfucker in charge," McDaniel expanded. Kasperek laughed. Mathis had heard that one before and just groaned. "What about you, John?" McDaniel asked.

"What about me?"

"You want to learn more about your M-16?"

"Don't have one," Kasperek retorted. "I got an M-79."

"Bloop gun," McDaniel said with a nod. "Pretty simple weapon. You know how to use it and clean it?"

"More or less. Good enough for Army work."

"All right, I'll let you slide. Bill, go get your weapon."

With a theatrical sigh Mathis got up, put on the poncho, and ran through the rain to get his weapon. When he returned he found McDaniel and Kasperek discussing the musical significance of The Mothers of Invention. They broke off the conversation and slid chairs around to a small table while Mathis removed the poncho. At McDaniel's direction, Mathis took a chair opposite him and laid the gun down on the table.

"Okay," McDaniel said, "what caliber is the M-16?"

"5.56," Mathis answered, having seen the label on a box of ammo once.

"Not exactly," McDaniel explained patiently. "The caliber is point two two three, slightly bigger than a .22-caliber squirrel gun. The bore is 5.56 millimeters, which is much smaller than the 7.62 of an M-14 or M-60, or AK-47 for that matter. The theory is that the smaller size permits a higher velocity and thus a longer range and better accuracy."

24

"Okay," Mathis said, looking to Kasperek for support. Mathis had no intention of ever firing the rifle, since his job normally did not put him into a combat situation. His job was to sit at a desk in a secure room and listen to enemy radio operators, so he saw no real need to learn about the weapon. Kasperek just shrugged.

"And why do you need to know this?" McDaniel asked rhetorically. "Well, this base camp is roughly two acres in size, on top of a mountain that the VC control the rest of. We are surrounded here, with no way out except by helicopter. When—and notice I said when, not if—the VC decide to attack us here, it is incumbent on all of us to know how to defend ourselves. I don't want to be the only guy who knows how to shoot back. So pick up that rifle and take it apart."

For the next hour Mathis—and Kasperek—disassembled and reassembled the M-16 with increasing efficiency and ease, while McDaniel lectured them on how the weapon operated and what to do when it jammed, which, he explained, happened often. He told them to not put more than eighteen rounds in the twenty-round magazines to avoid weakening the spring, to avoid putting it on full auto to conserve ammo, and to always keep it clean and well-oiled. They found some weapon-cleaning supplies in the clerk's desk and McDaniel had both of them thoroughly clean and lubricate the weapon twice each, to ensure they knew how to do it. Finally, around midnight, McDaniel concluded they were at least minimally trained and left to go to bed.

Mathis noticed that the rain had stopped, and now a sharp breeze blew through the semi-open sides of the building, making it seem cooler than it really was. He left the rifle on the table and returned to his seat behind the typewriter, taking a minute to call in a sitrep to Tay Ninh. Kasperek moved his chair back to where he could lean it back, and popped a new tape in the eight-track. The long slow introduction of Vanilla Fudge's version of "You Keep Me Hangin' On" thumped from the tinny speaker.

Hanging up the field telephone, Mathis asked Kasperek, "Do you think he's right? The VC will attack us up here?"

"Well," Kasperek said, pursing his lips and nodding thoughtfully, "he is a green beanie, and knows all sorts of combat shit. But they never have before, at least as far as I know. A couple probes, but nothing serious."

"Yeah, and we've got barbed wire and bunkers all around, right?"

"Well, only one strand of concertina, and the bunkers are really just wooden sheds, so I'm not sure how much resistance we could actually put up. But like I said, they've never attacked before, so why would they now?"

It occurred to Mathis that this site had, up until now, been only a radio relay station, and had not really impacted the enemy forces in the area. Once the intercept operation began, the site would be far more important and detrimental to the communist war effort. But as long as they didn't know about it, the site should be okay. He hoped. He got up and walked over to the table to retrieve his rifle, and then returned to the desk and leaned the gun against the desk in easy reach. Better safe than sorry.

Conversation lagged as they listened to the music, but soon Mathis found himself nodding off, so he got up and began to pace the room. "I like their version of this," Mathis said. The Fudge was playing a cover of the Zombies' song, "She's Not There."

"Yeah, me too," Kasperek said, and then, perhaps because of the song's lyrics, asked, "You got a girlfriend back home?"

"Me? Naw. I was dating a girl, but she dumped me when I enlisted."

"Oh, wow, that's fucked up."

"Tell me about it. How about you?"

"Huh-uh," Kasperek said, shaking his head slowly. "I didn't date much in high school."

"How come?"

"I don't know. It's a small town, not a lot of girls my age, and I wasn't a jock or anything."

26

"I know what you mean. I didn't do so good with the ladies either."

Kasperek looked at him. "Why not? You're not a bad-looking guy."

Mathis appreciated the compliment, especially because he had never considered himself attractive. He thought of himself as average—medium height, medium weight, dark brown hair, blue eyes, totally unremarkable. "I was a late bloomer," he told Kasperek. "Small for my age until I was nearly eighteen, and had to wear braces for three years. I was kind of a geek. Got good grades in school, too, which didn't help."

"Did you play any sports?"

Mathis scoffed. "Are you kidding? I was too small until my senior year, and then it was too late. I never really cared about sports anyway. I liked to read and listen to music."

"Yeah, me, too," Kasperek agreed. "I was too skinny for anything but track. I tried out for that, but it just seemed too boring."

Mathis thought about commenting on Kasperek's looks, but decided that would seem too faggy. Kasperek wasn't bad looking, but he wasn't any Cary Grant, either. Thin, mousy brown hair, a nose a little too large, he wasn't going to be a movie star, but he wasn't ugly, either. Mathis thought about telling Kasperek more about his own history with girls, which was not as exciting as he had implied. He had been on very few dates in high school and junior college, and none had led anywhere. He was too shy with girls, and had questioned the motives of any girl who would go out with him. The girl who had dumped him just before he enlisted had only gone on three dates with him, and had kissed him passionately on the second date. On the third date he asked her to go steady, and she immediately dumped him. Devastated and confused, he had decided to join the Army, in part just to get away from an awkward situation. He obviously didn't understand women, so an all-male environment like the Army had a strange appeal.

While he already had found Kasperek to be an amiable and understanding companion, he decided to withhold any further confessions about his love life. The reality was that he was a virgin, and that was not something guys bragged about. It didn't sound like Kasperek had gotten laid, either, but he didn't really want to know. If Kasperek wasn't a virgin, too, that would further degrade Mathis' opinion of himself as a man.

Instead, Mathis changed the topic of conversation to cars, a subject young men always turned to when they didn't want to talk about anything personal. They debated the relative merits of the GTO versus the Roadrunner, agreed that automatic transmissions were for girls, and described the ideal car they would buy when they got back to the world. Kasperek swapped out the tapes, plugging in Jefferson Airplane's *Surrealistic Pillow*. The psychedelic sounds and obscure lyrics of "White Rabbit" echoed in the room. Mathis wasn't sure what the words actually meant, although it seemed clear they referred to the use of drugs. He had never used drugs, and didn't intend to, since doing so would violate his security clearance, but he was fascinated by the images and freedom they implied. From the tape player Grace Slick's haunting voice advised, "Remember what the dormouse said—feed your head."

* * *

Mathis rolled over on the cot and draped his arm over his head, trying to block out the shaft of sunlight that had awakened him. It didn't help. Try as he might, he couldn't go back to sleep. After staying up all night on CQ, he and Kasperek had gone to one of the bunkers to sleep, to avoid the noise of the day-time billets. This bunker—or shed, more appropriately—was on the west side of the mountain, and the sunlight streaming in through the gun port meant it must be late afternoon. Giving up, Mathis raised his arm and opened one eye to look at his watch.

"What time is it?" Kasperek asked from the cot a couple feet away.

"Nearly four," Mathis answered groggily. "I feel like shit."

"You don't smell so good, either," Kasperek joked.

"Hey, I showered last week, whether I needed it or not." Mathis uncurled and sat up, keeping his bare feet from touching the dirty floor. Bending over, he found the socks he had left stuffed in his boots and pulled them on, before sliding his feet into the boots without tying them. Across from him Kasperek was lying back on his cot to pull on his fatigue pants. Mathis had slept in his uniform, but Kasperek had stripped down to his boxer shorts, and was now trying to get dressed without touching the floor with his feet. Mathis stood up, stretched, rubbed his eyes, and sat back down on the cot to tie his boots.

"We won't be able to sleep tonight," Kasperek predicted as he put his socks and boots on.

"Oh, I can sleep any time," Mathis told him. "Even coffee and Cokes don't keep me awake."

"I'll have problems," Kasperek said as he pulled on his shirt. "Maybe we ought to go to the club this evening, have a few beers. That'd help me sleep."

"We can go hang out, but I don't drink beer."

"Why not?" Kasperek looked at him suspiciously.

Mathis started to make an excuse, like he didn't like the taste or something, but decided to tell Kasperek the truth. He had grown to trust the other man in the few short days he had known him. "I'm LDS," he said. "Mormon. Sort of."

"Sort of?"

"Well, Jack Mormon, as we call it. I was raised in the faith, but kind of fell away from it."

"How come?" Kasperek looked at him expectantly.

"Long story. When I was a kid we lived in Utah, but my dad had some argument with the elders about the tithes, so we moved to Colorado. He went to work at Coors, and we mostly stopped going to the temple. Mom tried to take us, but Dad wouldn't let her. I mean, we were still pretty religious, but not directly associated with the church. You know? I mean, I'm not supposed to drink anything with caffeine, but I do. I don't smoke, but that's more because I just don't like the idea. And I curse, but the Army did that to me. I don't know, I might rejoin the church someday, become a missionary. That's why I volunteered for language school."

29

"Mormon, huh?" Kasperek said, nodding. "Never knew any Mormons before. Least that I know of. I don't think there's many Mormons in Canada, are there?"

"Canada?" Mathis looked at Kasperek in surprise.

"Yeah, I'm Canadian," Kasperek announced.

Mathis squinted his eyes at him. "You do know that this is the United States Army, right?"

"I know. My family lives in up-state New York, because that's where my dad worked. We moved there when I was in junior high. After I graduated from high school, all my friends started getting drafted, so I decided to join up. That way I can get U.S. citizenship."

"No shit?" Mathis marveled. "All the guys I knew were talking about going to Canada to avoid the draft, and you come from Canada to join up. That's bizarre."

Kasperek shrugged. "There are times when I question my decision. Like the first day of Basic Training. Or every day on this godforsaken Rock."

Mathis chuckled. "Yeah, I know what you mean. When I joined up for language school, they told me I would be taking German or Russian. Instead I end up in Vietnamese, and sent over here. I wanted to see Europe, and instead I see the asshole of the world."

They heard a scuffling on the rocks outside, and then the door in the side of the bunker opened and McDaniel stuck his head in, looking around as his eyes adjusted to the relative dimness of the interior.

"Hey, Two-dan," Mathis greeted him. McDaniel stepped in, ducking his head to avoid the low door frame.

"What the fuck are you two doing in here? Bunker duty doesn't start until sundown."

"We came down here to get some sleep," Mathis told him, standing up.

"Yeah," Kasperek said as he stood up as well, "it's quieter and darker here than in the billets."

"Okay," McDaniel allowed, "as long as you two weren't fooling around or anything."

Mathis gave him a disgusted look. "Eat shit and die!" he said with mock anger.

"So why were you looking for us?" Kasperek asked him. "Hoping to join a circle jerk?"

"Fuck off," McDaniel rejoined with a smile. He took off his beret and ran his fingers through his straw-colored hair that was longer than Army regulations normally allowed. "I wanted to tell you about what's on TV tonight."

"Old re-runs of Gunsmoke?" Mathis asked. The Armed Forces Viet Nam network broadcast whatever shows they could get for free from the major American networks, which meant re-runs, public TV documentaries, and old movies.

"Ed Sullivan, the one with the Doors."

"The Doors?" Kasperek blurted. "Cool! I want to see that. How do you know?"

"They were advertising on the radio. It's on at eight. I figured we could go watch it at the club."

"Yeah, let's do that. See if we can get Bill here drunk." Mathis scowled at Kasperek, while McDaniel just looked puzzled. "He doesn't drink," Kasperek explained, "because he's a Mormon."

"Better than being a Canadian," Mathis riposted, poking Kasperek in the chest with one finger.

"What the fuck are you talking about?" McDaniel asked, frowning and shaking his head.

"Bill's a jack-off Mormon," Kasperek crowed.

"That's Jack Mormon," Mathis protested. "And this idiot's a Canadian, who didn't have to join the Army at all."

"A Mormon? A Canadian? Are you shittin' me?" McDaniel was clearly astounded and confused.

"Yeah," Mathis admitted, "I'm Mormon, but I'm not a fanatic about it. John's still an idiot, though, for enlisting."

"Hey," Kasperek interjected, "it was my patriotic duty."

"Bullshit!" Mathis said with a laugh. "You just wanted to have the fun, travel, and adventure." That was the euphemistic expansion of the FTA graffiti seen all over Viet Nam, an abbreviation which in fact stood for 'fuck the Army.'

"Whatever," McDaniel grumbled. "Come on, let's go get in line at the chow hall."

The "club" was actually no more than a billet hooch with tables and chairs instead of bunks. At one end was a hand-made bar tended by one of the Vietnamese KPs, stocked with beer, sodas, and small bags of chips. Mounted above the bar was the TV, a large 21-inch portable with genuine wood-grain vinyl around the sides. Up here on the mountain it got great reception with only a rabbit-ear antenna, so the black-and-white picture was sharp and clear of any snow. The room was crowded with GIs, some standing, most sitting at tables. The majority was smoking, and almost all had beers in their hands, but a few, like Mathis, clutched cold cans of Coke or orange soda. Mathis, McDaniel, and Kasperek were seated at a table close to the TV, in anticipation of the evening's entertainment. Currently an old episode of *Combat!* was on, which almost everyone was ignoring.

"Who's that?" Mathis asked, nodding in the direction of a short stocky Asian man leaning against the wall on the other side of the room. He was wearing baggy jeans and a white dress shirt.

McDaniel took a drink of his beer, than set the can down on the table. "That's Park, the generator mechanic. Korean."

"Don't mess with him," Kasperek advised.

"Why?" He looked harmless to Mathis, smiling broadly at the other men as he chugged one beer after another.

.

32

"He's kind of strange," Kasperek said, pausing to take a drink of his own beer. "He's got an M-60 he likes to shoot off the side of the mountain some times. I heard he bought it on the black market."

"He's got his own machine gun?" Mathis marveled. "For God's sake, why?"

"Why not?" McDaniel answered reasonably.

"I also heard he's actually Korean CIA," Kasperek added.

"Bullshit!" McDaniel said dismissively. "Why would the Korean CIA care about this shithole?"

"Good point," Mathis agreed.

Up on the TV Mathis saw it was showing a reenlistment commercial, which brought out a few boos and catcalls from the crowd in the room. Finally the opening credits of the Ed Sullivan show appeared, and the room quieted down a little.

"Here we go," McDaniel said enthusiastically. "I'm getting another beer. You want one, John?"

"Might as well," Kasperek said.

"Get me another Coke while you're up," Mathis told him. McDaniel got up and went to the bar, returning to the table with their drinks just as Ed introduced a juggling act. More performances followed, all of which Mathis found dull or even annoying. Finally, after a nervous unknown comedian named Rodney Dangerfield sweated through his set, Ed announced the Doors, and the club erupted in cheers. The band appeared against a backdrop of wooden doors handing from the rafters, and swooped into their moody song, "People Are Strange."

Although he had never seen them before, Mathis had read about them, and could identify all the band's members. "Morrison looks stoned," he commented.

"Probably is," McDaniel said. "He'd have to be on drugs to write songs like that."

After the song ended, the band segued into "Light My Fire," which brought another cheer from the men in the club, as well as from the audience in the studio. As the music swelled, both audiences went quiet so they could enjoy the driving tempo and soaring melody. When the song was finally over and the show ended, everyone returned to their drinking and conversations.

"Yep, he said it," Mathis remarked.

"What?" Kasperek asked.

"'We couldn't get much higher'. I read that Sullivan told them to change that line, because it was drug-related. Morrison said he would, but didn't."

"Fuck him if he can't take a joke," McDaniel said. "That was so fuckin' far out. You got that album, John?"

"I asked my folks to get it for me," Kasperek answered. "I hope it gets here soon."

All three men turned their heads when they heard angry shouting from the back of the room. Two soldiers, one black, one white, were pushing and shoving each other while calling each other increasingly offensive names. Both were obviously drunk, and the guys around them were trying to calm them down, without success. Suddenly Park appeared, stepped between them, and shoved both of them backwards so hard they crashed to the floor on their butts. "Shut up!" Park roared, and scowled down at the two men menacingly. When they didn't immediately try to get up, he turned to head for the door, the crowd parting in front of him like the Red Sea in front of Moses. The room was silent until Park had exited, slamming the screen door behind him. Conversation resumed, but at a much lower level than before. Now Mathis understood what Kasperek had meant about the Korean.

* * *

"On your feet!" McDaniel's booming voice brought Mathis out of a deep sleep, leaving him momentarily disoriented. He blinked his eyes rapidly as his mind cleared and he remembered where he was. He and Kasperek had pulled guard duty in this bunker until midnight, and had decided to just stay there and sleep rather than find their way back to the billet in the dark. Standard practice on the mountain was that odd-numbered bunkers posted guards from dusk until midnight, and even-numbered bunkers were manned from midnight to dawn. They were in bunker number Five, facing west toward Tay Ninh. There were twenty perimeter bunkers arranged around the camp in an irregular oval, with number One facing directly north, and the others numbered counter-clockwise, with the final bunker, twenty, just to the east of number one. It was pitch black inside the bunker, and Mathis groggily sat up on the cot and placed his stocking feet on top of his boots.

"What?" he asked in annoyance. McDaniel flicked on a flashlight and shined it on the ceiling to illuminate the interior of the bunker. Now Mathis could see John Kasperek sitting up on his cot, his knees drawn up, rubbing his eyes.

"The shit's hit the fan," McDaniel announced ominously. "The gooks are attacking all over Nam."

"Here?" Kasperek asked nervously.

"Not yet," McDaniel told them. "But they might. We've got to be ready for 'em."

Mathis leaned down and picked up one of his boots, turned it over, and shook it vigorously to dislodge anything that might have crawled into it during the night. "They're attacking everywhere?" he asked as he slipped his foot into the boot and picked up the other to check it as well.

"Yeah. We think it's because it's Tet."

Mathis remembered reading something in the Stars and Stripes newspaper about Tet, the Vietnamese New Year. "I thought there was supposed to be a truce or something," Mathis said.

"Yeah," Kasperek joined in. "No fighting today."

"Well, I guess the VC lied," McDaniel said. "Big surprise."

"So is the whole camp on alert?" Mathis asked, lacing up his boots.

"Should be," McDaniel said with disgust, "but I don't think they are. We heard about it on our net, and our team chief went to tell the CO, but it doesn't look like he's going to do anything about it. I came to warn you guys, so at least somebody's awake."

"Thanks, I guess," Mathis told him, standing up and wandering over to the poncho-shrouded machine gun that jutted out of the gun port. It was a huge fifty-caliber M2 machine gun mounted on a tripod, and the poncho was supposed to protect it from the rain and dust. He bent down and looked around the gun out at the distant city of Tay Ninh, seeing only a few lights twinkling. "Nothing happening at Tay Ninh," he noted aloud. He felt Kasperek and McDaniel come up on either side of him and crouch down to look through the narrow opening as well. As the three men silently looked out at the moonless night, a green flare rose in an arc in the distance and died, and then more flares rose in the air.

"That's the base camp!" Kasperek whispered anxiously.

"No shit," McDaniel agreed. "I can see tracers. Green and red." American weapons fired red tracer rounds, but the communists used green tracers. At this distance it was hard to distinguish what was going on, but Mathis could also see brief flashes as artillery or mortar rounds exploded.

"Holy shit!" Mathis breathed. He pulled the poncho off the fifty-cal and gripped the dual handles at the back of it. "How does this work?" he asked plaintively. Kasperek brushed past him to collect his grenade launcher and the ammo vest filled with rounds. McDaniel talked Mathis through the process of loading and charging the machine gun, and warned him to fire only short bursts to avoid overheating the barrel. Mathis was getting nervous, and gripped the wooden handles of the gun so hard his knuckles hurt.

"You got it?" McDaniel asked.

"I hope so," Mathis answered doubtfully.

"I gotta go warn the other bunkers," McDaniel announced, and darted out of the bunker.

"What are we supposed to do now?" Kasperek asked, sounding a little desperate.

"Beats the shit out of me," Mathis replied. "Just be ready, I guess." He found a more comfortable positon behind the fifty and stared out at the darkness. Somewhere down the slope were bushes and trees that could hide an entire army of Viet Cong, but in the pitch blackness of a moonless night, he couldn't see anything but vague shapes, black on charcoal.

"Can't see shit," Kasperek complained beside him.

"Think we'll launch some flares?" Mathis asked, referring to the camp's internal defenses.

"I'm sure they've got illumination rounds for the mortars, but I don't know if anyone knows how to fire them." Kasperek had shown him the mortar pit earlier, and told Mathis that they only had three mortarmen assigned up here, and all three were fucking new guys with no experience.

"What about here in the bunker? We got any hand flares?"

"Not that I've ever seen," Kasperek told him. "There's trip flares out beyond the wire, but they've been there a long time, and might not even work anymore."

"Terrific," Mathis grumbled.

"You guys up?" a voice called from outside the bunker.

"Yeah, Top," Kasperek answered. Apparently he had recognized the voice of the company first sergeant, Robinson. The man stuck his head in through the door.

"Gooks are really active tonight. Keep an eye out." First Sergeant Robinson was the oldest guy on the mountain, short and wiry, his close-cropped hair steel gray. To Mathis he was a leaner, meaner version of Mr. Booker.

"Can we get some flares up?" Mathis asked.

"Working on it," Robinson replied, and then disappeared.

A few minutes later they heard the sound of a mortar round being launched, and then suddenly a pale blue light bathed the exterior of the bunker, throwing deep shadows that wavered as the parachute flare swung and descended. Now Mathis could actually see the rocks and bushes outside, the single strand of concertina wire glistening. He couldn't see any movement, but the swaying light source made it hard to tell. He gazed at the shadows, squeezing the gun handles tightly, ready to fire at the first hint of danger. He realized with regret that while McDaniel had taught him how to strip and clean his M-16, he had never actually fired it before, just as he had never fired this fifty-cal. Learning to shoot through OJT—on-the-job training—was not the best way when your life is at stake.

The first flare sputtered out, leaving the mountain in darkness again for a moment until the next flare was launched. As the jumble of rocks and bushes was again revealed, Mathis heard a single rifle shot somewhere off to his left. It was immediately followed by shouts of "Cease fire!" that were repeated and echoed around the perimeter.

"What the fuck," Kasperek said.

"Somebody got a little antsy, I reckon," Mathis told him. "Nervous in the service."

"I wish they wouldn't scare me like that. Well, startle, not scare, I mean."

"Me, too," Mathis assured him. He was just as scared as Kasperek, and wanted him to know that there was no shame in it.

They heard footsteps outside, and Mathis tensed up, fearing enemy infiltrators were sneaking up on them. Instead McDaniel ducked inside, and in the flickering illumination from the flare Mathis saw the gleam of McDaniel's grin.

"You guys staying cool?" he asked.

"Sure," Mathis lied. "What's going on?"

"The usual cluster-fuck. Some guy over in eight saw a ghost or something. Tay Ninh radioed they were under attack, said they couldn't help us right now. Not that we need help. No sign of a probe or anything."

"That's good," Kasperek said.

"Kinda makes you wonder why, though," Mathis mused.

"The gooks got bigger fish to fry than us," McDaniel said. "But. . .they might just be waiting to hit us later, for some reason."

"But we're alert now," Kasperek argued. "Wouldn't it have been better to attack earlier?"

"Well, yeah," McDaniel agreed, "but who knows what they're thinking? Inscrutable Orientals, and all that shit."

"Speaking of which," Mathis said to McDaniel, "what do the sidgees think?" Since the mercenaries were native Vietnamese, Mathis suspected they might have insights, or even insider knowledge, of what was really going on.

McDaniel shrugged. "They're pretty calm about the whole thing. They went to their alert stations, but they don't seem worried about an actual attack."

"Uh-huh," Mathis said, chewing on his lower lip.

"Now that you mention it," McDaniel said, changing his grip on his rifle, "I better go back and check on 'em. Make sure they're not getting drunk or playing grab-ass. You guys take it easy." With that he ducked back out of the bunker and slipped away into the night.

Mathis and Kasperek resumed their posts at the gun port, watching the bouncing shadows of the rocks and bushes in front of them as successive parachute flares were launched and then died, and stealing glances at the distant sparkle of tracers and flares at the Tay Ninh base camp. Mathis wondered what time it was, but couldn't read the hands on his watch. Regardless, it was still hours until dawn.

THREE

Mathis was in the Pagoda, staring at the walls of the empty room that was destined to be the ASA SCIF, someday. The Tet Offensive of the previous week had thrown the entire country into chaos, and their little construction project here on Nui Ba Den was on an indefinite hold. Mathis had been amazed and appalled by the news footage shown on AFVN, and the stories and photos in the

Stars and Stripes, especially since he knew that both outlets always played down such events to avoid causing morale problems among the troops. If what he saw and read was bad, he knew the reality must be much worse. And it somehow seemed unreal and detached, because life here on the mountain was virtually untouched by the battles raging down below. Sure, there were interruptions in the daily flow of supplies and restrictions on travel to Tay Ninh, but those were only minor annoyances. For Mathis it meant yet another day with nothing to do. He knew he should be grateful for the opportunity to just sit back and relax, but his religious upbringing had instilled in him a strong work ethic, and he felt guilty about his indolence.

He had volunteered to pull guard duty whenever he could, and he helped out in the orderly room when there was typing or mail sorting to do, but these were not really what he felt he should be doing. He had spent hours talking with Booker, drawing up plans and discussing the optimal placement of the equipment, but that had gotten old. Booker had flown back to the Tay Ninh base camp as soon as that option had been reopened, leaving Mathis on the rock to sit and twiddle his thumbs. Booker had said he was going down to try and get the project back on track, but Mathis suspected the warrant officer just wanted to get off the mountain and spend time at the O club and PX.

"Old Mother Hubbard," a voice behind him intoned, referring to the emptiness of the room. Mathis glanced back to see Kasperek in the doorway, smiling at him. In one hand he held his M-79 grenade launcher, although he carried no ammo for it. Since the Tet mess, he had decided to carry it wherever he went.

"Thought you were working," Mathis said.

"Just got off. With Carson back, we've got more guys than we really need right now."

Mathis checked his watch, and saw it was not quite ten in the morning. "So what are you going to do now?" he asked.

"I don't know," Kasperek said. "Play a round of golf? Go to the beach?"

"Yeah, right!" Mathis scoffed. He looked around the vacant room. "I feel as useless as tits on a boar hog."

"Don't sweat it, man. Pretty soon you'll be up to your ass in work and be complaining about too much to do."

"Yeah, I know, but it's still a pain. Usual Army bullshit: hurry up and wait."

"I talked to my platoon sergeant," Kasperek said, "and he says I can help you guys set up your equipment, if it ever gets here."

"Cool," Mathis said, nodding in approval. "They'll probably give us some shit about you not having the right security clearance, but I can deal with that. They won't be up here, and we will, so . . ."

"Fuck 'em if they can't take a joke," Kasperek finished the thought for him.

"Right. I need a Coke." Mathis picked up his M-16, which had been leaning against the wall near the door, and he and Kasperek went down the hall and out of the Pagoda, squinting against the bright sunlight. They had just started down the uneven rocky path toward the club when they ran into McDaniel coming the other way, holding a heavy canvas bag in one hand and his M-16 in the other.

"There you are," McDaniel greeted them. "Drop your cocks and grab your socks, boys, we got training to do."

"Training?" Kasperek asked, coming to a halt.

"We don't need no training, Drill Sergeant," Mathis protested with a hillbilly accent.

"Yes, you do," McDaniel said cheerfully. "I just got the okay from the base commander to conduct some live-fire training." He held up the bag. "Five-point-five-six and M-79 rounds. You two are going to learn how to actually shoot those weapons you're carrying."

Mathis' mood brightened. Now he had something to do, something that was both useful and fun. He had still never fired an M-16, and worried about his lack of experience if he ever needed to. He also knew that John had never fired his M-79 here in Nam, and only fired a grenade launcher once in Basic. "Where?" he asked McDaniel.

41

"Down by the cave." On the north side of the camp, near the reservoir, there was a cave just below bunker twenty. A wide draw spread below it, with scattered small bushes and rock outcroppings. "We won't be able to zero your sixteen, but at least you can familiarize yourself. A zero doesn't mean much up here anyway, since you can't see anything coming more than about a hundred yards away."

Mathis and Kasperek followed McDaniel down toward the billets, then around the Special Forces hut and past the reservoir crater, scrambling down through the rocks to the cave opening. It wasn't really a cave in the geologic sense; it was actually an old lava tunnel that only went back in for about thirty feet. A semi-flat shelf jutted out in front of the opening, and McDaniel set the bag down next to a pile of rocks at the edge of the shelf.

"First we'll do some familiarization," McDaniel announced, reaching into his bag and pulling out a single short fat M-79 round. "Is that a full magazine?" he asked Mathis, nodding toward his rifle.

"Yep," Mathis answered proudly, "with eighteen rounds in it."

McDaniel handed the M-79 round to Kasperek. "Lock and load, gentlemen. The firing range is now hot." While Kasperek broke open his weapon and slid the round into the wide breach, Mathis pulled back on the charging handle of his rifle and let it spring forward with a clack, then tapped the forward assist with the palm of his left hand. "Keep your weapons pointed up and down range," McDaniel reminded them, unnecessarily. Mathis raised the rifle to his shoulder, pointing it down the mountain, and out of the corner of his eye he observed Kasperek doing the same. Still using the officious tone of a drill sergeant, McDaniel bellowed, "Ready on the right? The right is ready. Ready on the left? The left is ready. Commence firing!"

Remembering at the last minute that his weapon was still on SAFE, he flipped the switch and pulled the trigger, and he was surprised by the recoil that caused the barrel to rise a couple inches. Beside him Kasperek fired his M-79 with a loud "pomp" sound, and Mathis paused to watch the fall of the grenade that arced out over the side of the mountain, exploding with a flashing crunch a couple hundred yards down the draw, throwing up a small cloud of dust and leaf debris. Mathis fired again, holding the forward hand guards more tightly to control the recoil, and hearing the clink of the empty shell casing as it bounced against the rocks off to his right. Behind him McDaniel handed another M-79 round to Kasperek. Mathis fired three more rounds, and he watched this second grenade go even further than the first before exploding in the distant trees.

"Cease fire," McDaniel told them laconically, no longer playing the drill sergeant. "Why don't you two switch weapons, so you can be familiar with both types?" They did so, and spent the afternoon firing off rounds and experimenting with both weapons. McDaniel threw some empty beer cans down the slope so they would have targets, and showed them how to use the folding sight on the M-79. After a couple hours they had fired off all the ammo McDaniel had brought, so they headed back to their billet.

"Well," McDaniel told them as they trudged up the hill, "you two will never be experts, but at least I think you can now hit the side of a barn two times out of three, from the inside."

"Gee, thanks," Mathis grumbled jokingly. "But I am glad I know how to fire this thing now."

"Me, too," Kasperek joined in. "It's actually kind of fun. Almost makes me wish the gooks would attack. Almost."

"Be careful what you ask for," McDaniel warned. "Meanwhile, get those weapons clean, and I mean spic and span. I'll come by to inspect them after dinner. Got that?"

"Yes, Drill Sergeant," Mathis and Kasperek shouted simultaneously before breaking into laughter.

* * *

The glare from the setting sun was almost blinding. Mathis shaded his eyes with one hand as he swept his gaze over the vast plain of Tay Ninh Province. Directly overhead was a layer of clouds seemingly only a few hundred feet above the peak, but the clouds didn't stretch to the horizon. The horizontal sunlight played on the underside of the overcast, and spots of yellow and orange mottled the grey and white blanket in a pattern that was undeniably beautiful. Viet Nam would be a beautiful country, Mathis thought, if it weren't for the war going on. He was awkwardly standing on the slope just beneath the bunker, shirtless, trying to get up the motivation to fill yet another sandbag, when he heard the scuffling of boots behind him.

"About done?" Kasperek asked as he came around the side of the wooden shed that pretended to be a bunker. He was carrying a small package and a few letters. Mathis and Kasperek had decided to better fortify their bunker, and for the last two days had been filling sandbags and piling them neatly along the front and side walls of the small building. They planned to put a layer on the roof, too, although they weren't entirely sure the structure could withstand the weight.

"No thanks to you," Mathis jibed good-naturedly. Kasperek had been called upon to work a short shift in the Pagoda after supper, but had more than carried his own weight earlier in the day. Due to the rocky nature of the mountain top, it had been difficult and frustrating scraping up enough dirt and sand to fill the dark green bags, and they had had to venture down the slope to find loose soil, fill the bags, and then haul them back up to the bunker. It was back-breaking work, but Mathis consoled himself with the knowledge that it was good exercise, and it gave him something to do while they still waited for the SCIF engineers to arrive.

Kasperek stood beside Mathis and squinted out toward the west. "Getting too late to do any more," he suggested.

"I thought you'd say that," Mathis replied with an exaggerated accusatory tone. "Anything to get out of doing any real work."

"Fuck you and the horse you rode in on," Kasperek responded mildly. Mathis, although bone weary from the labor, felt a wave of good feeling wash over him. He was glad Kasperek had returned, for they had already developed a very good friendship. Growing up, Mathis had not had a lot of close friends; his religion, and his father's disputes with the church, had left him in a no-man's land from which he had turned inwards. Books, movies, and music had been his closest friends, and the Army hadn't really changed that up until now. Here, on this wind-blasted god-forsaken mountaintop he now had two close friends, and it was a wonderful experience.

"Well," Mathis told him, turning to climb up the slope to the side door of the bunker, "since you're so lazy, we might as well call it a day. Tomorrow you can do all the heavy lifting while I supervise."

"Don't count on it," Kasperek warned him with a chuckle, following him into the interior dimness. "Here, a couple of these letters are for you." He handed the envelopes to Mathis, who was pulling on his shirt, and then he started ripping the paper off the package. Mathis looked at the return addresses, and saw that one letter was from his mother, and the other from his little brother. He knew from experience that neither would contain any real news— just vague ramblings and neighborhood gossip, and maybe comments on something they had seen on TV about Viet Nam, asking him if he was involved. As always, there was no letter from his father. Still, any mail was welcome, regardless of how innocuous it was.

"All right!" Kasperek exclaimed, pulling a small flat box out of the package he had received. He held it up for Mathis to see. It was an eight-track tape, still in its cardboard sleeve, printed with the moody cover art of the Doors album—Jim Morrison's face was most prominent, with a far-away look in his eye, while the other members of the band were in the background. Mathis was as pleased as his friend. They had both heard the singles derived from the album, but knew there were songs they hadn't heard, and the single versions were undoubtedly abridged. "I'll go get the player," Kasperek said, dumping the empty box the tape had come in on his cot, along with a couple letters he didn't even bother to look at.

"Get Two-dan, too, he'll want to hear it," Mathis told him, taking the tape from Kasperek to examine the information on the back. "And get me a Coke. I'm dying of thirst."

"Shall I peel you a grape, too, sir?" Kasperek joked.

"If you don't mind," Mathis said with a smile.

"Back in a minute," Kasperek told him and ducked outside into the fading light. Mathis sat down on his own cot and read the song list. The last cut listed was "The End," a song he had read about but never actually heard. It was a long song that didn't get played on the radio, both because of its length and because the lyrics were suggestive. Mathis wanted to hear it and judge for himself. A cool breeze wafted through the open door, cooling and drying the sweat on his forehead. Evening breezes were common up here, so at first he took no notice, until he heard the first plops of rain on the roof. The patter quickly developed into a roar as a downpour erupted from the low-handing clouds. Incongruously, the fading rays of the sun still burned through the falling water and lit up the interior of the bunker through the gun port. Mathis got up and went over to kneel beside the fifty-cal, watching the sun set below the horizon through a curtain of water rushing from the roof. It was somewhat surreal.

"Shit!" Kasperek complained as he burst into the bunker, followed closely by McDaniel. Both men were soaking wet, as neither had taken time to put on a poncho. Kasperek had a large bulge under the front of his shirt, and McDaniel was holding his M-16 in one hand and a can of Coke in the other, while he hugged two cans of beer under his arm. McDaniel propped his rifle against the wall and then handed Mathis the Coke while he set the two beers on the ledge below the gun port. Kasperek pulled the eight-track player from under his shirt and wiped it off with the blanket from his bunk. "God damn!" Kasperek groused, "I hope the water didn't get inside and short it out. Maybe I ought to open it up and see."

"It's okay," McDaniel assured him. You put it under your shirt before it had a chance to get really wet.

"Yeah," Mathis agreed, "and we want to hear the album."

Kasperek turned the device over and over in his hands, examining it closely in the remaining light streaming through the gun port. "Okay," he finally acknowledged, "I guess it'll be okay. Give me the tape."

As dusk turned to night they listened to the album, nodding along to the beat and drinking their beverages. Mathis was really pleased that the album version of "Light My Fire" was longer than the single version, and all three wondered at the mysterious lyrics of

"The Crystal Ship." But it was "The End" that really sucked them in, and none spoke throughout the twelve-minute piece with its dark and dangerous lyrics. The spoken part of the song was like poetry by Edgar Allen Poe, describing a patricidal killer and implying an incestuous relationship with his mother. Mathis was particularly intrigued by the repeated lyric, "This is the end, my only friend, the end." After the last chord the tape continued to run in silence for a minute, so Kasperek hit the stop button.

"That shit is weird," McDaniel commented.

"But it's so cool," Mathis enthused, totally taken by the psychedelic sound and bizarre lyrics.

"What do you think it means?" Kasperek asked.

"Who the fuck knows?" McDaniel replied. "Morrison was probably higher than a kite when he wrote it."

"I really like it," Mathis told them. "I don't know what it means, but I like it. Let's hear it again."

"Yeah," McDaniel said, nodding his head. Kasperek reached over and hit the play button, and after a moment, the first song, "Break On Through," began. Mathis leaned back against the wall and closed his eyes, letting his ears and mind absorb the guitar chords, the electronic organ melody, and Jim Morrison's soulful singing. Totally immersed in the sounds, he was wafted away from the reality of the war, the mountaintop, and all his cares. He was one with the music, and joyful that he was sharing it with his friends. For those few minutes, he was truly happy.

FOUR

Due to the turmoil following the Tet Offensive, the engineers assigned to build the SCIF didn't arrive on Nui Ba Den until late February. After Mathis and Booker showed them the room in the Pagoda and explained what they needed, the two men, civilian contractors, began taking measurements. Mathis was a little annoyed by this, feeling it was unnecessary since he had already compiled those figures, and their results matched his exactly, but suppressed his anger. Booker kept telling the men how the electronic equipment would have to be situated, even though these two men were only assigned to seal up the windows and add a door, so Mathis finally suggested Booker fly down to Tay Ninh to check on the status of that equipment, which was being shipped from Arizona. The engineers thanked him later.

Inevitable delays in acquiring the necessary materials and equipment and getting them flown up to the mountaintop slowed the process of securing the room, but by mid-March it was almost ready for use, except for the door. Security regulations required that it be a steel door in a steel frame, and while it had taken a while to have the door made and installed, that requirement had finally been met. Then the problem arose of the way to lock that door. Normally a SCIF required a combination lock, but the difficulty of acquiring and installing such a lock at Nui Ba Den could not be easily overcome. Long-distance arguments ensued between the construction company in Viet Nam and the security people at NSA in Maryland, taking weeks due to the slow mail delivery and time differences. Mathis and Booker refused to get involved, and spent their time assembling and arranging the tables and desks that had arrived weeks ago, long before the room was ready.

While the door lock controversy raged on, Mathis and Kasperek helped Booker erect the antennas on the roof of the Pagoda and run the cables down into the SCIF, still empty but for the furniture. Until the door could be locked, none of the radios and recorders could be brought up from their secure storage in Saigon, as that equipment was itself highly classified. After an initial reluctance due to a concern about security clearances, Booker had allowed Kasperek to help out with the initial stages of the setup, and had grown to accept the electronically knowledgeable Canadian as a fellow signal maintenance technician. His not-so-veiled hints that he would have to boot Kasperek out of the room once the radio equipment began to arrive had become less and less frequent, and he began to discuss placement and hook-up of the devices with both Mathis and Kasperek without reservation. Mathis was pleased that his friend was now included in the preparations, even though he was, as Booker phrased it, "a damn furriner."

After a hard morning stringing antenna cable and running it through holes in the walls, Mathis and Kasperek returned to their billet to clean up and grab some lunch. When they entered the long canvas-roofed building they saw McDaniel at the far end, sitting on Mathis' foot locker reading *The Stars and Stripes* newspaper. "Hey, Two-dan," Mathis called to him as he strolled down the center aisle between the bunks. McDaniel glanced up at them, made a show of looking at his watch, and folded the paper.

"About damn time, you two," he scolded. "I been waiting at least ten minutes."

"Didn't know we were on a schedule," Kasperek remarked disparagingly.

"Maybe not," McDaniel acknowledged, laying the paper on Mathis' bunk and standing up to greet them. "But time's awastin'. We got places to go, things to see, and people to do."

"Like what?" Mathis asked.

"We're going to do a combat patrol, with guns and shit." McDaniel saw Mathis' puzzled look. "I got permission. We're gonna go outside the wire and see if we can scare up some Victor Charlies."

"What do you mean 'we', paleface?" Kasperek asked, raising his eyebrows.

"You, me, Bill, and Hung."

"Hung?" Mathis enquired, forcing himself to pronounce the name the way a non-Vietnamese speaker would, like the past tense of 'hang.'.

"One of my sidgees," McDaniel explained. "So get your weapons, helmet, and ammo. Better take a canteen, too."

"But. . .why?" Kasperek asked. "What the fuck would we want to go outside the wire for?"

"Gooood training," McDaniel drawled. "You two need to learn how to be real soldiers, not remfs."

"I'm quite happy being a rear-echelon mother-fucker," Mathis boasted primly.

"Yeah, yeah, you know you want to do it."

"Can we have lunch first?" Kasperek moaned. "I'm starving."

"Yeah," Mathis agreed. "Don't want to get shot on an empty stomach."

"You won't get shot," McDaniel assured them. "I won't allow it. But go ahead, you pussies, have your lunch. Meet me down at the team hooch in half an hour. And be ready to do some serious boonie humpin'."

* * *

"Watch your ass, this shit is sharp," McDaniel warned them. He had just clipped the baling wire holding together two coils of the concertina wire and let them spring apart. The Slinky-like concertina was razor wire, with triangular metal blades studding the heavy wire strands, far more dangerous than ordinary barbed wire. McDaniel handed the wire cutters to Hung, the Vietnamese CIDG soldier in tiger-stripe fatigues who stood beside him. Mathis and Kasperek were standing next to Bunker 2, not far from the Special Forces hooch and just below the mortar pit. They had stood back and watched as McDaniel had first ensured that the detonator blocks in the bunker had been disconnected from the electrical wire leading out to the Claymore mines deployed in front of the bunker. Mathis had a flutter in his stomach that he hoped was just a natural reaction to his lunch, but a slight tremble in his knees belied that.

"Come on, move it out," McDaniel ordered them while he stepped through the opening in the wire right behind Hung, who scrambled down the slope with remarkable dexterity. Mathis hesitantly moved down the slope to follow, stumbling over the uneven ground and loose stones, his M-16 gripped tightly in his hands. Behind him Kasperek slipped when a rock rolled out from under his foot and he bumped into Mathis' back, almost sending him into the dangling end of the razor wire.

"Watch it!" Mathis yelped.

"Sorry!" Kasperek replied. "Fuckin' rock moved."

"Take it easy, guys," McDaniel said in a calm voice. "It's no big deal. We make these patrols all the time, and ain't seen a gook yet." He waited for them about five yards past the wire, just above where the first low bushes began. Hung had already scouted ahead, occasionally high-stepping over unseen obstacles. When they came up beside the Green Beret, they stopped and awaited further instructions. While the side of the mountain was relatively steep, it wasn't dangerously so, and yet Mathis felt he was in a precarious position.

"There are trip flare wires out here, so watch your step," McDaniel warned them conversationally. "I'll point them out to you, so just be careful when you step over them, like Hung's doing."

Mathis saw Hung waiting down below about fifteen yards, grinning up at them. When McDaniel had introduced them to Hung at the team hooch, Mathis had pretended to not understand the conversation in Vietnamese between McDaniel and Hung. Hung had made some disparaging remarks about Mathis and Kasperek, and McDaniel, with a sly look at Mathis, had agreed with him. Mathis, for his part, had to put on a blank face while slightly seething inside at the insults. But he had also appreciated the humor of the situation, and when Hung wasn't looking he furiously scowled at McDaniel, causing the sergeant to laugh out loud.

As they picked their way down the rocky slope, McDaniel pointed out the Claymores and trip flares for them to avoid. Mathis couldn't help noticing that the mines and flares were weathered and fairly obvious. He surmised that the Viet Cong would have no trouble locating and disabling them, assuming they were even still functional. Hung moved ahead of them, keeping about ten yards distance as he scouted the route. "We should all be spread about five yards apart," McDaniel told them over his shoulder, "but in this terrain, you two would probably get lost and end up in Cambodia or something, so stay close."

"Roger that," Mathis replied. He felt some comfort and safety in being close to McDaniel, who was a trained combat soldier with true fighting skills, unlike him and Kasperek. Mathis found himself squinting and scanning the landscape around him, his hands tight on the rifle, ready to drop to a prone position at the slightest provocation. He also found himself crouching as he walked, and forced himself back fully upright like McDaniel, who was strolling like he was on a nature hike.

"Where'd Hung go?" Kasperek asked anxiously. They had stumbled and skidded down the mountainside about thirty yards, where the low brush had given way to small stunted trees, and only when Kasperek spoke was Mathis aware that the Vietnamese had disappeared.

"Right over there," McDaniel said nonchalantly, nodding toward their right. Mathis searched the foliage with his eyes, and finally caught a glimpse of movement as Hung crept through the trees. "Don't worry about him, he knows what he's doing." Following Hung's route, McDaniel veered to the right and led them across the slope, dodging around the small trees and large bushes and starting to distance himself. He was far more nimble on the rough terrain than Mathis and Kasperek, who were stepping slowly to avoid sliding down the hill while they dodged the roots and bushes. McDaniel glanced back and saw they were falling behind, so he stopped and waited for them to catch up.

"Look at that view," he said expansively, waving a hand toward the plain below them that stretched out to the horizon. Here the trees below them were blasted and even more stunted than the ones they had just walked through, affording them a wide view of the distant terrain. They were looking straight north, and there was little to see but endless forest, unbroken by roads or fields. "Somewhere over there is Cambodia," McDaniel remarked. Mathis took in the view for a moment, fighting off the touch of vertigo caused by seeing such a distance while standing on a steep slope. A breeze had come up, and occasional gusts threatened to knock him off balance, further heightening his sense of imbalance.

McDaniel turned and looked up slope, back toward the camp, and Mathis and Kasperek did the same. Mathis could just barely see the top of Bunker 2, but none of the other bunkers were visible. A small square cupola was visible off to the left, just peeking above the shoulder of the mountain top, which Mathis finally recognized as the top of the SF team hooch. To the right he could see the antenna masts that surmounted the Pagoda, although the building itself wasn't visible. This, he realized, was the view that any attacker would have of the base camp. While the enemy wouldn't be able to see much, he thought, that meant they, too, would be difficult to detect from above.

"Break's over," McDaniel announced. "Let's keep moving." Briefly adjusting his beret, McDaniel resumed the patrol, heading in the direction Mathis had last seen Hung. Mathis marveled at McDaniel's ability to follow Hung's trail, for he could see nothing to indicate the young Vietnamese had passed this way. He glanced back to make sure Kasperek was keeping up, and saw his friend managing at least as well as Mathis, his M-79 held in one hand while the other waved around to help him keep his balance.

"Up there's the cave," McDaniel told them without stopping, pointing his M-16 uphill with one hand. Mathis looked but couldn't see anything but a rough stone outcropping. They had spent a couple hours at the cave doing their live fire practice, but from down here everything looked totally different. Because he was looking up instead of down, he tripped on a rock and went down to his knees, reaching out to grab a bush for support. Kasperek helped him stand back up, and together they hurried forward to catch up, since McDaniel had apparently not noticed the mishap. A few minutes later Mathis noticed that they had been angling down the hill, and they were now completely out of sight of the base camp. The trees here were no longer so stunted, often as much as ten feet tall and fuller. Now Mathis could use his left hand to lean against the tree trunks and keep himself from slipping down the hill even farther. Watching every step and looking for trees to support himself, he almost bumped into McDaniel when the man suddenly stopped. Looking past McDaniel, he saw Hung kneeling and examining the ground.

"What is it?" Mathis asked, moving uphill to stand beside McDaniel. Kasperek moved downhill to take a position on McDaniel's left.

"Hung found something," McDaniel said softly. Hung poked at the ground with one finger, picked up a small fragment of something, and held it up close to his face. Then he wiped it off his fingers on a rock and stood up.

"Rice," Hung said in Vietnamese. Mathis forced his expression to remain neutral and waited for McDaniel to translate.

"There's some rice," McDaniel explained. "Must have been left by the VC." In Vietnamese he asked Hung how long it had been there, and then translated the answer. "Says it was from last night. Probably just a couple guys keeping an eye on us."

"They're this close?" Kasperek asked, a note of concern in his voice. Mathis found himself looking around nervously, searching his surroundings for any evidence of enemy activity.

"Sure," McDaniel said. "They control the whole damn mountain, except for the top. The guys that were here last night are probably sleeping it off now in one of the caves."

"There are more caves than the one up there?" Mathis asked.

"Yeah, I hear this mountain is riddled with caves. That's where the gooks spend most of their time, I reckon. That's why the Army doesn't even try to take the rest of the mountain. I mean, look at this terrain." He waved his left arm to encompass the steep slope, rocky ground, and heavy forest. "Can't use tanks or APCs, the gooks all in caves, it'd be worse than Okinawa. And for what? We've got the top, and that's all we really need, so fuck 'em." He nodded at Hung, who had been looking at McDaniel expectantly, and the Vietnamese took off, vanishing into the trees like a ghost.

After a moment McDaniel followed, and Mathis and Kasperek fell in behind.

Soon they came to a ravine running down from the top. Trees on either side shaded the shallow banks, but rain runoff had left occasional patches of dusty earth between the rocks. Hung was waiting for them, pointing down at one of the sandy places. Mathis came up beside McDaniel and stared at the ground like everyone else. It took him a minute, but finally he saw the faintly squiggly lines in the dirt. It looked like the tread marks from a tire, but there was no way any vehicle could have been here. Even a bicycle would be almost impossible to maneuver in such tight and steep confines.

"Ho Chi Minh sandal," McDaniel told them. Mathis had heard of them—sandals made from old car tires, popular with the Viet Cong and liberal college protestors in the States. McDaniel looked down the ravine, and then up toward the top of the mountain. "We better head back up," he said, motioning to Hung to start up the ravine. As the group began climbing, Mathis found himself now at the back of the formation, because Kasperek has quickly fallen in behind McDaniel. Mathis kept looking behind him, feeling very vulnerable as they made their way upwards. Each time he thought he heard a sound behind them, he would spin around and sweep his rifle barrel back and forth, looking for a target, but he never found one. McDaniel just kept climbing, chuckling to himself, but Kasperek seemed almost alarmed as Mathis. Despite the increasing strength of the wind, Mathis was bathed in sweat when they finally reached the concertina wire. The coils were stretched across the ravine, leaving almost a two-foot gap between the lower edge of the wire and the sandy bed of the runoff.

While he paused to catch his breath, Mathis saw that Hung had already reached the far side of the wire and was sitting on a rock, smiling down at them. He also noticed that he could not see any of the defensive bunkers. In fact, he could not see any man-made structures from this vantage point, and it occurred to him that this area was a significant weak point in the camp's defenses. If he couldn't see the bunkers, than it stood to reason that those manning the bunkers at night wouldn't be able to see anyone approaching up this ravine. He worried about the implications of this as he low-crawled under the concertina that McDaniel was lifting with the barrel of his M-16. It wasn't until he was twenty feet further up the slope that bunkers came into view on his left and right. The trip flare wires were even more obvious here than over by Bunker Two. The jumble of rocks along the edge of the summit provided plenty of places to use for cover if someone were trying to sneak into the camp along this route. It was only when they had passed between the bunkers, which stood over fifty yards apart, that they could see the rest of the camp off to their right. Directly ahead was the helicopter landing pad, the rectangular concrete with its painted markings being swept clean of dust by the rising wind.

The three soldiers paused at the edge of the pad, letting the wind cool their bodies. McDaniel told Hung to go back and repair the concertina wire where they had descended, and Mathis caught a flash of resentment on the Vietnamese's face as he turned to comply.

"Wouldn't that be a good infiltration route?" Mathis asked McDaniel, nodding toward where they had just been. He figured out that the top of the ravine began between bunkers eighteen and nineteen.

"Fuckin' A," McDaniel agreed. "We've told the CO that's a weak spot. He says that Division won't give him any more resources." McDaniel shrugged as if he wasn't sure that was true.

"And we know the VC are scouting around down there, right?" Kasperek chimed in. "I mean, we saw the rice and the footprints."

"What are you gonna do?" McDaniel said with exasperation. "I guess everyone figures that if they haven't attacked before now, they aren't going to. They've had plenty of chances. Maybe we're just not important enough to bother with."

Mathis turned his back to the wind, which was actually starting to chill him, despite the fact the sun was still only midway down the western sky. Clouds were building in the south, and the cool wind probably presaged another rain storm. "Well, let's hope they don't change their minds," Mathis asserted. But a thought popped into the back of his mind that caused him to begin worrying. Up until now, the Nui Ba Den base camp had existed only for radio relay, and while that was important to the allied operations, it didn't directly threaten the communists. The establishment of an ASA intercept site, however, would provide intelligence that could be immediately and directly used to identify and attack enemy formations, and if the VC or NVA became aware of the site's operations, that might give them a reason to rethink their dismissal of the camp's importance.

"So," McDaniel asked, "do you two feel like real soldiers now?" As a matter of fact, Mathis did consider their little sojourn somehow enlightening and empowering, but he wasn't going to admit that to McDaniel.

"It was okay," Mathis admitted, affecting an air of disinterest.

"It was kinda cool, actually," Kasperek said. "I haven't done anything like that since Basic."

Mathis, encouraged by Kasperek's enthusiasm, admitted, "Yeah, it was kind of fun. Like when I played Army as a kid."

"Only now the bad guys are using real bullets," McDaniel reminded him.

"Good point," Kasperek said. "So what now?"

"Time to clean our weapons. A clean gun is a happy gun." McDaniel gave them a stern look.

Mathis and Kasperek both groaned, then sighed with resignation. Together the three headed back to the billet. After evening chow they went back to the bunker and listened to Kasperek's eight-track. They played the Doors tape twice, with McDaniel playing air guitar, Kasperek pounding imaginary drums, and Mathis playing air electric organ along to "Light My Fire," while all three sang along with Jim Morrison. While listening to the mournful dirge "The End," they debated the meaning of the lyrics, and guessed at what Morrison was screaming in the spoken part that began, "Mother, I want to . . ." For Mathis it had been a very gratifying day: he had braved the possibility of enemy contact and survived, and he had enjoyed a real camaraderie with two guys he really liked. For being stuck on top of a mountain in Viet Nam, life wasn't all that bad.

FIVE

"Shit mother-fuck god-DAMN!" Mr. Booker cursed, stomping his feet to try and shake off some of the water. He had just come into the Pagoda, where Mathis and Kasperek had been waiting for him, his poncho dripping. Outside the rain was coming down in sheets, driven by a strong wind that mostly defeated any attempt to stay dry under a poncho. Mathis' pants below the knees were soaked through, and the rest of his uniform was at least damp. He had hung up his poncho on a nail and was wiping water from his face with his sleeve, which wasn't much dryer than his pants. Kasperek, who had been on duty since midnight, was completely dry. He handed Booker a brown towel.

"How come I didn't get a towel?" Mathis complained to him.

"You aren't an officer and a gentleman," Kasperek told him blandly.

"Yeah," Booker agreed, pulling the poncho over his head and splattering Mathis and Kasperek with drops of water. Then he rubbed the towel over his face and neck, muttering more curses under his breath. The other radio operators in the Pagoda ignored all three of them, their ears covered by bulky headphones and their hands tuning the big radios in front of them, searching the airwaves for any radio traffic that needed relay.

Booker hung the towel around his neck and walked down the short hall to the SCIF. The steel door had been painted dysentery green and sported a hefty hasp from which hung a huge combination padlock. Just below the hasp was a lever door latch with a key-slot in the base. This was the compromise that had been reached on securing the SCIF, which had a misleading name stenciled on the door: RADIO RESEARCH. Mathis and Kasperek stood back while Booker pulled out his wallet and retrieved a small slip of paper with the combination on it. Having the combination written down was a security violation in itself, but Booker had said he wasn't going to depend on his memory when he had more important things to think about. Holding the paper in two fingers of his left hand, he lifted the padlock and began twirling the knob back and forth. After two unsuccessful tires, he finally got it right, pulled the lock open with a snap, and unthreaded it from the hasp. "Your turn," he said to Mathis, stepping back from the door.

Mathis already had the key in his hand, and stepped forward to unlock the handle, pushing it down with the key still in the slot to unlatch the door. When the door came open, he withdrew the key and returned it to his pocket. From the outside, the door could only be opened with the key, another stage in the security protocol. As yet, only Booker had the combination, and Mathis had the only key, although both knew these restrictions would have to be relaxed once they were in full operation.

Booker pulled the door all the way open, and the three men stared at the pile of boxes and crates that filled the small room, some piled on the tables they had set up before, but most just stacked in the middle of the room. The equipment had arrived on a Chinook late the day before, and had been piled into the room haphazardly before being locked up for the night. They now faced the daunting task of unpacking everything and setting it all up, running power cords and signal lines to all the components and testing them. And all of it had to be done with the door closed.

"Are you sure it's all right for me to be in there?" Kasperek asked, shaking his head with doubt.

"It's okay with me," Booker said, and then turned to Mathis. "How about you, Bill?"

"Sure," Mathis said.

"Fuckers were supposed to send me a tech to help out," Booker complained, pushing into the room and edging around a pile of boxes. "Now they say he's got crotch rot or something. Probably got the clap. Anyway, I can't do it all by myself. I'm a fucking officer, you know."

"You don't have to, John" Mathis assured him. "You've been up all night. Aren't you tired?"

59

"It was a slow night," Kasperek said. "I caught a few Z's at the desk."

"Sleeping on the job, huh?" Booker said without any hint of condemnation. "Well, let's get started. Bill, close the door."

Mathis and Kasperek had followed Booker inside, and while Kasperek scooted along between a table and the stacks, Mathis drew the door shut and threw the two bolts that were mounted above and below the handle. Booker had disappeared behind the stacks of wooden crates on the left, and Kasperek was moving boxes so he could make the turn on the right. Closing the door had shrouded the room in semi-darkness, but Mathis found the wall switch and turned it on. A long fluorescent tube on the ceiling blinked into life.

"John," Booker called from across the room, "turn on the fan. Shit! The rain's coming in the god-damn window." High on the wall opposite the door was a narrow horizontal slot that allowed outside air into the room. The engineers had filled in the existing windows in the office, leaving only this opening at the top of one. It was barred and screened for security, but there was no glass, and by stretching his neck Mathis could see the rivulets of water running down the interior wall below it. On the right wall, after filling in the window there, the engineers had bricked in an exhaust fan. Kasperek, stretching across a table, reached up and switched it on, and with a whir it began sucking out the stale air of the room and drawing in the dampness of outside.

"Maybe we should put up an awning," Mathis suggested loudly, so Booker could hear him over the exhaust fan.

"Something," Booker agreed, coming back into sight. He put his hands on his hips and surveyed the many boxes in the room. "How the hell are we going to do this?" he asked rhetorically.

"One at a time?" Mathis offered, not very helpfully.

"As good a plan as any," Booker sighed. "Let's get this table cleared off first, then we can put the equipment we unpack on it until we're ready to start hooking shit up."

And so they did. After restacking many of the boxes and crates, they opened the bigger ones first, pulling out the radios, recorders, and other equipment and stacking them neatly on the tables while they shoved the packing materials out into the hall. Despite the exhaust fan the room became stifling, and although the rain had halted, the humidity remained extremely high. All three had stripped off their shirts while they ripped open boxes and pried open crates. The good news was that as they pushed the bulky packing materials out the door, the room became less crowded. The bad news was that the hallway had become almost impassable.

Mathis was closest to the door when they heard the knock, so he slid the bolts back and opened the door a few inches. Standing amidst the packing debris were Captain Ashbrook and First Sergeant Robinson.

Ashbrook smiled tentatively and asked, "How's it going?" Mathis could see that Robinson was scowling at all the mess.

"It's going, sir," Mathis said, and then turned his head to look for Booker. "Mr. Booker," he said loudly, "the CO and first sergeant are here."

Booker came over to the door, picking up the towel Kasperek had given him and wiping his face with it before draping it around his neck. He slipped out the door into the hallway, followed by Mathis. Both were still shirtless, their dog tags swinging from their necks.

"Morning, sir," Booker greeted Ashbrook, pushing aside some empty boxes to make room for himself and Mathis.

"Making progress, I see," Ashbrook said, nodding toward the piles of cardboard, wood, and shredded paper.

"Slowly but surely," Booker replied.

"What are you going to do with all this stuff," Robinson asked, clearly not happy with the mess.

"I'm not sure," Booker admitted. "Any suggestions?"

"I guess we could burn it," Robinson said judiciously. "If you don't need it for anything."

"Sounds good to me," Booker said with a smile.

"Good idea, First Sergeant," Ashbrook said. "Can you get a detail to take care of that?"

"Right away, sir," Robinson replied, but Mathis could tell that the first sergeant would have preferred that Booker and Mathis cleaned up their own mess.

"Thank you," Ashbrook said. He turned back to Booker and said, "Didn't I see Specialist Kasperek helping you in there?"

Mathis had been worried about what the captain might have seen through the crack in the door. Because they had allowed Kasperek in the SCIF, it would be hard to deny Captain Ashbrook entry. But Booker was good about thinking on his feet.

"Yes, sir," Booker said with assurance. "My technician wasn't available, but we were able to get Kasperek an interim clearance, just for the initial setup. I hope you don't mind."

"No, no, that's fine. Anything we can do to help." Mathis imagined he could see the wheels turning in Ashbrook's head. The captain could quiz Kasperek later and maybe find out what was really going on in this room. Mathis would have to warn Kasperek about how to handle Ashbrook's inquiries. And it was a short-term problem anyway. Once they actually began their intelligence-gathering operations, Kasperek would no longer be allowed inside, since he didn't have the proper clearance. He didn't even have the "interim clearance" Booker had lied about. He and Booker had violated all sorts of security protocols, but they had gone with the old dictum that it was easier to ask forgiveness than to get permission.

As soon as Mathis and Booker were back in the SCIF, they resumed unpacking, with Mathis telling Kasperek about what had been said in the hall. "John, Ashbrook knows you've been in here helping us, and he's okay with it. But I'll bet you he'll be asking you about what's going on in here."

"Why?" Kasperek asked, his forehead creased in puzzlement.

"Cause he's an asshole," Booker commented acidly.

"No," Mathis interjected, "because he's not allowed to know what goes on in here, and it pisses him off. The regular Army guys hate the ASA, because we won't tell them how we know things or what we do behind the green door."

"You mean, like the song?" Kasperek was referring to the fifties' pop song in which the singer wonders what goes on behind the green door. It was not entirely a coincidence that the door to this SCIF had been painted green, even though the stated reason was because it was the only paint the Army could supply.

"Exactly. So if he asks, just tell him the truth, but only the minimum truth you can get away with. We have radio equipment, recorders, a typewriter, and some electronic equipment you aren't sure about."

"And maybe drop a hint that you heard us talking about submarines," Booker offered with a grin. Mathis chuckled and nodded in agreement.

"Submarines?" Kasperek was obviously confused.

"Don't ask," Mathis told him. Kasperek just shrugged and went back to unpacking.

The next time Mathis opened the door to put some trash in the hall, he noticed that most of the waste that had been piled up there before was now gone. The first sergeant had been as good as his word, and Mathis was glad, because he had feared that he and Kasperek were going to be responsible for disposing of the discarded materials.

"Most of the trash is gone," he reported to Booker when he closed the door.

"Good," Booker said from behind a radio where he was hooking up cables. Then the warrant officer raised his head and sniffed the air. "Is that smoke?" he asked, looking around the room anxiously. Kasperek sniffed a couple times and then said, "Yeah, I smell it, too."

"Shit!" Booker said, jumping up from behind a table. "We can't have a fire in here!" He darted around the room, searching behind the equipment and shoving boxes around, and Kasperek and Mathis joined him, trying to track down the source.

63

"Wait," Kasperek called out, "here it is." Mathis looked over and saw Kasperek leaning forward across the table under the high narrow window, inhaling deeply. "It's coming in from outside."

"What the fuck?" Booker complained, rushing out the door. In a couple minutes he was back, shaking his head with disgust. "Those idiots are burning all our trash just outside the building. Couldn't carry it just another fifty feet before they lit it up. Jesus H. Christ!"

Like Kasperek, Mathis didn't say anything. There was little open area on the peak, and they had probably used the only available location to burn the stuff, so Mathis wasn't upset. The smoke coming in the window was only an occasional wisp, and not really a problem. Mathis was just happy it wasn't him doing the work.

By later afternoon all the equipment had been unpacked and arranged on the metal tables that lined three walls of the room. File cabinets and a bookshelf filled the spaces on either side of the door, along with a large electric paper shredder. The center of the room was a jumble of rolling office chairs, made of grey-painted metal with gray-green thin vinyl cushions. Mathis pushed the chairs under the tables as far as they would go, but the tiny room was still jam-packed and would be even more crowded when it was fully manned.

"Cozy," Mathis remarked as he surveyed the room.

"Cramped, I'd say," Booker responded. "Glad it's you going to be working in here, and not me."

"What?" Mathis said with feigned indignation. "You're not going to stay in here with us in case anything doesn't work right?"

"I'm going back to Japan," Booker told them. "If anything goes wrong, you're just SOL."

"Gee, thanks, sir."

"Actually, if there are any electronic problems, you can get John here to fix them. He knows what he's doing." Booker clapped Kasperek on the shoulder.

"Uh, there's the little problem of his clearance," Mathis reminded him. "As in, he doesn't have one."

"Well, get him one," Booker said dismissively. "That's not my problem."

Mathis just rolled his eyes, and Kasperek chuckled.

"Let's lock it up," Booker told them, heading for the door. "I want to take a shower before supper."

Mathis and Kasperek grabbed their weapons and followed Booker out into the hall. Kasperek held Mathis' rifle while he found his key and locked the handle, and then Booker hooked the big padlock on the hasp and twirled the dial a couple times. Mathis took his M-16 back as they exited the building, where he noticed an old 55-gallon drum a few feet away, still smoking. The drum had a number of ragged holes punched in it, and was blackened with soot. All the packing trash had been shoved into the barrel for burning, and the last of it was still smoldering. Mathis made a mental note that the barrel would be a good way to destroy the classified trash the intercept site would generate once it was in full operation, if they had not been supplied with a shredder. For that matter, the paper shreds themselves would have to be burned, so it could still be useful.

While Booker headed to the officers' quarters, Mathis and Kasperek slowly wound their way down the path to their billet.

"Thanks for helping, John," Mathis said sincerely. "If you hadn't, we'd still be working."

"No sweat, Bill. It was kind of fun. I got to mess with equipment I've never seen before."

"Well, forget it." Mathis saw Kasperek's expression, and hastened to explain. "No, seriously, forget about everything you saw. Booker didn't care about your lack of a clearance, and frankly, neither do I, but tomorrow the rest of the guys will get here. One of them will be the security guy, and he'll take such things very seriously. If he finds out we had an uncleared person in there, he'll get his panties in a wad and raise holy hell. So don't ever mention that you were in there."

"Captain Ashbrook knows I was there," Kasperek pointed out. "What if he tells that guy?"

Mathis hadn't thought about that. "Shit. I don't know. Let's just hope he doesn't." They walked a little further, passing the operations building. "I wonder if I *could* get you a clearance," Mathis mused.

"How would you go about that? I'm Canadian, you know."

"Yeah. I probably couldn't. And it would take weeks even if I could. Man, I'm sorry."

"Not your fault," Kasperek sympathized. "I don't mind. While you're in there working hard and sweating your ass off, I'll be out here in the fresh air enjoying myself."

Mathis gave him a sour look. He was already dreading the stifling working conditions he knew would exist with five or six guys crammed into that little room with only one small window. As if to emphasize the difference, a cool wind sprang up as they reached the billet, flapping the tail of his shirt and cooling his face. He had been here on Nui Ba Den for three months, a long time to be basically unsupervised and pretty much free to do whatever he wanted, but now that was all going to end. It was a depressing thought, although he admitted he would like to get back to doing what he had been trained for.

Later that evening, they were relaxing in their corner of the hooch, after going to chow and then checking mail at the orderly room. Kasperek had taken off his boots and shirt and was reclining on his bunk with his knees drawn up, reading a letter from home. Mathis sat on his cot with his feet on the floor, his elbows resting on his knees, while he read the latest issue of *The Stars and Stripes*. Or tried to read. Mostly he just thought about what the next few days might be like, and how his relationship with Kasperek would be changing. They had become very good friends, sharing a love of rock music and similar views on life. They both liked McDaniel, too, although the Special Forces soldier was a lot more hard-core than they were, as well as being a real NCO. The three of them had become true buddies, talking for hours while they listened to Kasperek's eight-track, and Mathis felt like they were the closest

66

friends he had ever had. He felt more kinship with them, and especially with Kasperek, than he ever had with his own brothers. It was a very gratifying sensation, and he hated the fact that he would have to start keeping more secrets from his friends, as well as spend more time separated from them.

Kasperek folded his letter and put it back into the envelope. "So who all is coming tomorrow?" he asked.

Mathis folded the paper and laid it down beside him. "There'll be an E-7 named Johnson. He's the site supe. And five or six guys like me, to do the work. And a civilian." The civilian was actually a representative from the National Security Agency, but Mathis wasn't allowed to reveal that.

"A civilian?" Kasperek asked, a hint of disbelief in his voice.

"Yeah," Mathis lied, "he's a contractor, works for Raytheon." Mathis saw the look on Kasperek's face, and realized his friend knew he was lying, but also understood why.

"And the E-7's in charge? No officer?"

"Yep," Mathis said, glad the subject had been changed. "We don't need no stinkin' officers. I've met him. He's an SFC, not a specialist. He's okay, knows what he's doing."

"Are the other guys, uh, like you?" Kasperek asked, raising one eyebrow. Mathis understood that Kasperek was asking about them being linguists.

"Some of them, sort of," Mathis replied vaguely. He wasn't actually revealing anything, he rationalized, even though he felt sure his friend knew exactly what he meant.

Mathis considered the fact that he would no longer have any real authority, either. Up until now, Booker had been his nominal supervisor, but in fact Mathis had made most of the decisions and was in charge of the SCIF. No one actually reported to him, and he couldn't give orders, only suggestions, but it was a small taste of responsibility, and he kind of enjoyed it. Tomorrow, however, he would be just one of the crew, doing the bidding of Sergeant Johnson and the NSA rep. On the one hand, it would be nice to be relieved of any responsibility, but on the other, he would again just be a pawn in the game. He was a little conflicted about that.

* * *

The next morning the summit of the mountain was totally enveloped in clouds, delaying the arrival of the rest of the ASA team. Mathis and Booker walked up to the Pagoda through the cool swirling mist and checked out the SCIF again, to make sure it was ready. After locking themselves inside, Booker rechecked power and antenna connections, powered up the equipment briefly, and straightened everything. Mathis just stood in the middle of the room and tried to visualize how the site would function when fully manned. Just inside the door on the left were two filing cabinets and the shredder. On the left wall were two intercept positions, or poz's, as they were normally referred to. Each had a big radio and a reel-to-reel tape recorder. The back wall, under the slit window, had two tables set up as desks, one with an intercept radio and one with a small bookshelf. These would be the supe poz and the traffic analysis poz. On the right wall, under the ventilator, was a transcription poz, holding a typewriter and a tape recorder, and a Morse poz, holding an HF intercept radio and another tape deck, along with a Morse sending key. Between the Morse poz and the door was a tall bookshelf that would also function as a tape rack. Two of the shelves were already full of blank 7-inch tape reels, each inside a yellowish-tan envelope with labeled lines to be filled in when the tape was used.

At each position there was a headset plugged into either the radio or recorder by a thick coiled cord. The headphones were bulky grey plastic with black vinyl ear pads, uncomfortable to wear and having dubious sound quality, but they were very rugged. They looked a lot like the headsets Mathis had seen in movies about World War II bomber crews, and suspected they were, indeed, war surplus. Under each of the tables that held a recorder was a big metal foot switch that could start and stop the recorder; the switch under the transcription poz was slightly different, in that it had two buttons, one to move the tape forward, and one to reverse it. Once the site became operational, two voice intercept operators would man the positions on the left, spinning the dials to search the airwaves for any enemy radio broadcasts. If and when they found something, they would start the recorder while simultaneously taking notes on yellow legal pads of what they heard. The traffic analyst (TA) would attempt to analyze the information and reconcile it with the existing intelligence on enemy units in the area. When the intercepted signal went down, the tape would be passed to the transcriber, who would listen to the broadcast again, stopping and rewinding as necessary, while typing up a full transcript in Vietnamese, and then gisting the conversation into English.

The TA would then compile all the information and write a brief report, which would next be encoded and handed to the Morse operator. The Morse operator, colloquially known as a ditty-bopper, who was also scanning the ether to pick up enemy broadcasts, would switch to the appropriate frequency and send the encrypted message on the Morse key in front of him. The recorded tape would be appropriately labeled and put on the shelf, to be sent to Saigon later, along with the typed transcript, in a secure courier bag. It had been difficult to squeeze in all the necessary tables and equipment, and one thing that was missing was a separate desk for the NSA representative. Mathis was sure he would hear about it when the NSA rep arrived, but space limitations were more important than bruised egos. The rep would just have to find a seat wherever he could. It was unlikely all the poz's would be occupied at one time anyway, since the manning was the bare minimum that the ASA could get away with, despite the fact that the site was supposed to be operational twenty-four hours a day. Mathis knew he was in for some long hours.

By mid-afternoon the sky had cleared, so Mathis and Booker went down to the helicopter landing pad to await the arrival of the Chinook carrying the ASA guys. Mathis turned his back and closed his eyes to protect them from the dust and grit stirred by the helicopter blades as the big machine settled onto the pad. Once the rotors spooled down to an idle, Mathis and Booker rushed to the back of the chopper as the crew chief lowered the loading ramp. A couple of the soldiers from the base camp were there to help also, and they quickly unloaded the gear and pointed the new arrivals up the slope toward the orderly room. Mathis took just a moment to shake the hand of Sergeant First Class Johnson, the site supervisor, and waved to a couple of guys he had seen before in Japan, before hustling everyone away from the Chinook so it could return to base. While the chopper roared away, Mathis noticed the civilian who stood there, looking a little lost. He was chubby, with glasses and longish black hair, and he was wearing black slacks and an incredibly ugly brown and orange plaid shirt. He was clutching a large leather satchel to his chest. Must be the NSA rep, Mathis said to himself.

Mathis took one end of a foot-locker-sized plastic case that was padlocked shut while SFC Johnson took the other, and they joined the line of men carrying duffel bags and boxes across the saddle in the direction of the orderly room. Up ahead Mathis could see Booker carrying a large civilian suitcase and walking beside the civilian, who looked both bewildered and angry.

"I don't think he wants to be here," Johnson commented dryly, looking toward the civilian.

"What's his name?" Mathis asked.

"Carson Weller," Johnson answered. "Says he went to Harvard. He'll tell you all about it, if you let him."

"And he's our rep?" Mathis asked, not happily.

"Afraid so."

When they reached the orderly room, everyone set down their loads just outside and regrouped. Johnson had the enlisted men go inside and start in-processing with the company clerk. "We need to get some of this stuff into the SCIF and lock it up," he told Mathis. "Sir," he said to Booker, "can you get that box over there?" He pointed toward a green metal file box whose lid was also secured with a padlock. "Mathis and me'll get this big one, and Mr. Weller here can carry his bag, I guess. If you'll lead us to the SCIF."

Weller rolled his eyes and shot an angry glance at the burly sergeant. "The 'radio room'," he corrected. He was right, Mathis acknowledged, but disliked the way Weller had handled it. They weren't supposed to call it a SCIF in mixed company, since that might hint at their real purpose in there.

70

"Right," Booker said, bending down to lift the metal box. It appeared to be heavier than he expected, but he shifted it around in his arms until it was secure before walking up the path toward the Pagoda. "This way, gentlemen," he said. "Just follow the yellow brick road."

Inside the Pagoda they set down their burdens in the hallway while Booker and Mathis made a big show about unlocking the door to the SCIF, mostly for Weller's benefit. Mathis dragged the big plastic case into the room, while Johnson brought in the metal box and placed it on the table that held the Morse equipment. Weller lugged in his satchel and plopped it on the TA position's desk. "So I'll be here?" Weller asked, although he made it clear it wasn't actually a question.

Mathis shrugged. "Actually, that's the TA poz. We're going to have to share, I think."

Weller frowned, but didn't say anything.

"We can work it out in the morning," Mathis suggested. "We need to get you all signed in and get you places to sleep. Supper will be in about an hour."

"I suppose," Weller grumbled. He took a look around the small room, frowning at the window above the desk he had appropriated. "That's not secure," he announced.

"We have to have ventilation for the equipment," Booker told him. "We couldn't get air conditioning. The window's got bars and screening. It's the best we could do under the circumstances."

Weller sighed theatrically. "I suppose. We'll just have to keep our voices down when we're in here."

"That's what we'll do," Sergeant Johnson agreed heartily. "So let's go get checked in. What's for chow tonight, fellas?"

"It's steak and lobster night, isn't it?" Booker asked Mathis innocently.

"I believe you're right, sir," Mathis replied, nodding earnestly.

"You wouldn't be puttin' me on, would you?" Johnson scoffed as they filed out of the room.

71

"Would we do that, Sarge?" Booker asked as he locked up the door. "No, I think you're really going to like it here on the mountain. It's just like a resort, sort of."

"Now I know you're shittin' me," Johnson laughed as they left the Pagoda.

Mathis brought two beers and a Coke back to their table and passed the beers out to Kasperek and McDaniel. The club was filling up, and the noise level totally drowned out the TV.

"So where are your new buddies?" McDaniel asked after taking a first long swig from the can.

"Getting settled, I guess," Mathis replied, talking loudly to be heard over the roar of conversation around them. After they had locked up the SCIF, Booker had taken Weller to the officers' hooch, and First Sergeant Robinson had been waiting at the orderly room to meet Sergeant Johnson and show him to the NCO hooch. Mathis had helped Kerrigan, the company clerk, find bunks for the rest of the guys, and then after dinner he had given them the nickel tour of the base camp. He had suggested they join him at the club, but all had preferred to unpack and get cleaned up.

"So how are they?" Kasperek asked. "Nice guys?"

Mathis shrugged. He would have liked to describe them to his friends, but he was afraid that in doing so he might let slip something about their real jobs and why there were here. "They're okay." He looked Kasperek in the eye, and John nodded in understanding.

"Spooks," McDaniel scoffed quietly. Mathis gave him a warning look. McDaniel had learned a lot about the ASA when he was at the language school, and had only grudgingly agreed to keep his mouth shut about Mathis and his associates here on the Rock.

"Sergeant Johnson's a pretty good guy," Mathis told them. "Not like most lifers. I think he'll be all right. Weller, the civilian, is kind of a tight-ass. But he's not in my chain of command, so fuck him. I don't know all that much about the rest of them yet." He thought about the other guys, wondering how they would be to work with. Albertson, the traffic analyst, was kind of a surfer dude; not a

72

linguist, but not a jerk, either. The other two Vietnamese linguists hadn't said much, and Mathis had only met one of them, McIntosh, before. McIntosh, a small black kid with glasses and the unfortunate first name of Delbert, was very educated, but maybe not all that street smart. Farley, the other Vietnamese linguist, was a big pudgy guy who liked to brag about himself. Davies, a Cambodian linguist, had been with Mathis on the hearability test last June; Mathis had not warmed to him then, and didn't expect to do so now. The last new arrival was Kelso, a short muscular guy whose hairline was already receding, and who seemed to have a chip on his shoulder. He was their only designated Morse intercept operator, although Sergeant Johnson, who was originally also a ditty-bopper, could back him up when necessary.

"Guess you're going to be busy now, huh?" Kasperek asked.

"Looks like it. Technically, we're supposed to operate around the clock, but we just don't have the manpower to do that. Still, I'll probably have to be in the radio room a lot, and every day."

"It's tough when you have to work for a living, huh, Bill?" McDaniel jibed.

Before Mathis could respond, the room suddenly went quiet. He looked up and saw that Park, the Korean generator mechanic, had just entered. Today he wore a sweatshirt with the sleeves ripped off and baggy shorts that revealed muscular legs. Stomping over to the bar, he bought four beers and then carried them over to a table where two soldiers had been playing cribbage. When he sat down the two Americans greeted him politely but warily. Park popped open one of the beer cans and drained it in one long swallow. When he reached for the next beer, one of the guys at his table looked at his watch, affected a look of surprise, and gathered up the cards and cribbage board so he and his friend could leave. Park ignored them as they departed, reaching under his shirt to pull out a folded up newspaper which he proceeded to spread out on the table. Mathis saw that it was in Korean, and Park ran one finger down the page as he read, sometimes grunting angrily and other times laughing out loud. Gradually the rest of the guys in the room resumed their conversations, but at a much lower volume than before.

73

"So John and most of these other guys are wearing the Electric Strawberry," McDaniel said, pointing at Kasperek's shoulder patch. The 25th Division's patch was in black and olive drab on the jungle fatigues, but on dress greens it was a red taro leaf with a yellow outline and a big yellow lightning bolt down the center, earning it the nickname. McDaniel punched Mathis' shoulder patch. "What's this one called?"

The dress version of the patch was a light blue background with a yellow outline and an eagle's talon gripping three yellow lightning bolts. Mathis had just heard from one of the newly-arrived ASA guys the latest nickname, and he proudly announced it to the others: "Screaming Yellow Chicken-Fuckers." All three burst out laughing. Then Mathis began singing, to the tune of SSG Barry Sadler's pop song, "The Ballad of the Green Berets." "No silver wings upon our chest; we are not America's best. One hundred men will test today, but not a one from the ASA." The self-deprecation went over well, and the laughter continued.

"There are more words to it, but I've forgotten them," Mathis admitted. He was actually proud to be in the ASA, but the rest of the Army held them in low regard, and they had found that putting themselves down often made life easier.

McDaniel got up and went to the bar for more drinks, and when he returned Mathis steered the conversation away from his job. Instead they discussed rock music, the Church of the Latter Day Saints, Canada, and Special Forces training. They kept glancing over at Park, but the Korean never got belligerent, and when he folded up the newspaper and left, they decided to call it a night themselves.

SIX

The next few days flew by, with Mathis spending twelve to fourteen hours a day in the SCIF. Mr. Weller and Sergeant Johnson had several low-key arguments about scheduling and priorities, as each obliquely asserted that he was in charge of this operation. A deal was worked out that left only two men in the SCIF at night. Meanwhile the enlisted men got to work, scanning the frequencies for traffic and learning how to differentiate between ARVN and communist radio operators. Their first day of operation was May 1, May Day, the world-wide communist holiday, and all Mathis picked up was a couple of NVA radio operators exchanging drunken insults. The following days the traffic was more military, and as Mathis and the other two Vietnamese ops got the feel of things, the quantity and quality of intelligence began to grow. Davies was tasked with finding Cambodian traffic, but he kept insisting that all he was hearing was crap, administrative traffic and bullshit, and nothing worth reporting. Mathis secretly wondered if that were true, or if Davies simply didn't want to bother finding any real intelligence.

After making minor adjustments to the equipment the first few days of operation, Mr. Booker declared they were good to go, and he took the next chopper out. Sure enough, the following day one of the radios stopped working, and Booker couldn't be located. After a long discussion about security clearances, Mathis convinced Weller to allow Kasperek in to fix the radio. First, of course, they had to totally cease operations and cover everything in the room with large black cloths that Weller had brought along for that specific purpose. "The room must be totally sanitized," Weller had insisted. When Kasperek had been allowed in to work on the radio, Weller had watched him like a hawk, as though the electronics technician was a spy and a thief. It had taken Kasperek only about half an hour to find and correct the problem, and Weller had quickly ushered him out without so much as a "thank you."

75

Later that evening, when Mathis dragged himself into the billet and plopped on his cot, he had apologized to Kasperek for the way Weller had treated him.

"Well," Kasperek commented, "you said he was a prick, and you were right. Glad I could fix it, though."

"Yeah, me too. They should have assigned us a cleared sig maintenance tech, but I guess they didn't have any to spare."

"Well, I'm here if you need me. Maybe next time I'll just fix it with my eyes closed, so you don't have to put those sheets over everything."

"Sure, that would work." They both laughed. Mathis was truly glad he had met John Kasperek. Despite the differences in their backgrounds, education, and their MOS's, they had developed a real kinship. He had never had a friend for whom he had felt this deeply before, and their relationship had really helped him survive the dread and discomfort of Viet Nam. He truly felt closer to John than he did to his own siblings, although, he admitted to himself, that wasn't saying all that much. He and his siblings had always gone their separate ways, and while they didn't fight amongst themselves, they didn't share much either. And that made his relationship with John even more special, as he was sort of the brother Mathis wished he had always had.

"What's the date today?" Mathis asked while he fed the six-ply paper into the tractor-feed of the typewriter.

"The eleventh," Weller answered from the next table, where he was scribbling away on a yellow legal pad.

"Thanks," Mathis said and started typing. "11 May 68. Another day in Paradise." When he finished typing the header to the transcript, he slid the headphones over his ears and started the tape recorder. After a minute of tape hiss, he heard Farley's voice as he had recorded the tape identification data, and then the low static of dead air. Mathis glanced down at the handwritten notes Farley had stuck inside the tape jacket. According to Farley, the tape contained a brief conversation between two NVA radio operators about an

76

upcoming visit to a whorehouse. Although that was hardly of any intelligence value, Mathis thought it might be an interesting diversion from the mundane crap he usually heard. Then he heard the first radio call, and began typing.

The first thing he noticed was that the two speakers, who were using generic call signs, were not North Vietnamese, but more likely to be Viet Cong. Their accents and vocabulary pegged them as being from South Vietnam. After establishing the initial call-up, he decided to listen to the entire tape once before going back and typing the actual conversation. While he listened, he concluded that Farley was at least partially correct—the two men were laughing and talking very crudely about women in general, and later about a specific woman "in the village" who was very skilled at sex. The first part of their conversation, however, had seemed to be more serious in nature. Rewinding to the beginning of the tape, Mathis began typing every word, pausing the tape every few seconds and rewinding as needed to ensure he got the exact phrasing. Although the recording was less than five minutes long, it took Mathis over two hours to get it all down on paper. The transcript was four pages long, and when he was done he tore along the perforations at the bottom of the last page and began separating the copies.

"Mr. Weller, I think you ought to see this," he said, handing one of the fan-folded transcripts to the NSA rep.

"What's up?" Weller said, taking the sheets and starting to read.

"I'm not sure. I'd like to get your opinion." Mathis had learned through experience that it was always important to get a second opinion, and to not prejudice the other person by telling them what you thought you heard. He waited expectantly while Weller read through the transcript. Weller considered himself to be the best Vietnamese linguist of the group—possibly the best in the world, if you accepted his own description. Finally Weller laid the paper down on the table and looked over at Mathis.

"So?" he asked.

"That first part, where the guy talks about assaulting the virgin on Monday."

"Yes?"

"I think he's talking about here, Nui Ba Den."

"No," Weller said, shaking his head. "He's talking about sex. Pure and simple. Yes, I know Americans call this mountain the Black Virgin, as did the French, but that's due to a misinterpretation of the legend. It's more accurate to call it the Dark Lady or the Black Widow."

"I know that," Mathis insisted, "but many South Vietnamese have adopted the Western version of the legend. The tone of his voice when he says it is serious, not like he's joking about sex, like they do in the rest of the cut."

"Okay, let me listen to it," Weller condescended, and rolled his chair over to the transcription table. Mathis handed him the headphones and scooted the foot control over to where Weller could operate it. Pushing his chair back to get out of the way, he watched the civilian take a minute to re-familiarize himself with how the recorder worked. Finally Weller got the hang of it and began listening, stopping and rewinding several times. Mathis wasn't convinced Weller was all that good with aural Vietnamese, having learned it in college mostly from books, but he was supposed to be their resident expert.

After ten minutes of listening, Weller pulled off the headphones and shrugged. "I understand why you might think that's what he's saying," Weller said, "but I cannot totally agree. Literally, he says he will climb on top of a maiden and do nasty things. In the context of the rest of the conversation, we have to assume that he is talking about sex."

"I just don't think so," Mathis argued. "The way he says it, it sounds like he is using euphemisms for a military attack, and the rest of the conversation is spontaneous, either to disguise what he said initially, or just inspired by the first part." The problem, Mathis knew, was the lack of articles in Vietnamese grammar. In English "a virgin" and "the virgin" had totally different connotations, but those distinctions were missing in this case. The written transcript couldn't show what was truly implied, and the emotional content of

78

the phrase Mathis heard when he listened to the tape was entirely subjective.

"Regardless," Weller told him, rolling his chair back to the other table, "it's not clear enough to report. We would look pretty silly if we reported to NSA that we were about to be attacked, when actually it was just an off-hand remark from a randy radio operator."

"But what if you're wrong?" Mathis persisted.

"Look, Mathis, if they really are going to attack us, there will be other indications. Why don't you monitor that freq and see if you can pick up any other traffic that mentions this mountain? Then we can send out a report."

Acknowledging defeat, Mathis finished filling out the tape jacket, rewound the tape and inserted it into the jacket along with a copy of the transcript, and put it on the tape rack in the section for tapes to be sent back to Japan for further research. Then he switched chairs and went to the vacant intercept position, put on the headphones, and listened to the static.

When Sergeant Johnson came in to relieve Weller for lunch, Mathis waited until Weller was gone before broaching the subject with his supervisor. Johnson wasn't a linguist, so he had to take Mathis' word for how the conversation should be interpreted.

"I see where you're coming from," Johnson told him, "but really, our hands are tied. Weller has final say on any report that goes out of here, and I can't override him. Besides, by the time the report went through all the channels, it would have already happened. I'll go ahead and send some kind of advisory, so at least if you're right, you can say I told you so."

"Thanks, Sarge. But what about warning the folks up here?"

Johnson grimaced. "That's really a problem. Even if we were sure, we couldn't tell these guys. I mean, they'd want to know how we know, and we just can't tell them. And if we told them and nothing happened Monday, they'd never trust anything we tell them again. It's a pisser, but that's the nature of the business."

Mathis knew Johnson was right, but it didn't make it any easier. His shoulders slumped.

"By the way, when you go to lunch, stop by your hooch and get your helmet and rifle" Johnson advised.

"How come?"

"The battalion commander for 125th is coming up this afternoon to do an inspection. Captain Ashbrook wants everyone standing tall and looking sharp. For a change."

"He's not coming in here, is he?" Mathis asked, raising one eyebrow.

"Oh, no, he can't. But he might be still be around when you go to evening chow."

"Okay, sure thing, Sarge." There was a knock at the door, and Mathis got up and opened it just enough to peek around the edge. McIntosh was standing there, almost unrecognizable with his helmet on and M-16 in hand. Mathis let the black kid in, glad that he was here to relieve Mathis so he, too, could go to lunch. "Back in a few," he told Johnson, and left the room.

* * *

The sun was hanging low in the west when Mathis got off duty that day. He and McIntosh had rolled through the frequencies all afternoon, seeking out any calls that might support Mathis' premise, but with no luck. There were, in fact, few communist radios on the air at all, and those were mostly administrative in nature. It was Saturday, after all, and the Viet Cong, like the ARVNs, often took the weekends off. Weller had signed out around four, and around five Mathis told McIntosh he could go to chow, and not to bother coming back afterwards, since Mathis wasn't hungry. That had left just Mathis and Kelso, the ditty-bopper, in the SCIF until the night trick showed up. Farley arrived around six, and Mathis told Kelso he could go ahead and take off while they waited for Albertson, the TA. Mathis briefed Farley on the day's events, then had to suffer through yet another of Farley's fantastic stories about himself. His favorite was about how he was an airline pilot before being drafted, and he would tell these adventure-filled tales of flying 707's around the world. If you believed Farley, he was also the son of a Navy admiral, and his brother was an agent for the CIA. What wasn't

80

explained was why Farley, with such an illustrious background, was a lowly E-4 sitting on a mountaintop in Viet Nam. Mathis was relieved in more ways than one when Albertson finally appeared.

As he trudged down the path toward the billets, Mathis noticed the other soldiers in the area were no longer looking sharp for the colonel; none had helmets or weapons, and most were bare-chested. Clearly the battalion commander was no longer on site, and discipline had receded accordingly. When he entered his hooch he found McDaniel and Kasperek sitting on Mathis' cot listening to the eight-track perched on Kasperek's bunk, the eerie strains of the Rolling Stones' "2000 Light Years From Home" washing over them. Kasperek stood up when Mathis approached, making room for him to drop his rifle and helmet on the cot with an exaggerated sigh.

"Bad day at the office, Bill?" McDaniel asked. Mathis nodded. "Could be worse," McDaniel noted. "You could be humpin' the boonies with the grunts."

"At least I'd get some fresh air that way," Mathis responded.

"I'm sure it could be arranged," McDaniel threatened mockingly.

"So what happened?" Kasperek inquired.

Mathis picked up his helmet and hung it on a nail, and propped his rifle against a post, so he could sit down on the end of the cot. "Just the usual bullshit," he told them. Kasperek picked up the eight-track and moved it to his foot locker so he could sit on his bunk.

"Anything we need to know about?" McDaniel asked with forced casualness. McDaniel had a pretty good idea about what Mathis did when he was working, but also knew Mathis couldn't talk about it. Mathis looked at McDaniel with a totally blank face for a moment.

"No, I guess not," Mathis hedged. "You guys got anything going on Monday?" he asked, as if he were changing the subject.

"Not that I know of," McDaniel said. "Just the usual. Why?"

81

"No reason. Boy, I could sure use a Coke right now. John, you got any of those cookies left? I missed chow."

McDaniel stood up. "I'll make a beer run," he announced, and walked out. Kasperek moved the eight-track to the floor and opened his foot locker to dig out a box of stale home-made chocolate chip cookies his mom had sent him. Mathis had scarfed down three of the cookies by the time McDaniel returned with beers for him and Kasperek and a Coke for Mathis. After they had all enjoyed the first few swallows of the cold drinks, they sat in silence for a minute, not sure what they could actually talk about.

"You might want to talk to your boy Farley," McDaniel told Mathis.

"Why? What's that douche-bag done now?"

"He's been talking to the sidgees. Telling them all this crap about how he's a pilot and his brother runs the CIA or some shit."

Mathis groaned. "Yeah, he tells us that shit, too. Does he really think we believe it?"

"Well, the sidgees appear to. Worse, he's talking to them in Vietnamese. I thought he wasn't supposed to do that."

"Mother-fuck!" Mathis bitched. "He knows better than that. That stupid son of a bitch. I'll have Sergeant Johnson straighten his ass out." All of the linguists had been reminded repeatedly not to reveal their Vietnamese language skills to anyone up here on the Rock, and especially not to the sidgees or the Vietnamese KPs. It wouldn't take much for the Vietnamese to put two and two together, and figure out what Americans who spoke Vietnamese were doing locked in that radio research room every day. And if the South Vietnamese on the Rock knew it, it was a good bet that the VC would hear about it sooner or later. Mathis fumed for a minute, and then changed the subject again.

"So how did the big inspection go?" he asked.

"No big deal," McDaniel said. "Him and his cronies just walked around and looked at everybody doing busy-work."

"Yeah," Kasperek joined in, "I talked to Kerrigan when I went to check mail. He said the colonel thought everything was 'outstanding,' and said we were all doing a terrific job up here."

"Like he'd know," McDaniel groused. "This is the first time he's been up here in months."

"Kerrigan did say the captain asked about additional troops and better defenses, and the colonel said he would look into it."

"Well that's very nice of him," Mathis said scathingly. "Maybe he'll form a working group to discuss the possibilities."

"And four years from now. . ." McDaniel suggested.

"We haven't had any contact with the VC for over a year," Kasperek said. "I guess he figures, if it ain't broke, don't fix it."

"But what if he's wrong?" McDaniel asked with a meaningful look at Mathis.

"I guess we'll find out the hard way," Mathis responded. He gave his two friends a meaningful frown, and they nodded in understanding.

"Did he come by your radio room?" Kasperek asked.

"Yeah, but we couldn't let him in. Weller made Sergeant Johnson go out and talk to him in the hall. I guess Johnson made up some bullshit to appease the guy. He said the colonel was kind of pissed that he couldn't come in. But, oh, well."

"Couldn't you have put all those black sheets over everything?" Kasperek asked.

Mathis shrugged. "We were busy. And Weller doesn't have much respect for Army officers anyway. They didn't go to Harvard, you know."

"I don't have much respect for most officers either," McDaniel stated, "but not because they didn't go to Harvard. They're just assholes."

"Good point," Mathis agreed.

* * *

Sunday was a quiet day at work. Mathis had been scheduled to work the night trick on Sunday, and thus have the second part of the day off, but Farley had decided he liked working that graveyard shift and had volunteered to do it every night. Mathis suspected Farley preferred working nights because there was less work to do, it was cooler in the SCIF, and he could probably sleep at his poz and get away with it. But that was okay, because Mathis hated having to stay up all night and try to sleep in the heat of the day with all the noise going on. Mathis didn't pick up any useful intelligence that day, although he did overhear some American Army guys talking about going into Seoul to go drinking. It was obviously skip, the occasional bouncing of a radio signal off layers of atmosphere that carried it far beyond its normal range. He had been listening to guys in South Korea, thousands of miles away, and while it was interesting and entertaining, it wasn't useful.

Although he didn't hear anything more about a possible attack on Nui Ba Den, Mathis continued to worry about it. He listened to the tape again, thinking maybe he had misheard or misinterpreted something, but it still sounded to him like a threat. He even had McIntosh listen to it. McIntosh agreed with Mathis, but Mathis could tell he was just agreeing to be agreeable, which didn't really help. By the end of the day Mathis had almost convinced himself that the recording wasn't quite what he thought, and there was no imminent danger. Almost.

Monday was a much busier day in the SCIF. First Infantry Division troops had busted up an ambush in the Michelin rubber plantation the other side of Dau Tieng, and there was a lot of NVA radio traffic as the communists disengaged and withdrew into the surrounding forests. Meanwhile Davies had picked up Cambodian traffic about a big NVA supply column coming down the Ho Chi Minh trail, and that became the top priority. Weller and Albertson kept hovering over Davies, snatching his notes as soon as he finished a page so they could compose intel reports and code them so Kelso could send them to Saigon via Morse. Mathis kept trolling the ether for Vietnamese calls, dismissing most when they turned out to be ARVNs or ruff-puffs, the Vietnamese equivalent of the National Guard. Because of the hubbub around him, Mathis almost missed the calls that were actually Viet Cong. He had just rolled onto a freq and had missed the initial call-up, so he couldn't be sure who he was listening to, but the content was definitely significant and operational. The two speakers were discussing ammunition requirements for that night, when they would be going "up." One of the speakers insisted he would need more mortar and RPG rounds. When the other voice asked if Bangalore torpedoes would be needed, the first guy said the wire wouldn't be a problem. They would just cut it or crawl under it. The second speaker promised to get the ammunition that had been requested, and asked that the first speaker meet him tonight at the bottom of the hill "at the usual time and location." They then signed off, and Mathis checked that the tape recorder had been running before ripping off his headphones and shouting at Weller.

"I got it! They're coming tonight."

"What?" Weller complained, looking up from what he had been writing.

"I've got it on tape," Mathis insisted. "They're attacking here tonight."

"Do the transcript," Weller told him. "I've got to finish up this report on Cambodia. It's high priority right now. Might need to be a CRITIC."

Mathis made claws of his hands in frustration. He quickly rewound the tape, jerked the reel off the machine, and took it over to the transcription poz. After threading the tape through the other machine, he pulled on the headphones and began typing. Despite his growing sense of urgency, he reversed the tape every few seconds to hear the phrases again and again, to make sure he was getting the conversation down exactly as it was spoken. He used his dictionary to double-check the translation of several words, noting the various meanings each word could have based on tone and context. There was no doubt in his mind that they were discussing an attack up a hill, and the only "hill" within fifty miles was Nui Ba Den. When he finished typing, he listened to the tape again without stopping, while he read what he had written. It all matched. He pulled the pages out of the typewriter and separated the copies into neat piles. He pulled off the headphones just as Weller handed his completed report to Kelso to start keying.

"So what have you got?" Weller asked tiredly, as the sound of electronic dits and dots filled the room.

"Here," Mathis told him, handing him the white copy of the transcript. "Two guys discussing the ammo needs for the attack up the hill tonight."

Mathis held up a hand for silence as he read through the transcript. "There's no mention of Nui Ba Den here," he commented after finishing.

"There's no other hill or mountain for miles around," Mathis pointed out.

"But it could be skip from somewhere up north," Weller argued.

"It wasn't skip," Mathis insisted. "Wait a minute." He jumped up and ran to the tape rack, pulling out the tape from two days earlier to check the writing on the jacket. "It's the same freq as the one I transcribed before, about assaulting the virgin." He held the tape jacket up for Weller to see.

"Let me listen to this one," Weller said, sitting down at the transcription poz. Mathis put the older tape back and fidgeted while Weller listened and read the transcript again.

"What's going on?" Albertson asked quietly, to avoid disturbing Weller.

"The VC are going to attack us tonight," Mathis whispered hoarsely.

"Where?"

"Here!" Mathis told him. "Right here on Nui Ba Den."

"No shit?" Albertson blurted out, a look of real alarm on his face. "Are you sure?"

"Calm down," Weller said, setting the headphones on the table and turning the chair to face them. "We can't be sure of that."

"What else could it be?" Mathis demanded. His hands were in front of him, shaking and alternately clenching into fists and spreading his fingers.

"I don't know. Let me think about it." Weller picked up the transcript and read through it again, while Mathis shifted his weight from one foot to the other and back, and Albertson tapped his pencil on a legal pad, ready to start composing a report.

Weller put the paper back on the desk and rubbed his eyes with both hands. "Okay. All right. That is certainly one way to interpret this." He pulled his hands from his eyes and placed them in his lap. "But it's not one hundred percent. It could be skip, or maybe there's a hill we don't know about, or maybe they're just, I don't know, referring to something as a hill that isn't. I mean, they don't call it a mountain, and this certainly is a mountain, not a hill."

"Yeah, but. . ." Mathis complained, unsure how to convince Weller of what he was more than certain. "We still need to warn people of the possibility."

"Agreed," Weller said, nodding. "Albertson, start a report. We'll send it up the chain. Tell them it's possible there will be an attack on Nui Ba Den tonight."

"We need to warn the people up here," Mathis said.

"The report will go to Saigon, and they'll sanitize it and send it down to the commander here."

"Yeah, if they agree with our interpretation," Mathis said with disgust. "And even then, it will have to go through USARV, Corps, Brigade, Division, and Battalion before it gets to Captain Ashbrook. That could take several days."

Weller shrugged. "You're right. But what else can we do? I was given very strict instructions about what we can reveal to the commander here. If we even hint to him that we think there might be an attack, he would very reasonably want to know why, and we absolutely cannot tell him how we know. Even if he believed us, he would have to report it up the chain of command, and our real purpose up here would become public knowledge. The Agency would be calling for our heads."

"Aaah!" Mathis groaned, kicking the table leg. "And what about us?"

"Yeah!" Albertson chimed in anxiously.

"We'll just have to take suitable precautions," Weller blithely suggested. "I'm sure Captain Ashbrook has contingency plans for such an attack, and he can call for support from Tay Ninh. With all those bunkers and mines and such, I don't think the Viet Cong could overrun this place. It would just be a probe, I imagine."

Mathis wanted to continue arguing, but knew it was futile. He understood, far better than Weller, the true state of the camp's defenses. He took a deep breath, and sat down at the intercept poz. Jamming the headphones on, he began searching the airwaves for anything that would confirm his belief about the attack, or, perhaps, prove he was worried for no reason.

SEVEN

Burned out and worried, Mathis signed out of the SCIF around four, telling Weller he had to get ready for bunker guard duty, which wasn't entirely untrue. While he and the other ASA guys had been exempted from such duties, he knew that Kasperek had it, and he intended to pull the duty with him. The sense of impending doom had been growing all afternoon, and he just couldn't shake it.

When he came down the aisle of the billet hooch he saw Kasperek stretched out on his bunk, apparently asleep. Mathis came up quietly and laid his helmet and rifle down on his own cot, not wanted to disturb his friend. Without opening his eyes, Kasperek said, "Got off early, huh?" Then he rolled over and sat up, smiling at Mathis.

"Yeah," Mathis told him, "I'm going to take bunker guard with you tonight."

"You don't have to," Kasperek said. "Chuck Yoder's on with me. He's one of the Manchus." The Manchus were members of the Fourth of the Ninth Infantry, guys who were assigned as security up on the rock. Although it was supposed to be a full company of experienced infantrymen, there was only about a platoon-sized element, and they were mostly FNGs, the standard abbreviation for fucking new guys.

"I know," Mathis said, sitting down on the edge of his cot, "but I just think, you know, that maybe I'd like to be in the bunker tonight." Kasperek looked at him with raised eyebrows, but didn't say anything.

"At ease, gentlemen," McDaniel announced as he walked up, as if he were an officer. He smiled broadly as he sat down on Kasperek's foot locker. "About ready for another delicious dining experience?"

Mathis tried to smile back, but the changing expression on McDaniel's face indicated his forced cheerfulness wasn't succeeding.

"Uh, so what's happening?" McDaniel asked, his gaze shifting from Mathis to Kasperek and back.

"Oh, uh, Bill's going to take bunker guard duty with me tonight," Kasperek said lightly.

"He is?" McDaniel exchanged looks with Mathis and Kasperek, and Mathis could see in their eyes they understood what that meant. "Interesting," McDaniel said, chewing on his lower lip. "Did you hear about last night?"

"No, what?"

"The guys at Bunker Fifteen said they heard movement, saw something going on between them and Fourteen. The requested illumination, but didn't get it."

"Why not?" Mathis asked, feeling a little perturbed.

"Don't know. Maybe didn't want to wake up the mortar guys, or maybe didn't believe the guys in the bunker. Nothing else happened, so maybe it was just an animal."

"I've never seen any animals on the mountain," Kasperek said.

"Me neither," McDaniel replied, "but that doesn't mean there aren't any. Lions, or tigers, or bears, oh, my."

"Yeah, right," Kasperek scoffed.

Mathis looked over at the ammo bandolier hanging from the corner of his cot. It was one of the thin green cotton items that came in every can of 5.56 ammunition, a row of six pockets that held one magazine each, with straps at each end that could be tied around one's waist. Mathis' bandolier held only three magazines, the other pockets empty and useless. "I wish I had more magazines," Mathis mentioned conversationally. He raised one eyebrow at McDaniel.

McDaniel nodded. "I could probably find some for you. I'll go look after dinner."

"Thanks," Mathis told him. "No hurry." The tone of his voice, however, betrayed the fact that there was in fact an immediate need. McDaniel's forceful nod showed he understood that need.

"Well," Kasperek said, standing up, "let's go get in line before all the good food's gone."

"There's going to be *good* food?" McDaniel asked with feigned surprise. They all chuckled, but more from force of habit than genuine good humor.

* * *

After dinner McDaniel went back to the SF hooch to look for M-16 magazines, while Mathis and Kasperek got their gear and headed for Bunker Five. Along the way they stopped at the ammo bunker and drew a case of M-79 rounds to keep at the perimeter bunker, "just in case." Due to their having eaten early, they arrived at the wooden building long before sunset, the time they were officially supposed to begin their guard duty. With sunlight streaming in through the gun port and the open door, they did a little cleaning and straightening, pushing the cots to the back and setting the ammo next to the gun port where it would be readily available. Mathis removed the poncho from the machine gun and folded it neatly, and then checked the gun out and fed in a belt of ammo. Nothing was said about why they were doing this; both men were in sync about the sense of danger that hung in the air around them.

A figure momentarily blocked the light coming in the doorway, and Mathis looked up expecting to see McDaniel, but instead there was a short heavy-set soldier in full battle gear.

"Specialist Kasperek?" the guy asked, his young voice querulous.

Kasperek looked up from M-79 ammo box he had just opened. "Oh, hey, Chuck," he greeted the young man.

"I thought it was just you and me in here tonight," the kid said, looking at Mathis.

"Yeah, well, Bill's going to be here, too. Bill, this is Chuck Yoder. Chuck, this is Bill Mathis, one of the ASA guys." Mathis reached out to shake Yoder's hand. Yoder took off his helmet and set it down on the sill of the gun port. He was a PFC, and he looked even younger than he sounded; his black hair, although short, was sticking up in various directions.

"ASA?" Yoder asked, looking at Mathis curiously.

"Army Security Agency," Mathis told him.

"Like MPs?"

"Oh, no. Uh, we make sure communications are secure. You know, checking radios, supplying call signs and code books, shit like that."

"Oh, yeah, sure," Yoder said confidently, although his expression betrayed his confusion.

"Chuck just got here last week," Kasperek explained.

"But I've been in-country nearly three weeks," Yoder boasted. "Went through training at Cu Chi, and orientation at Tay Ninh, before they sent me up here."

Mathis turned away to hide his smirk. Talk about an FNG! But at least, since he was infantry, he should know how to use his weapon.

"So how do you want to work the guard roster tonight?" Yoder asked.

"Since this is Bunker Five," Kasperek told him, "we only have to be on guard until midnight. After that we can sleep here or go back to the billets, whichever. Bill and I plan on staying up all evening, but if you want to hit the rack earlier, that's okay."

"Okay," Yoder said. "I'm not tired, so I'll probably stay up, too."

All three turned as McDaniel appeared in the doorway, his arms loaded down. He pushed into the bunker and dumped his load on one of the cots in the back. He turned to look appraisingly at Yoder, who Mathis saw was staring at McDaniel with a touch of awe, his gaze centered on the green beret McDaniel was wearing.

"Chuck," Mathis said, breaking the spell, "this is Sergeant McDaniel. Two-dan, this is Chuck Yoder, one of the Manchus."

92

McDaniel extended his hand. "Glad to meet you." After a quick shake, McDaniel turned back to the cot and picked up three M-16 magazines to hand to Mathis. "This is all I could find," he said apologetically. Mathis took them, and saw that all three were already loaded with rounds.

"Thanks," he said. Every little bit helps."

"How many mags you got?" McDaniel asked Yoder.

Yoder touched the bandolier tied around his waist, as if mentally counting them. "Uh, six, I guess."

McDaniel nodded. "Usually you infantry guys carry twelve or fourteen in a Claymore bag."

"Yeah, if I was out in the field, I would," Yoder insisted unconvincingly. "But here, not so much."

"I picked up a case of M-79 on the way over here," Kasperek told McDaniel, pointing to the box on the floor.

"Outstanding," McDaniel said approvingly. "I brought you guys something you can use tonight." He retrieved a small black suitcase from the cot, unsnapped the latches, and pulled out a starlight scope. "Know how to use it?"

"I do!" Yoder chirped. "We were trained on it at Fort Polk, and again at Tay Ninh." He reached out and took it from McDaniel, turning it over in his hands as he examined it.

"Good," McDaniel said, "then you can show these two commo pussies." Mathis wasn't offended, because he understood that McDaniel was trying to build up Yoder's confidence and bring him into the team. Besides, McDaniel had shown him and Kasperek how to use the starlight before.

"Hello?" a voice called from outside. There was some scuffling as several men scrambled down the rocky path to the bunker door and crowded inside the small building. Mathis recognized Captain Ashbrook, the company commander, Captain Starr, the executive officer, and a third officer he didn't know. First Sergeant Robinson stayed just outside the door, in deference to the crowded conditions, holding a clipboard. When he got a better look at the third officer, Mathis could see he was a first lieutenant named Gretchen.

"Are you gentlemen all set for the night?" Ashbrook asked pleasantly.

"Yes, sir!" Yoder answered brightly.

"And there's four of you assigned here tonight?" the lieutenant asked dubiously.

"No, sir," McDaniel told them. "I'm just visiting, bringing them this starlight."

"Well, thank you for doing that, Sergeant," the Starr said with false heartiness.

"No sweat, sir. Uh, how can we help you?"

"Oh, we're just following up on the colonel's inspection Saturday," Captain Ashbrook told them. "Looks like you've got things well in hand here." He turned to usher the others out of the bunker. They had to pause while Robinson made some note on his clipboard, and then the group climbed back up the slope and walked away toward the next bunker.

"Good timing for us," Kasperek commented when they were gone. "We were looking pretty good for a change."

"Yeah," McDaniel said. "Most of the other bunkers probably don't have anybody in them yet. Or have guys drinking and smoking."

"Not my problem," Kasperek joked.

Because it was so stuffy in the bunker, all four, at Kasperek's suggestion, went outside and climbed onto the roof of the bunker to sit and watch the sun settle toward the horizon while they talked. As always, the discussion soon turned to rock music. With the officers going around inspecting, Mathis was glad Kasperek had decided to leave his eight-track player back at the billet. Yoder, it turned out, liked country-western music, which the rest of them despised, so after a while he made excuses and went back inside. The other three debated the religious significance of the title and cover for the Rolling Stones' album, *Their Satanic Majesties Request*, reaching no

94

real conclusions and further darkening the mood as they awaited nightfall.

"There it goes," Mathis remarked sadly, watching the glaring orange ball of the sun start to dip below the horizon.

"How sure are you?" Kasperek asked. Mathis knew he wasn't talking about the sunset.

"On paper, maybe fifty percent. But my gut tells me at least ninety-five percent."

"Some of the sidgees are acting goofy," McDaniel noted. "If that means anything."

"Goofy how?" Kasperek asked.

"I don't know exactly. They're always kind of goofy, but today it seemed different. They were cleaning their weapons without being told to. Shit like that."

"You know that one KP with the big ears," Mathis said, "the one that pushes the other KPs around all the time? At chow today he wasn't yelling at them like usual. He was even helping clean the tables."

"Definitely odd," Kasperek agreed. "Maybe he got chewed out after the colonel's visit."

"Maybe."

The conversation lapsed while they watched the upper edge of the sun slide beneath the haze and disappear completely. It was now officially dusk, and Mathis felt a rising sensation of fear, excitement, and gloom starting to surge through his body. It was a bizarre feeling, one he couldn't explain. He felt a tremendous dread of what he was sure was about to occur, but at the same time he looked forward to it. It was kind of like how he felt standing in line before the first time he rode a roller coaster. He wanted to tell his friends about it, but couldn't. It was too personal, and might bring derision.

"I better go jack up the sidgees," McDaniel announced suddenly, rising to his feet. "You guys stay awake tonight."

Mathis stood up as well. "Yeah, I forgot to check mail. I better do that before it gets too dark."

Kasperek remained seated. "Why don't you stop by the club and get us some sodas?" he asked Mathis. "Get one for Yoder, too." Kasperek leaned back so he could dig in his pocket for some crumpled MPC notes.

Mathis waved him off. "I got it. You can pay next time."

Mathis and McDaniel climbed up toward the Pagoda, and then separated as McDaniel went left to go around toward the SF hooch, and Mathis headed across the camp toward the orderly room. He passed between the officers' hooch and generator shed, where the diesel generator was roaring its monotonous song of power, weaving his way between the big rocks that cluttered this side of the camp. On one of the bigger rocks near the orderly room someone had long ago erected a huge wooden cross, now weathered and slightly off kilter. Mathis idly wondered if an American had set it there, or if maybe it was from before the Army had occupied the site, maybe put there by Vietnamese Catholics during the French regime. Regardless, the cross reminded him of his own religious convictions, jumbled as they were. Should he consider himself a Mormon, a Christian, or an agnostic? Did it really matter? As he had been reminded more than once, there were no atheists in foxholes. As long as he believed in God, he should be okay.

When he entered the orderly room, he stamped his boots to get rid of some of the dust, but the soldier behind the desk held one finger up to his mouth in a shushing signal and tilted his head over toward the switchboard, where the lieutenant Mathis had met just a little while ago was holding a telephone handset up to his ear while he punched buttons and plugged wires into the switchboard, saying "Hello?" over and over. Lieutenant Gretchen, Mathis told himself, wondering if the man's name had caused him much grief growing up.

"Just checking mail," Mathis said quietly. The man behind the desk had buck sergeant stripes, but Mathis didn't really know him. The Charge of Quarters, or CQ, for the night. Over at the table sat the CQ runner, reading a comic book. Mathis went to the mail sorter and checked his box, finding it empty.

"Damn it!" Lieutenant Gretchen cursed, slamming the handset down on the small table. "I've got to call Tay Ninh." He stood up and strode toward the door. "I'm going to the commo ops building to see what the problem is," he told the CQ as he left.

"Good luck with that," the CQ said after the officer was gone.

"No comms with Tay Ninh?" Mathis asked him, a touch of worry in his voice.

"Not right now," the sergeant said. "Nothing new. Shit goes out all the time."

Mathis nodded and started to leave, but then stopped. "Flag's still up," he said, referring to the American flag flying on the pole outside the building.

"Craig, go take it down," the sergeant told the CQ runner. It was supposed to come down at sunset, but here on the Rock it was done without ceremony. Craig followed Mathis out of the building and went over to lower the flag. Mathis walked down the path between the billet buildings until he reached the club. When he stepped inside, the cigarette smoke hung like a noxious cloud under the canvas roof, and the rumble of conversation filled the room with a miasma of noise. The TV over the bar was showing an old Jimmy Durante Show rerun that was being ignored by all. Mathis got a Coke, an Orange, and a 7-Up at the bar, putting them in his pants cargo pockets to leave his hands free for his M-16. He was the only one with a weapon, but no one seemed to be concerned, assuming that he was on his way to guard duty. Which he was, he realized. He left the club and made his way back up the hill toward the Pagoda, the SF hooch off to his right, the Operations hooch on his left. When he made his way around the Pagoda, he saw the strobe-like light flickering through the ventilation fan of the SCIF, and wondered if the guys inside were actually intercepting something, or just hanging out. Sergeant Johnson and Farley were on duty tonight, but he doubted Farley was working; he was probably just sleeping with his headphones on, unless Johnson kept after him.

With the sun having dipped below the horizon, the ambient light was fading rapidly. Mathis had to really watch his step as he made his way through the jumble of rocks to the bunker. The lights of Tay Ninh were twinkling on as the vast plain below became shrouded in darkness. Mathis pushed open the door to the bunker, where Yoder and Kasperek were barely visible, sitting on the cots, and he stepped in to prop his rifle against the wall next to the gun port. He passed out the sodas and then knelt at the gun port, staring out at the gathering gloom.

"Anything happening?" Kasperek asked, using his church key to open his soda. He passed the opener to Yoder.

"Not much," Mathis said. "That lieutenant that was here earlier was in the orderly room trying to call Tay Ninh, but couldn't get through."

"Not surprised," Kasperek said. "The multichannel is real sensitive, goes out all the time."

Mathis took the opener from Yoder and punched open his Coke. "Not a good time for it."

"They'll get it working pretty soon, I'm sure," Kasperek said. "And we've got all those VHF radios. It's not like we're cut off or anything."

"I guess," Mathis said. He took a drink and gazed out the gun port, searching the dark shapes of the rocks and bushes just down the slope from him. Nothing seemed out of place or abnormal. Then he heard the distant bangs and rattles of gunfire. ""Someone's shooting," he said, picking up his rifle. Kasperek and Yoder rushed to the gun port. The noises seemed to be coming from somewhere way down the mountain. Mathis could make out single shots and occasionally a staccato burst of automatic fire.

"Sounds like AK's," Yoder said authoritatively, although Mathis wondered how the new guy could possibly know that.

"Pretty far away," Kasperek remarked. "We hear that every once in a while."

"You do?" Mathis asked with a note of disbelief.

"Oh, yeah. I figure they're just testing their weapons, or target shooting. There's no ARVNS or GIs on the mountain other than up here, so they can't be having a firefight."

"Shouldn't we report it?" Yoder asked.

"You can," Kasperek told him. "You'll have to run all the way over to the orderly room, since we don't have a phone here. But they won't do anything about it."

"They won't?"

"What are they gonna do? What can they do? Sure as shit not going to send out a patrol, and can't call in artillery if they don't know where the gooks are."

Although the inside of the bunker was now totally dark, Mathis could tell that Kasperek was looking at him intensely. Despite what he was saying, Mathis suspected that his friend thought that maybe this time they actually should report it.

"Well, maybe we better," Mathis said finally. "Chuck, you want to do it?"

"Sure," Yoder said enthusiastically. He grabbed his helmet and rifle and ran out of the bunker. Mathis and Kasperek didn't say anything when he left, just returned to staring out the gun port at the nearby rocks, and the almost invisible plain sprawled out below.

"Looks like we got a moon tonight," Mathis said after a few minutes.

"Oh, yeah?" Kasperek said, leaning down so he could look up at the sky.

"Behind us," Mathis told him. "If you look real hard, you can see the shadow of the mountain on the paddies." With his finger he drew a triangular pattern in the air, tracing the barely distinguishable outline of the mountain's shadow stretching across the darkened fields and forest below.

After a moment Kasperek said, "Yeah, okay, I see it now. Must be pretty bright tonight."

"Which is good, I guess."

"For us, or them?"

Mathis just shrugged.

Yoder bounced in the door. "Told 'em. They said they had heard about it from other bunkers, too. Wrote it down in the CQ log."

"That's it?" Mathis asked.

"Like John said, there's not much else they can do. Especially with comms down to Tay Ninh."

"Well, we tried," Kasperek said.

EIGHT

"I'm gonna get a Shelby GT350," Yoder declared. The inside of the bunker was now pitch black, although Mathis could barely make out Kasperek's outline at the gun port, silhouetted by the pale blue moonlight and myriad stars outside. Mathis and Yoder were sitting on the cots while Kasperek kept watch. They had been discussing what they all would do once they got back from Nam.

"A Ford!" Kasperek scoffed. "Fix Or Repair Daily. No, I'm getting a Roadrunner. With a four-twenty-six Hemi. Orange, with a black vinyl roof."

"I'm thinking about a Fiat 850 Spider," Mathis said. "Not real fast, but at least it'll turn corners."

"A Fiat?" Kasperek snorted. "Fix It Again, Tony."

"Yeah," Yoder jibed, "I hear they come with a basket on a rope that you drag behind you to catch all the parts as they fall off."

"I said I'm thinking about it," Mathis replied a little defensively. He knew the Fiat's reputation, but he really like the sleek little car's looks. "Or maybe an Austin Healey Sprite," he began, when he stopped at the sound of an explosion.

"What the fuck?" Kasperek yelped.

Mathis felt a lurch in his stomach, and electric current surged through his chest and shoulders. There was another crunching thud, seeming to come from the other end of the camp, followed by a scatter of small arms fire.

"Oh, shit!" Mathis groaned. "It's happening."

"What?" Yoder yelped. "What's happening?"

"It's an attack," Kasperek responded with a note of exasperation. "The VC are attacking the camp."

"Oh, uh, yeah," Yoder sputtered. "So what do we do?"

"You know how to shoot the fifty?" Mathis asked him.

"Kinda, yeah." Yoder jumped over and squatted behind the machine gun, swinging it back and forth on the tripod pintle. "Should I go ahead and start shooting?"

"Cock it first," Mathis said, trying to sound calm. Yoder pulled the charging handle back two times until a round was seated in the chamber. Then he pressed the butterfly trigger with his thumb, and the gun erupted in a pounding beat, spewing bullets down the mountainside in a steady stream. Mathis thumped Yoder on the shoulder until he released the trigger.

"Did you see something?" Kasperek barked.

At the same time, Mathis admonished Yoder, "Short bursts!"

"No! Yes." Yoder was excited and confused.

"Yes, you saw something?" Kasperek asked.

"No, I was just shooting, you know, suppressive fire."

"Okay, okay," Mathis told him, "but remember, just short bursts. And lower your aim. You were just shooting out into the air. If there's any VC out there, they'll be down in the bushes."

"Right," Yoder agreed nervously. "Right. Should I start shooting again?"

"Wait one," Mathis said, listening to the many sounds echoing in the dark outside the bunker. More explosions and rifle fire, sounding like they were at the east end of the base camp, were joined by machine gun and small arms fire coming from other areas. He could also hear shouts and panicked yelling. The bunkers to either side of theirs were silent, which was to be expected; they weren't supposed to be manned until after midnight. Mathis tried to remember what McDaniel had taught them, and what he knew about tactics from reading war novels in high school. None of that seemed to apply to this particular situation. And why, he wondered, was he now in charge? Because, he admitted to himself ruefully, he was the ranking soldier in the bunker.

"Okay," he finally told Yoder, "fire into the bushes, all across our front, short burst of five or six rounds. If anyone's out there, you want to force them to take cover. Roger?"

"Roger," Yoder said, regaining a semblance of confidence. He pulled the box with the M-79 rounds over behind the gun so he had something to sit on, and then began firing the machine gun just as Mathis had told him. The roar of the gun was deafening in the small building, and the reverberations caused a sprinkle of dust to rain from the ceiling. Mathis crouched down behind Yoder to watch the red streaks of the tracers that often bounced up into the sky as they hit rocks and ricocheted. Between bursts he directed Yoder on where to aim next, trying to choose a random pattern that would prevent the VC, if there were any, from predicting the next spray of bullets and thus advance on the bunker. In the back of the bunker he could hear Kasperek rummaging around, looking for more fifty cal ammo. A moment later a heavy metal box was dropped on the floor on the left side of the gun, and Kasperek unlatched the lid.

In the brief respite between burst of machine gun fire, Mathis detected a new sound coming from somewhere behind them. He whacked Yoder on the shoulder and urged him to cease fire for a minute.

"What?" Yoder asked, spinning his head back and forth to look for any incoming threats.

"Listen!" Mathis heard the sound again. It was a distant plonk that was barely discernable above the sound of rifle and machine gun fire. Two seconds later there was loud bang much closer to them. "Is that a mortar?" he asked no one in particular.

"I think so," Kasperek said uncertainly. "Sounds like one. And not one of ours."

They heard footsteps outside, and Mathis grabbed his M-16 and pointed it at the door.

"Bill, John, you in there?" McDaniel's voice was recognizable, despite being much higher pitched than normal.

Mathis released the breath he hadn't realized he had been holding. "Yeah," he shouted with relief. "Come on in."

McDaniel slipped inside, his dark figure briefly outlined by the moonlight outside.

"The shit's hit the fan," he informed them unnecessarily. "You guys okay?"

"So far," Mathis told him. "We been firing the fifty, but haven't really seen anything. What's happening out there?"

"From what I can see, the gooks penetrated up that ravine between Eighteen and Nineteen."

"Where we . . .?" Kasperek started to ask, and Mathis knew he was referring to their little combat patrol and how they had re-entered the camp up that ravine.

"Yep. Same-same. They blasted the bunkers with RPGs, and now they've set up a mortar on the chopper pad. Man, it's a cluster-fuck out there, everyone running around like chickens with their heads cut off."

"Should we keep firing the fifty-cal?" Yoder asked.

"Wouldn't hurt," McDaniel said, "if you've got the ammo. So far they're only attacking at that end of the camp, but God knows what they'll do next."

Yoder grasped the gun's handles and let off burst until the belt ran out and the gun clicked quiet. While he pulled a belt from the new can and set it in the feed tray, McDaniel asked, "Where's the starlight?" Mathis had completely forgotten about it. He rushed over to his cot and fumbled around in the dark until he found the case, unlatched the lid, and pulled the tubular device from the protective foam rubber.

"Here you go," he said, holding it out for McDaniel, who didn't take it.

"Bring it," McDaniel ordered curtly. "Let's go check things out." He opened the door and stepped through, holding it open for Mathis, who took a minute to tie on his bandolier of magazines and plop his helmet on his head before following him with his rifle in one hand the scope in the other. They scrambled up the path toward the Pagoda that loomed directly ahead. Mathis could see the narrow slit of light at the corner of the building that was the window for the SCIF, but as he watched the light went out. McDaniel veered left and approached the near north wall of the Pagoda cautiously, pressing his back against it as he scooted forward to the eastern edge. The three-quarter moon provided just enough light to help Mathis follow him. Between them and the rest of the camp was the Operations building; while situated slightly lower than the Pagoda on the mountain peak, it was high enough that its roof blocked their view. McDaniel moved farther to the left until they could see around the building, and Mathis kept up as best he could. Now that he had a clear line of sight to the east, he caught glimpses of tracers and the brief flash of explosions at the far end of the camp. He heard a noise behind him and spun, bringing up his rifle one handed.

"It's me," Kasperek whispered hoarsely. "Don't shoot."

"What about Yoder?" Mathis asked as McDaniel took the starlight scope from his hand.

""He's okay. I gave him a couple more boxes of ammo, told him to keep shooting." Mathis worried about leaving the young soldier alone in the bunker, but appreciated having his friend beside him even more.

"Over here," McDaniel ordered, moving to a pile of rocks about three feet high. Mathis and Kasperek followed him, and all three knelt down in the dirt to gaze out over the mountain top. From this location they could see virtually the entire camp, which Mathis now realized was shaped something like a human foot. They were located at what would be the ball of the foot, looking down toward the heel. The bunker they had come from was at the big toe, and a glint of water off to the left was at the instep. Rows of buildings-- the billets, club and mess hall—stretched across the sole to their right, with the orderly room being the last structure before the line of bunkers. As far as Mathis could tell, the fighting was so far limited to the heel area, around the helicopter landing pad. There was random firing from many of the perimeter bunkers, but the sound of AK-47s and explosives was so far limited to the chopper pad area.

McDaniel had placed his rifle on a rock and had been scanning the camp with the starlight scope. "Take a look," he said, handing the scope to Mathis. Mathis put his own rifle down so he could use both hands to steady the heavy device. Pushing the eyepiece against his brow to open the shutter, he was briefly blinded by the bright green image. He moved the scope in a circular motion until he was able to find a recognizable reference point, and then shifted the focus to the concrete rectangle of the chopper pad. He could see a number of people moving around in a cluster near the center of the pad. A few feet away from this assembly a smaller group crouched around a mortar tube, and as Mathis watched they fired a round.

"Incoming!" he yelled, and ducked down behind the rocks. McDaniel and Kasperek dropped as well, and the three waited for the round to come down, fearing the worst. With a sigh of relief Mathis heard the mortar round impact somewhere in the middle of the camp, and raised his head just enough to again observe the copper pad. He handed the starlight scope to Kasperek so he, too, could take a look.

"Looks like they're setting up a CP on the pad, along with the mortar," McDaniel said, sounding rather clinical to Mathis. "They've got a team blowing the bunkers. There's white smoke from Nineteen, Eighteen's gone, Seventeen's on fire, and they're hitting Sixteen right now."

"They're waving a flag," Kasperek announced. "Oh, shit! Another mortar!"

Again they ducked down until the round exploded, and this time it was much closer. There was a bright flash and they felt the concussion as the round impacted along the back wall of the Pagoda, only about thirty feet to their right.

"Give me the scope!" McDaniel demanded, reaching across Mathis. Kasperek handed it to him, and McDaniel rested it on a rock while he scanned the camp. Mathis clutched his rifle and peeked around the side of rock, trying to make out what was going on at the far end of the camp. The moonlight helped, but it was still just a jumble of dark shapes outlined against a starry sky, punctuated by tracer rounds and the flames from a burning bunker. A shower of sparks suddenly marked the flight of an RPG which slammed into the side of a bunker, number Fifteen, Mathis thought, and exploded, demolishing the back wall.

"John," McDaniel said urgently, "can you hit the chopper pad with your bloop gun?"

Kasperek rose up enough to look down the slope. "Should be able to," he said doubtfully.

"Do it."

"What about our guys down there?" Kasperek asked plaintively, raising the folding sight and aiming generally down range.

"There's nothin' but gooks down there now," McDaniel assured him. "We need to return fire, disrupt them."

Mathis watched Kasperek try to aim using the sight, but it was too dark for it to help. Finally Kasperek just estimated the range and fired, the explosive pumping sound assaulting Mathis' ear. A moment later they saw the round explode, far past the chopper pad, almost off the far side of the peak.

"Drop fifty," McDaniel said.

Kasperek broke open the gun, and the ejected casing popped out and clattered on the rocks. He pulled another round from his ammo vest and slipped into the wide breech before snapping the gun closed and raising it to his shoulder. Mathis covered his right ear with his hand when Kasperek fired the second time, and then waited for the round to fall. This time he saw a flash at the right edge of the chopper pad.

"Twenty left, fire for effect," McDaniel said, but before Kasperek could respond they heard the crack of incoming rifle rounds splitting the air above them and pinging off the rocks in front of them. All three huddled down behind the rocks, seeking protection from the incoming bullets.

"I think they know where we are," Mathis said blandly, trying to calm his own nerves.

"No shit, Sherlock," McDaniel replied testily.

A mortar round crashed on the roof of the Pagoda, and there was another large explosion from the other end of the camp, but the hail of lead directed at them ended.

"Want me to try again?" Kasperek asked, quickly reloading.

"Wait one," McDaniel said, easing back up to aim the starlight scope at the enemy. "I want to see what they're doing now." Mathis paused to get up his courage, and then slowly repositioned his body until he could see between two rocks. The mortar fired again, but the round fell among the buildings at the center of the camp. Another soon followed, while another RPG round was fired at a bunker on the southeast side of the perimeter. He could see figures darting around, but couldn't tell if they were friends or foes.

"An assault team is moving toward the billets," McDaniel announced. "They're walking the mortar rounds in front of them. I can see our guys running around in their shorts, and no one is returning fire."

"So what do we do?" Mathis asked.

"Shoot back. Looks like no one else is going to do it."

McDaniel laid the scope down on top of a nearby rock and picked up his rifle. "Aim for the pad," he said simply, and began firing single shots in a steady rhythm. Mathis aimed his own rifle as best he could in the dark, firing evenly spaced shots at the concrete rectangle that was barely visible in the dim moonlight. Kasperek launched another grenade before ducking down to reload. Mathis and McDaniel emptied their magazines, and Kasperek got off another round, before again dropping down to reload and avoid the scattered rifle fire that was now directed at their location.

"Are we doing any good?" Kasperek asked.

"Fuck if I know," McDaniel answered dejectedly. He slapped another magazine into his rifle, and Mathis did the same. McDaniel reached up to get the starlight scope, but it suddenly flew over their heads, bounced against a rock, and rolled down at their feet. Even in the minimal light, Mathis could see the lens was shattered.

"What are the fucking odds?" McDaniel cursed, kicking at the now useless object.

108

Anger surged through Mathis at this enemy success, and he rose up and began firing at the distant figures as fast as he could pull the trigger until the bolt locked to the rear, the magazine empty.

"Cool it, John Wayne," McDaniel said, pulling Mathis back down behind the rocks. "We gotta think this through."

"They must have called Tay Ninh for help, right?" Kasperek asked.

"Yeah, but what's Tay Ninh going to do?" McDaniel did not sound hopeful.

"Artillery?" Mathis said, knowing it was wishful thinking.

"They can't drop any rounds on the camp without hitting our own guys," McDaniel explained. "It's too dark to bring in choppers, and they sure as hell can't come up the side of the mountain to rescue us. I think we're on our own."

Another mortar round exploded on the roof of the Pagoda, and Mathis looked up to see the tallest of the antenna masts toppling over and crashing to the ground on the west side of the building.

"Son of a bitch!" Kasperek cursed, rising up enough to pop another M-79 round toward the chopper pad.

Mathis released the empty magazine from his rifle, pulled a full magazine out of his bandolier, and slapped it into place. Releasing the bolt, he edged up until he could just see over the top of the rocks they were behind and tried to make sense of the dim figures and flashes of light spread out before him. Two of the bunkers on the far edge of the perimeter, beyond the chopper pad, were burning, the flames licking the roofs of the wooden buildings and silhouetting the enemy soldiers on the concrete slab. There appeared to be two men operating the small mortar tube, and nearby a cluster of three men consulting and occasionally pointing up toward Mathis. An RPG was launched toward the billet buildings, but there was no explosion. A few seconds later there was a massive explosion over near the reservoir.

"Water purification hut," McDaniel said. Mathis hadn't noticed that McDaniel was now right beside him. "Satchel charge, probably." On his other side, Kasperek popped up long enough to fire another grenade down range. Mathis glanced over at McDaniel, whose blond hair shone in the bluish light of the moon, and became conscious of his own helmet pressing down on his head. With no cloth camouflage cover, the olive drab steel pot, while not shiny, was a readily identifiable feature even in the dark. In addition, it was heavy and had a tendency to fall down over his eyes at inopportune moments. Mathis decided that if McDaniel, a trained Green Beret soldier, didn't feel the need to wear a helmet, then neither would he. He pulled off the metal dome and dropped it to the ground.

"You might need that," McDaniel suggested mildly.

"Fuck it." Mathis responded. McDaniel just shrugged. Kasperek launched another grenade, so Mathis aimed his rifle as best he could and started shooting at the men on the chopper pad. It was too dark for the peep sight to be of any value, so he just looked across the top of the carrying handle and guessed at where the rounds would fall. McDaniel was doing the same, and Mathis grinned with satisfaction when he saw one of the men in what was presumably the command group stumble and drop to his knee. One of the others rushed to the wounded man's aid, while the other shouted orders and fired his AK up at the Pagoda. The men attacking Bunker Thirteen broke off their assault and began firing at the Pagoda area with their AK's, while the mortar team redirected their fire as well. Kasperek fired another M-79 round, and when he ducked down to reload a bullet ricocheted off the top of the rock where he had just been. Mathis and McDaniel both dropped as well, as more bullets snapped overhead, and a mortar round crashed just a few yards in front of their position.

"I think I hear my mother calling me," McDaniel joked. "I'm gonna go see what the sidgees are doing. You coming?"

"I ought to go see what's happening in the radio research room," Mathis told him. The SCIF was his appointed place of duty, after all, although this was hardly a good time to be there.

"I need more ammo," Kasperek said. "I'm going back to the bunker, make sure Yoder's okay."

"Okay," McDaniel said decisively, "meet back here in five minutes. And watch your asses."

The three waited until there was a break in the fire directed their way, and then scuttled away, keeping low and dodging from rock to rock. Mathis went to the Pagoda and rounded the northwest corner of the stone building, coming to a stop below the high slit window of the SCIF.

"Sergeant Johnson! You in there?" There was no immediate answer, and Mathis jumped when a mortar round exploded just around the corner. "Sergeant Johnson! Farley! It's me, Bill Mathis. Are you okay in there?"

"So far," came Johnson's voice. "What the fuck's going on out there?"

"VC are attacking the other end of the camp. They've got a mortar, and a bunch of RPGs."

"They coming this way?"

"Looks like it."

"We've lost all our comms," Farley yelled from within.

"They've knocked down the antennas," Mathis informed them. A mortar round exploded about twenty feet away, between the Pagoda and the bunker where Kasperek had gone, shrapnel and rock chips clattering against the wall of the building above him. Mathis crouched closer to the base of the Pagoda.

"What do we do?" Farley cried.

"Start destroying the documents and equipment," Mathis yelled over the noise of other explosions from down near the billets.

"That bad?" Johnson asked, his worried voice floating through the high window.

"It's that bad. Keep the door locked. I'll let you know when it's safe to come out."

"Roger that," Johnson replied. "What are you going to do?"

"Try and survive," Mathis told him succinctly.

Mathis leaned out from the wall and gazed down the front of the building. The windows and the front door were all shut tight, and he could just imagine the radio operators huddled inside. He

111

hoped they had some weapons with them. He briefly considered knocking on the door to see if they were all right, but worried that someone might be trigger happy. Instead he turned and made his way back to his previous position in the rocks. McDaniel and Kasperek were both still gone, and Mathis suddenly felt very alone and vulnerable. Squeezing into a narrow space between two of the boulders for added protection and a false sense of security, he peered over the top at the chaotic scene down slope.

The mortar had stopped firing, and Mathis could see figures darting forward amidst the billets. While he watched an explosion ripped apart one of the buildings, dust and debris flying into the air. Over on the right, along the perimeter, it appeared the bunkers there continued to be overrun and destroyed as the VC made their way up the southern edge of the camp. Amazingly, some of the buildings still had their electric lights burning, illuminating the soldiers who were running helter-skelter seeking a place to hide, many of them only partially dressed and virtually none carrying weapons. The random shafts of lights through windows, combined with the moonlight and flickering fires, made it almost impossible to distinguish with certainty the nationality of the running men he could see.

One man, who appeared to be wearing shorts and a t-shirt, carried a package in his arms that he tossed into one of the billets and then scampered away. Five seconds later the building erupted in flame and smoke. Mathis brought his rifle to bear, but the man who had tossed the satchel charge had already disappeared. Mathis told himself that if he had known for sure earlier that the man was a Viet Cong, he would have tried to shoot him, but in the confusion that reigned throughout the camp, identifying targets was almost impossible.

Mathis heard some small arms fire to his right, and then a small explosion, like a hand grenade. He stood up to see better, looking along the back of the Pagoda, past the officers' hooch and generator shed, toward the bunker line. What he saw threw him into an even greater panic. Another group of VC had come through the wire and were attacking the bunkers on the southwest side of the camp. Mathis caught fleeting glimpses of small men in shorts carrying rifles and RPG launchers, filtering in through the rocks between the bunkers, meeting little resistance. An RPG was fired, and the generator shed was blasted to bits, causing all the remaining lights in the camp to immediately go dark.

Mathis wanted to go hide somewhere, to just cover his head with his arms and whimper, but knew he couldn't do that and ever live with himself, assuming he lived through this night. He wished McDaniel or Kasperek was there to support him, but they weren't. So he raised his rifle to his shoulder and began firing, anything to try and stop the onslaught of the enemy that had now invaded the camp in at least two places. The destroyed generator shed had caught fire, perhaps from the diesel fuel, and the growing flames helped Mathis identify the Viet Cong soldiers who were now moving toward the officers' hooch. When he began firing at them, they took shelter in the rocks and returned fire. Mathis dropped into a crouch behind a rock himself and pondered his next move as bullets flicked through the air above him.

"Bill!" Mathis recognized Kasperek's voice behind him.

"Over here," Mathis said. Kasperek ran over and slid in the dirt to stop next to him. "They're through the wire over there," he told Kasperek, nodding toward the bunker line to their south. "Just blew up the generator shed."

"They're after the Pagoda," Kasperek asserted. "Have I got a shot?" He raised his M-79 to his shoulder and peeked over the rocks.

"I don't know," Mathis said. "They're like ants, running all over the place. And in the dark, it's too hard to tell the good guys from the bad guys."

"So what do we do?"

Mathis had been thinking about that, and didn't like the answer. "We've got to stop them, somehow. If they take the Pagoda, we're fucked." He looked over at his friend, and even in the semi-darkness, he saw that Kasperek returned his gaze with determination and agreement.

"I've got some canister rounds," Kasperek told him, patting the lumps on his ammo vest. The M-79 grenade launcher had a variety of rounds designed for it, beyond the normal explosive projectile; these included tear gas rounds and canister rounds, which were simply very large shotgun shells filled with BB-sized pellets. Canister was deadly, but only at close range. Mathis knew that if Kasperek was suggesting canister, that meant he was willing to take on the Viet Cong the hard way: face to face.

"That looks like a good spot over there, just below the far corner of the Pagoda," Mathis suggested, rising up just enough to look over the rocks. The enemy was no longer shooting in their direction, he noticed gratefully.

"Right behind you," Kasperek said as both jumped up and bean running toward the south, dodging rocks along the back of the Pagoda. Mathis heard bullets ricochet off the wall of the stone building, and wasn't sure if those were aimed at him and Kasperek, or just general fire aimed at the Pagoda. It didn't matter, he supposed, since he would be just as dead either way if one hit him. When he reached the spot he had intended, he sprawled in the dirt and realized there was far less cover than he had expected. Kasperek hit the ground beside him, and both men flattened themselves as bullets sprayed the rocks in front of them and pinged off the wall of the Pagoda behind them. There was little protection here, and the Viet Cong were far closer than Mathis had expected.

Mathis kept his head down, but raised his rifle and fired blindly over the low stones in front of him. Kasperek rolled onto his side to break open his gun, extract the HE round, and replace it with a canister round. In his mind Mathis ran through all the possible moves they could make, actions they could take, and likely outcomes; all appeared to be suicidal. He had led them to a precarious position where they were pinned down and in danger of being surrounded. From his training, and from his reading of books about historical battles, he knew that the best move tactically was to charge the enemy positions, to disrupt their advance and drive them back with sheer audacity. Knowing the best move and actually doing it were two different things, however.

A sudden burst of machine gun fire from their left startled Mathis and made him flinch as he tried to push his body down further into the ground. Then he noticed the fire wasn't directed at them, and it had a familiar sound to it. Kasperek had also flattened, and they looked at each other for a moment before cautiously raising their heads to take a look.

"Son of a bitch!" Kasperek gulped. "It's Park!"

Fifty feet away the Korean generator mechanic, dressed only in his baggy jeans, held an M-60 light machine gun at his hip as he fired around the corner of the officers' hooch. He was yelling something in Korean, and the tone implied his words were not complimentary. Tracer rounds were bouncing up into the sky from the rocks where the VC were hiding, which meant Mathis and Kasperek were no longer under fire.

"Let's rush 'em," Mathis said, secretly hoping Kasperek would dissuade him. Kasperek looked doubtful, but nodded his head. Without further discussion, both scrambled up into a crouch, looked around for anyone approaching, and then jumped over the rocks and jogged toward the enemy position, firing their weapons and yelling incomprehensibly.

Mathis saw Park look over at them in surprise, and then grin viciously and resume firing his machine gun, the belt of ammo feeding from a box clipped to the side of the gun. Mathis couldn't run, not only because of his innate terror, but also because the ground was so rough he had to pick his way among the rocks. Nonetheless, he kept up his barrage, firing sporadically at any suspicious lump in the terrain. Simultaneously, he made sure he didn't get ahead of Kasperek, who was firing canister rounds as fast as he could load them, which, admittedly, was not all that quick. As they came abreast of Park, he too began moving forward, still screaming imprecations over the pounding of the machine gun. Mathis noticed that Park was barefoot, and briefly wondered if the man's anger was due to the destruction of his generator, or just a general antipathy toward the communists.

When they reached the cleared area in front of the burning generator shed, the Viet Cong soldiers broke and ran, two running off to the right along the bunker line, and a third darting left to put the shed between himself and his attackers. Mathis fired at the two headed west, and saw one of them stumble before they disappeared behind more rocks. He turned to see Kasperek searching his ammo vest for more canister rounds, and Park shuffling more to the left, trying to spot the third VC. He heard what sounded like an M-16 firing, probably from one of the bunkers over there, and then the Viet Cong soldier swerved into view, apparently avoiding whoever was shooting over there. That was just what Park had been waiting for, and his machine gun erupted in a spray of bullets that almost cut the communist soldier in half, his body flopping onto the path like a broken doll. Park grunted in satisfaction, and then turned and nodded at Mathis and Kasperek, implying a job well done.

"I'm out of canister," Kasperek said.

Mathis released the empty magazine from his M-16 and reached for a full one. He patted the empty pockets of the bandolier until he found a magazine, realizing it was the only one left. "This is my last mag," he told Kasperek while he slipped it into the magazine well.

"Maybe the guys in that bunker have some," Kasperek suggested, pointing at the bunker on the other side of the generator shed, the one from which someone had fired an M-16 a few seconds earlier. Mathis looked around, and saw Park ambling back toward the officers' hooch. Beyond Park there were more explosions and small arms fire over toward the center of the camp, where all the billets were. Then a blast ripped through the Ops building, near where they had been only a few minutes ago. That was also where the ammo bunker was located, so their access to that was probably cut off.

"Let's hope so," Mathis said, leading the way to the bunker, whose roof was level with the path they were on. ""Don't shoot," he warned as they crept down toward the door in the side of the bunker.

"Halt!" a squeaky voice ordered from inside. "Who goes there?"

Mathis burst out laughing, the tension that had been building inside of him released in millisecond by the inane question.

116

"Nobody really says that anymore," he admonished between gales of laughter, bending over to catch his breath.

Behind him Kasperek was laughing as well, yelping "Who goes there?" in a puny mocking voice.

"Joe DiMaggio," Mathis managed to finally announce. "John Wayne. Don't ask me who won the pennant, because I fuckin' don't care about baseball."

The door of the bunker slowly swung open, and a scared voice apologized. "Sorry. We're kind of nervous in here."

Mathis scrambled down the slope and pulled the door open wider, stepping aside to make room for Kasperek. "How many guys you got in here?" Mathis asked, peering into the dark shadows of the bunker. Only then did he notice that the opposite wall of the bunker was missing, along with part of the front wall.

"There's three of us," the guy at the door said. "Alive, anyway. Another guy is dead."

Another voice from inside the bunker informed them, "A couple guys went out to hide in the rocks down by the wire. They didn't have weapons."

"What's going on out there?" a third voice asked.

"Gooks in the wire," Mathis said succinctly. "There's a bunch of them. They've got a mortar down at the chopper pad, and they're blowing the shit out of all the buildings. You guys got any extra ammo?"

"We got fifty-cal," the guy at the door said. "Our gun is jammed, so we can't use it."

"How about 5.56, or M-79?"

The guy shook his head and held up his M-16. "I've got a few rounds left in this mag, and then I'm out. We don't have any M-79."

"Fuck!" Mathis cursed quietly.

"I've got more at our bunker," Kasperek said, "mostly frag, a little canister."

117

"Better than nothing, I guess," Mathis told him. "But I need rifle rounds."

"What should we do?" the bunker guy asked plaintively.

"Stay here, I guess," Mathis told him. "If things ever get organized, we'll let them know you're here. But without ammo or weapons, you can't really help."

"Wanna try the ammo bunker?" Kasperek asked Mathis.

Mathis shrugged. Above them the firefight raged on, the rattle of gunfire punctuated by frequent explosions. There seemed to be no place safe on the mountain peak, and climbing down the mountain was out of the question. Maybe the guys in the bunker had the right idea, he thought. Just hide and wait it out. But there was a whole night ahead until there was a possibility of rescue or relief, which gave the gooks plenty of time to hunt them all down one by one. He and Kasperek could continue to fight back, but that put them at even greater risk of being killed or wounded, and for what? The camp was in total chaos, resistance to the incursion was sporadic at best, and as far as he knew, there was no viable defensive plan in place; therefore, the chances of driving the Viet Cong away were so slim as to be nonexistent. In other words, there was no good option, just a range of bad ones. He decided to keep fighting. At least then he would have something to be proud of, should he survive, and also have the satisfaction of taking a few of the gooks with him if he didn't.

"Yeah," Mathis finally said, "we can try the ammo bunker. If the gooks haven't gotten there first." Since they had seen the Ops building destroyed, and the ammo bunker was right next to it, he wasn't optimistic.

The two of them climbed up from the semi-destroyed perimeter bunker and found the path that led past the burning generator shed toward the ammo bunker, located between the officers' hooch and the now-destroyed operations building. The flames lit them up and made them perfect targets, so they ran in a crouch as bullets whizzed past them and pranged into the nearer rocks. The rounds were coming from several different directions, and Mathis wondered how many of them were fired by antsy

118

American soldiers shooting at anything that moved. They reached the dubious shelter of the partially destroyed officer hooch, pausing there in the lee of one of the remaining walls to let the incoming rifle fire die down. Somewhere on the other side of the hooch Mathis heard the distinctive chatter of an M-60, and surmised that Park was still taking on all the Viet Cong by himself.

Kasperek nudged Mathis to let him know he was ready, and together they sprinted across the rough ground to the ammo bunker, a low rectangular concrete structure with sloped sides. They plopped down on the south wall and looked around to assess the situation. The door to the bunker was on the west side, at the bottom of a staircase cut into the rock; if they could get there, they would be relatively safe from direct fire.

"I'll go first, and cover you after I get there," Mathis told Kasperek, getting into a sprinter's crouch. Before he could launch himself around the corner of the bunker, however, he saw something out of the corner of his eye: a small black cylindrical object that spun through the air from the east side of the bunker and clattered into the stairwell. Two seconds later there was an explosion that erupted from the stairwell, sending smoke and shrapnel flying. A Chinese Communist hand grenade, he realized, one that must have been thrown by someone very close.

"Shit!" he cursed, settling back against the rough concrete.

"We can't stay here," Kasperek insisted, pointing his M-79 at the southeast corner of the bunker. That's not going to help, Mathis thought, since Kasperek only had grenade rounds, useless at close range. But if that's all you have, then that's what you use.

"Back to Bunker Five," Mathis urged. At least there Kasperek could get more ammo, and maybe Yoder would give up some of his to Mathis.

"Which way?" Kasperek asked anxiously.

Mathis took a quick look to his left, but didn't see any movement along the east wall of the Pagoda, which was squarely between them and their bunker. He had to assume that some of the Viet Cong who had infiltrated between Seven and Eight were now approaching the south side of the Pagoda, so that route was out of the question.

"Back around the north side of the Pagoda," he told Kasperek. "We'll see if Two-dan is back where we were before. You ready?"

"Roger that," Kasperek affirmed.

Together they rose and sprinted for the jumble of rocks between the Pagoda and the now-burning ops building. Bullets split the air around them with nasty cracking noises. Mathis felt something catch his shirt-tail, and glanced back to see if Kasperek had tugged on it for some reason. Kasperek was two steps back and concentrating on studying the ground ahead as he ran, so it wasn't him. Mathis dismissed it from his mind; reaching the shelter of the rocks was his only priority now.

NINE

"Yoder!" Mathis called quietly. He and Kasperek were hunched down just above the bunker, trying not to draw the attention of any Viet Cong that might be in the area. Here on the west side of the peak the flickering light of the buildings that were burning was blocked by the Pagoda, so they had only the moon and stars to illuminate the rugged terrain. There were rifle shots and small explosions up around the Pagoda, but the bunker line here was strangely quiet.

"Yoder!" Kasperek said, louder than Mathis had done. "It's us. You in there?"

There was no answer. The door to the bunker was closed, but no machine gun fire emanated from the gun port. Feeling exposed, Mathis eased down the path to the door, sensing Kasperek right behind him. There was a wide area of flat dirt around the side of the bunker to allow the door to swing open, and Mathis pressed his back against the wall to the left of the door and motioned for Kasperek to slide past him and take a position on the other side. Kasperek obviously knew what Mathis intended, and reached across the door for the handle. He waited a moment while Mathis turned to face the door with his M-16 held ready at waist level. Mathis gave Kasperek a sharp nod, and Kasperek pulled the door open with a jerk.

Slowly swinging the barrel of his rifle from left to right, Mathis waited a few seconds for any response, but the inside of the bunker was deathly quiet. The fifty-cal machine gun, partially blocking what little moonlight seeped in through the gun port, sat unmoving and silent. "Yoder?" Mathis called out softly. There was no reply. He eased into the room, searching the barely-discernable shapes that littered the floor, but saw nothing that raised any alarm. There was something on one of the cots at the back of the bunker, but he couldn't tell what it was. Behind him Kasperek slipped into the room and fumbled for something laying on one of the two-byfours that formed the framework of the building. A soft click, and then a weak beam of yellow light sprang into life. Kasperek had found the bunker's flashlight, complete with dying batteries.

"Where'd he go?" Mathis asked rhetorically as Kasperek played the flashlight beam around the room, revealing only a pile of blankets on the cot and a glittering carpet of spent brass machine gun shells on the floor. Brushing the shells out of the way with his foot, Kasperek walked over and used the flashlight to examine the machine gun and the empty ammo cans beside it.

"He used up all the ammo," Kasperek said. "Maybe he went to get more."

"He won't be able to get in the ammo bunker," Mathis pointed out.

"Then maybe he'll come back here. Or not."

Both men froze when they heard the sound of boots on the path outside.

"Anybody in there?" McDaniel called out quietly.

"That you, Two-dan?" Mathis said with relief.

"Affirmative." McDaniel stepped in and looked around. Kasperek swept the flashlight around the room quickly to show McDaniel who and what was there, and then flicked the switch off. "Where's the other guy?" McDaniel asked.

"Don't know," Mathis admitted. "Maybe went to get more fifty-cal ammo."

"Won't help. The gooks are all inside the camp, and the fifties all point outside. I'm telling you guys, we are royally fucked."

"Some more came in over by Bunker Eight," Kasperek said. "We shot at 'em, but they were all over the place."

"Yeah," Mathis said, "and Park was there with his M-60, smokin' their asses. There's a bunch of guys hiding out in Eight, even though it's half destroyed. They don't have weapons or ammo."

122

"There's a lot of that going around," McDaniel said with disgust. "Bunkers abandoned, no one shooting back hardly. What a cluster-fuck."

"Any chance of help from the flats?" Mathis tried to keep his voice calm, but even he detected the squeakiness of fear.

"I heard some explosions down the hill a ways, might be arty from Tay Ninh, but what the fuck good does that do?"

"Yeah," Kasperek groaned. "They can't shoot up here without hitting us, and they can't bring in choppers in the dark."

"Not to a hot LZ," McDaniel agreed. "All we can do, I guess, is try to hold on until morning. What time is it now?"

Kasperek flicked on the flashlight to look at his watch. "Just after ten."

"Shit! Gonna be a long night."

"So what do we do meanwhile?" Mathis asked. He despised the whininess of his own voice.

"We gotta regroup and consolidate," McDaniel said authoritatively. "United we stand, and all that shit. Let's head to the SF hooch, join up with the rest of my guys, and find a place to make a stand."

"What about this bunker?" Kasperek asked. "Don't we need to man it?"

"What for? The gooks are all behind the bunkers now, not out front."

"Yeah, I guess so. But I need to get more ammo first." Kasperek found the M-79 ammo crate knelt down to replenish the rounds in his vest.

"I need more ammo, too," Mathis said. "I'm down to my last mag. And there's none here."

"There's some at our hooch," McDaniel assured him. "Come on, John, step it out. Time's awasting."

Kasperek rose as he stuffed the last shell into one of the pockets on the vest. "I'm getting mostly canister. Looks like that's what I'll be needing most."

"You got that right," McDaniel said. "So let's go."

They emerged from the bunker and cautiously crept up the path until they could see the Pagoda. Mathis noticed how dark and quiet the building was, and wondered if it had been taken by the Viet Cong. As if in answer, an RPG flared to life over to his right and streamed through the night leaving a trail of sparks and smoke before slamming into the front wall of the Pagoda, just a couple feet from the front door. Mathis ducked down, but not before the flare of the explosion partially blinded him for a minute. Beside him McDaniel rose up and snapped off a few rifle shots toward the area from which the RPG had been launched.

"Did you get him?" Mathis asked, blinking and squeezing his eyelids to try and restore his night vision.

"Doubt it," McDaniel said. "Fuckers are too quick."

"Building look's okay," Kasperek said. Mathis stared at the front of the Pagoda, willing his eyesight to clear. Aside from some smoke drifting away, he could see no damage from the RPG. Which wasn't surprising, he realized, since the Pagoda was built of stone and concrete, materials fairly impervious to the small shaped charge of an RPG, which was designed to penetrate a sheet of steel.

"Good thing it didn't hit the door," Mathis noted. "That could've fucked up their whole day." He was referring to the guys inside, and he was glad it wasn't him that was trapped inside that building, fortress though it might be. He wondered what weapons they had inside, fearing that there were probably very few. At least Sergeant Johnson and Farley, in the SCIF, had their rifles; it was one of the security measures that Mr. Weller had insisted upon. He had even hinted that should any of the ASA guys end up in a situation where they might be captured, they should avoid being taken alive. As far as Mathis knew, no one had taken that suggestion seriously.

With his night vision slowly returning, Mathis gazed at the dark shape of the Pagoda, outlined by the firelight from the middle of the camp, the three-quarter moon rising behind it, and the pinpoints of stars twinkling overhead. He blinked when he saw something he wasn't expecting. A small rectangular object rose in the air from behind the Pagoda, trailing some kind of loop. Tumbling through the air, it hit one of the few remaining antenna masts, and the loop caught on one of the cross-arms, causing the object to twirl around the mast, jerk to a halt, and swing slowly just above the roof. "Satchel charge!" Mathis guessed loudly, and ducked down while shutting his eyes. McDaniel and Kasperek understood and did the same, and just in time. A powerful blast of sound ripped through the air, and Mathis felt the shock wave wash over him. He looked up to see the antenna mast tottering and then crashing to the roof like a fresh-cut tree.

"Let's get out of here," McDaniel urged, rising to a crouch. Kasperek and Mathis followed as the athletic Green Beret soldier darted from rock to rock, following the line of bunkers to their left and maintaining a safe distance from the embattled Pagoda on their right. While they circled around the shoulder of the peak, Mathis kept glancing to his right at the many fires that now burned in the center of the camp. It looked like all the buildings were either on fire or knocked flat, and small figures danced between the flickering flames like devils in a Hieronymus Bosch painting, throwing satchel charges and firing their assault rifles. The Viet Cong were everywhere, it seemed, and only this small northwestern corner of the camp remained in American hands. Mathis had to really struggle to tamp down the rising panic he felt. They were trapped on a mountain top, surrounded and infiltrated by a ruthless foe known for his skill at night operations, and had no chance for rescue until morning. It was a recipe for terror.

Just as they passed above Bunker Three, a flash from down the hill signaled another RPG launch, one that struck Bunker Two and blew the roof off. Mathis hoped there was no one in that bunker at the time. He dived to the dirt behind a rock, and saw McDaniel and Kasperek take cover together behind a larger outcropping.

"Fuck!" McDaniel cursed in a hoarse whisper. Mathis felt the same way. Just when they thought they were avoiding the enemy, he suddenly appeared in a new location. Mathis raised his head just enough to see over the rock in front of him, and saw several figures

125

darting up the hill past the destroyed bunker. Small men in shorts and sandals, some with white shirts, others with packs on their backs, were scrambling up the side of the hill in the direction of the Pagoda. Most carried AK-47s, but one had an RPG launcher. Mathis counted six men, but there could have been some he missed in the dark. He ducked his head, glad that so far he had not been seen by the men running up the path that crossed in front of him, but he could still hear them chattering away in Vietnamese. One even had a transistor radio on, blaring the discordant tones of local music. He could pick out only a few of the words they were speaking, which seemed to be mostly directions and encouragement. He looked over at his friends, and McDaniel gave him a patting motion with his hand, indicating he should stay down. Mathis had no trouble complying with that request.

Praying that this new group of enemy soldiers would quickly pass, Mathis hugged the ground and fought down his fears. Unfortunately, he heard the squad stop and the leader order the others to quiet down. Then one of the Viet Cong shouted out in Vietnamese, "We are here!"

From somewhere on the other side of the Pagoda a voice yelled, "Why are you so late?"

The nearer voice replied, "Jacques hurt his ankle. He went back down."

Jacques?! Mathis wondered about that for a moment, and then decided the man must have had a French father back in the fifties. He also marveled at the lack of noise discipline the Viet Cong were displaying. Apparently they were so sure of their success they saw no need to be discreet.

"Send three men to the west," the distant voice ordered. "Destroy those bunkers and then attack the stone building from that side."

"Understood," the nearby leader answered, and then named the men who were to carry out the order. Now Mathis was really worried, for those three men would have to pass very close to him and the other two, if not right through them. He looked over at the huddled dark shapes of McDaniel and Kasperek. Kasperek had not understood the Vietnamese, and showed no different reaction than the ongoing concern for his own safety. McDaniel's eyes, however, were wide with worry, and he and Mathis stared at each other, trying to mentally convey some plan of action.

"This way," a voice said in Vietnamese, the scuffling of sandals signaling the approach of the three men designated to attack the bunkers. Mathis, McDaniel, and Kasperek were directly between the Viet Cong and bunker three, their apparent first target.

"They're coming!" McDaniel whispered to Kasperek, and signaled to Mathis by raising his rifle. Mathis understood. They had no choice but to jump up and start shooting, knowing it would give their position away. Mathis nodded and drew up his knees in preparation for a scramble to his feet.

"Now!" McDaniel shouted, and Mathis pushed himself erect, holding his M-16 at his waist and searching the darkness for a target. A few feet away the first of the Viet Cong stopped in his tracks, astounded by the sudden appearance of armed Americans jumping up from the rocks. Mathis pulled the trigger, and then again and again, firing from the hip but not knowing where the bullets were really going. Kasperek moved up on his left side and fired his M-79 from the shoulder, the blast of canister pellets hurling forward like a deadly hailstorm. Just beyond Kasperek McDaniel stood shoulder to shoulder, sighting down the barrel of his M-16 as he pulled off round after round in metronomic rhythm. Mathis had only a vague mental image of figures behind the first man diving to the ground, because the first man was still standing, his AK half raised, while his body jerk and juddered from the blows of multiple bullets. Finally he just collapsed in a heap, at the same time Mathis felt his bolt lock to the rear, signaling that his gun was empty.

Kasperek was nervously inserting a fresh round into his M-79, and McDaniel had stopped firing to look for a fresh target. Mathis felt helpless, standing exposed, with no ammunition for his rifle. He scanned the jumble of rocks in front of him, looking for any movement. Maybe they had killed all three men, he told himself without conviction. Beyond the fallen Viet Cong the Pagoda provided a black backdrop that made distinguishing the shapes before him difficult. The moonlight helped, though, and Mathis saw

127

a silvery shape rise from behind a cairn, a long tube with a bulbous end perched on the figure's shoulder, aimed right at him.

"RPG!" Mathis shouted, diving to his right and banging his knee as he sought shelter in the rocks. He felt more than saw that Kasperek and McDaniel had jumped the opposite direction, just before the rocket was launched. At this range it was only a split second between the firing of the rocket and the blast when it hit the rocks where Mathis had been standing only moments before. He had closed his eyes, but still saw red when the round exploded; worse, he was buffeted by the concussion of the explosion and felt something hit the side of his head like he had been swatted with a baseball bat. He blacked out.

He didn't know how long he had been unconscious, but it didn't seem to have been more than a minute. He found himself lying on his back, staring up at the stars, which were revolving disconcertingly in the sky, making him dizzy. He shut his eyes, but it didn't help—he felt the earth turning beneath him, and mental images were whirling through his mind. Blindly he stretched out his left hand and grabbed at the ground, trying to reassure himself the mountain wasn't actually moving. Compounding his discomfort, his ears rang with a high-pitched whine that blotted out all other sounds. He thought he heard someone call his name, but didn't know how to respond; his lips were dry and his tongue was stuck to the roof of his mouth. Opening his eyes again, he saw the pinpoints of light spinning like they were in a whirlpool, and his head felt like it was stuffed with helium, trying to float away. Quickly he squeezed his eyes shut again and lay as still as he could, hoping that would calm the turmoil.

Mathis jerked awake. How could he have fallen asleep? Where was he? His momentary disorientation fled as his memory returned with a rush. He was still lying in the dirt, but the stars were no longer in motion above him. Looking down along his nose, he could see the moon glowing brightly, and he noticed that the shrill whine in his ears had faded, although not completely disappeared. He lifted his head from the dirt, hoping to look around himself, but the movement sent his brain roiling and the sky spinning again, so he slammed his eyes shut and dropped his head back into the dirt. The motion had also caused an intense throbbing on the side of his head, just above his left ear. He willed the dizziness to go away, with limited success, and reached up to gingerly touch the side of his head with his fingertips. Wincing, he found that even the slightest pressure on his scalp sent flashes of pain throughout his body, and his fingertips were now wet and sticky.

"Shot in the head," he whispered. "Now I'm really fucked."

Despite the pain and his own misgivings, he gently probed around his head, trying to determine the extent of the damage. The soft exploration revealed a huge swelling under his hair, one with a small hole in the center that was still leaking blood, albeit at a very slow rate. Wiping his hand on his pants leg, and keeping his eyes shut, he slowly raised himself to a sitting position. With some surprise, he noticed he still clutched his rifle in his right hand, useless though it might be. His head still swam, so he kept his eyes closed as he waited for the nausea and vertigo to abate. Meanwhile, he felt the drip of blood on his left ear, so he slowly tilted his head over to keep it from running inside.

"Where are the guys?" he wondered aloud, keeping his voice to what he hoped was a whisper. In the back of his mind the fact that he was talking to himself seemed a little disturbing, but he couldn't help it. "Did they get hit? Guys? You there?" There was no answer, but he was now aware of the ambient noise, such as it was. There was scattered small arms fire, seeming to come from far away, and occasional explosions, so the battle for the camp raged on. "I need to help. I need ammo." Mathis opened one eye for a second, to judge the effect. Things were still moving around him, but now at a much slower pace. He opened both eyes and watched the nearby rocks and the distant stars and moon waver back and forth, not really staying in one place, but not totally spinning away either.

Gathering his legs beneath him, Mathis rose to a standing position, but immediately sat down hard on a nearby rock. He was still too unsteady to be walking, but he knew he had to move somewhere, although he wasn't sure where. "Okay, what do I do now?" He looked around, ignoring the apparent motion of his surroundings, and considered his options. To his right the dark bulk of the Pagoda loomed, and occasional shots from that direction told him it was still under siege. He faced down the hill toward the rest of the camp, where he could see damaged buildings, many of them on fire; one exploded as he watched. On his left should have been McDaniel and Kasperek, but in the foreground there was nothing but rocks and dirt. Further away was the SF hooch, a large rectangular shape at the edge of the peak, around which he caught the occasional flash of tracers, some red, some green. That was where they were headed when the RPG hit, he remembered. "Maybe I should go there, too."

Using his rifle like a cane, Mathis pushed himself back up and paused to let things settle down. Unsteadily he began shuffling forward, struggling to maintain his balance as he maneuvered between the rocks on the narrow path that led to the SF hooch, wondering what he would do when he got closer. The hooch seemed to be under attack, so how could he slip through the enemy lines without getting shot by either side? "Something will turn up," he told himself. And something did, but it wasn't good.

Mathis had closed to within fifty yards of the hooch when a whooshing noise erupted on his right and an RPG streamed through the air toward the building. The rocket hit a big butane tank positioned against the south wall, and the flash of flames seared Mathis' eyes a split second before the pressure wave hit him and knocked him to his ass. Blinking rapidly to clear his vision, Mathis watched the SF hooch go up in flames. It was like the time his dad had put too much lighter fluid on the barbecue before tossing a lit match at it. The fire engulfed the hooch in an instant, and he could see figures jumping from windows and running out the door as rifles fired in every direction.

"Fuck me!" Mathis complained quietly. Still sitting in the dirt, a sharp rock poking him in the ass, he released the magazine from his rifle and checked it. It was still empty. He patted his bandolier, and found only two magazines, both equally empty. He wondered if McDaniel and Kasperek had been in the SF hooch when it was hit, and if so, had they escaped. He wanted to go look for them, but walking around with an unloaded gun was hardly a good idea. He had to get ammo somewhere. The ache in his head suddenly flared, and he grabbed his forehead and squeezed his eyes shut until the pain subsided again. He needed medical attention, too, he realized.

"There's first aid stuff in the orderly room," he reminded himself out loud. "Maybe some ammo, too." Now he had a purpose, a destination that might solve his problems. His thinking was still muddled, but he was pretty sure that going to the orderly room might provide some solutions. He staggered to his feet and turned around to face the south side of the camp. "How do I get there from here?" he asked. To his right sat the Pagoda, still under attack. Directly ahead was the Ops building, now burning fiercely, and beyond it the officers' hooch, broken and half collapsed. Between them was the ammo bunker. Further to the left was the line of billets, some burning, none intact, with rifle fire scattered throughout. He would have to go east first, passing by the mortar pit, then turn south past the showers, picking his way along the path between the rocks and avoiding the enemy as best he could. "It's now or never," he encouraged himself, and began stumbling toward the distant burning buildings, his head fuzzy and his balance intermittent.

TEN

The mortar pit was silent and untouched. Beyond it the SF hooch crackled and popped as the flames devoured the building and set off stray rounds of ammunition inside. The combination of moonlight and firelight showed that the mortar was still covered with canvas; no attempt had been made to use it against the Viet Cong who were ravaging the camp. Mathis sat down on a rock at the edge of the shallow depression, striving to clear his brain of the nagging pressure and drift that kept him from thinking clearly. Scattered images of his friends Kasperek and McDaniel flitted through his mind; he wondered where they were, but shied away from accepting the possibility that they had been killed. He reconsidered the advisability of searching for them, but had no idea where to start, and the sound of shots around the burning buildings made the prospect too risky for someone who was essentially unarmed. No, the orderly room was the best bet, he decided. If there were an organized resistance effort in the camp, surely it would be centered there.

Back on his feet, he turned south, picking his way along a meandering path lit by the flames of the Ops building on his right and the burning billets on his left. Ahead was a pile of broken lumber and corrugated tin, and it took Mathis a few seconds to realize the heap had formerly been the camp's showers. Even that innocuous building had been blown up in the Viet Cong's frenzy of destruction. When he came abreast of the shattered remains, he could see the glint of water spewing in the air from a broken pipe. The stream of water somehow reminded him of his head wound, and he reached up and touched it, harder perhaps than he had intended. His finger was like a butcher knife, making him jerk his hand away like he had touched a hot stove. A wave of nausea overcame him and he stepped backwards, dropping his rifle and sitting down hard in the dirt. With his left hand clenched in a fist, he rubbed the right side of his head with his other hand as hard as he could, trying to

132

somehow ameliorate the throbbing pain on the left side. His eyes were shut, his teeth clenched, and his lips open as he sucked air in, willing the pain and dizziness to go away.

Drawing up his knees, Mathis crossed his forearms over them and laid his head down, tilting it to the left to avoid putting any more pressure on his wound. He remembered how he had learned to sleep in that position when he was in basic training, and wished he could do so now. The throbbing was too great for sleep, however, not to mention the ongoing battle for the mountain top. Gradually his equilibrium returned, so he took a deep breath, slid one knee beneath him, and wriggled to his feet, seeing the distant fires rotate slowly around him as his dizziness came back. Closing his eyes to shut out the apparent motion around him, he remembered his rifle was lying somewhere on the ground nearby. Keeping his eyes closed, he cautiously squatted down and probed his surroundings with his hands, brushing his fingers over dirt and rocks as he felt for metal and plastic. He was thinking that maybe when he found his rifle, he would go over and duck his head under that stream of water; that would wash his wound, cool his head, and offer him a much-needed drink.

He had just found the smooth surface of his rifle's stock when someone slammed into him and both went sprawling in a tangle of arms and legs. "Hey! Watch it!" Mathis was furious, opening his eyes to see what fool had just bowled him over. What he saw sent a surge of adrenalin through him. A young Vietnamese man was scrambling to his knees, the long tube of an RPG launcher clutched in one hand. Dressed only in khaki shorts, barefoot, he had a pack on his back that appeared to contain a couple RPG rounds. With the agility of a gymnast the boy—for he appeared to be in his teens— leaped to his feet and faced Mathis in a crouch, his eyes wide with fear and surprise. Mathis bounced up as well, and the two faced each other for moment without moving, neither sure what to do next.

Mathis saw the soldier take a deep breath, obviously preparing to shout for help, and he knew he couldn't let that happen. Jumping forward, he grabbed the boy's neck with his left hand and clamped his right over the kid's mouth, pushing him backwards until he tripped and both fell to the ground, Mathis still desperately clutching at the boy's head. Mathis heard the RPG launcher clatter on the rocks when the kid released it, and then felt blinding pain as the boy's now-empty right hand slapped the side of his head, right where he had been wounded. Roaring in pain and anger, Mathis slammed the boy's head against the ground and rolled over on top of him, trying to slam his knee into his opponent's groin.

With his left hand the kid reached up and scraped the side of Mathis' face, first trying to poke him in the eye, and then grabbing his right ear. He pulled and twisted at the ear, and Mathis instinctively rolled to the right to relieve the intense pain and break the kid's hold. As soon as Mathis was off him, the boy jumped to his feet and turned to run, but Mathis's left hand shot out and grabbed a thin ankle, sending the boy sprawling on his face. Mathis scrambled after him, leaping onto his back and grabbing him around the neck. The RPG rounds in the boy's backpack pressed against Mathis' chest, and he suppressed a thought about what would happen if one of them exploded, concentrating instead on his grip around the boy's thin neck. The Viet Cong child warrior clawed at Mathis' hands, his body squirming beneath Mathis' superior weight, but Mathis was relentless. With strength and ferocity he didn't know he possessed, Mathis dug his fingers into the skin and muscle of the boy's throat. His fingertips could feel the cartilage of a windpipe, and he tried to press it closed while maintaining the pressure on the sides of the kid's neck, remembering something he had read about carotid arteries there.

Mathis was now driven by powerful emotions—fear, anger, frustration, pain, and unfocused hatred. In the last hour his home, such as it was, had been attacked and violated, his friends and acquaintances killed, wounded, or missing, he personally had been wounded, and he wasn't going to get any sleep tonight. It was just too damn much. He squeezed even tighter, feeling the body under him begin to relax and then go limp entirely. Nonetheless, he kept throttling the boy until his fingers ached. Finally he let off on the pressure slightly, just to see what would happen. And nothing did. The boy didn't gasp for air, or moan, or show any other signs of life. Mathis released his hold entirely and flexed his fingers to relieve the stiffness. With a sigh he rolled off the body and lay on the ground

134

beside it, staring up at the stars. Idly he began counting the stars as he slowed his breathing, studiously avoiding any thoughts about what had just happened.

Mathis soon found that counting stars was entirely too difficult, for they seemed to keep moving around. His head was still swimming, and smoke kept drifting across his field of vision. The sound of gunfire and explosions rattled around in his brain, reminding him of where he was. When he tried to rub his forehead with his right hand, he discovered his arm was still partially trapped under the lifeless form of the dead boy. He jerked his hand free, wiped it on his pants for some reason, and then sniffed it. "Why did I do that?" he asked himself quietly. He glanced over at the dark shape beside him, just to make sure it hadn't started moving, and then looked back up in the sky, focusing on the moon. Despite the smoke in the air, he could almost distinguish individual craters, so bright and near did it seem. Then something flitted across the face of the moon, and Mathis blinked rapidly, unsure of what he had seen. A brief lull in the gunfire allowed him to hear the distant drumbeat of a helicopter. He couldn't believe it. Helicopters didn't fly at night. Did they?

A blinding flash of light made him close his eyes, the glare shining through his lids with an orange glow. He cracked one eye open, and saw the huge parachute flare drifting down from high in the sky. He opened the other eye and saw two helicopters, brightly illuminated by the flare, circling around the mountain top. High above the flare was what looked like a loach, the light observation helicopter shaped like an egg on a stick. Lower down, off to the south side, a Huey chopper cruised a few hundred yards away. As Mathis turned his head to follow the Huey, the machine gun on the side of the aircraft began spitting out shells, the bright red tracers streaming sideways and punching into the mountain somewhere below the peak, outside the wire perimeter.

"Fat lot of good that'll do," he commented sourly. But what else could they do? They couldn't fire on the camp, where the VC were, without hitting Americans. And they certainly couldn't land on the chopper pad, since it was the enemy's current base of operations. So all they could do it light the mountain up, both literally and figuratively. And Mathis wasn't sure that the flares were actually a good idea, watching another parachute flare burst into life above him. While the light helped the choppers, and revealed the enemy soldiers, it also shone on the Americans, making them even easier targets for the Viet Cong who ran rampant through the camp. That thought made him realize how precarious his own position was—lying on his back in the dirt, next to the body of a communist soldier he had just killed.

Mathis rolled left, over onto his stomach, and raised his head enough to look around. The flares had brought his surroundings into sharp relief, revealing how exposed he really was. Anyone within twenty yards could clearly see him, and with his uniform there would be no doubt as to his being an American soldier. He saw his rifle a few feet away, and low-crawled over to it. Until he found ammo for it, it was pretty much useless, but it would at least look intimidating. Rising up on his hands and knees, he looked to the south and saw the orderly room, one end of which had collapsed. He also could see two Viet Cong soldiers duck into the doorway, apparently seeking shelter from the light fire team above them.

A scattering of green tracers arced up toward the Huey from the chopper pad, and the helicopter swerved right, seeking altitude and distance. Mathis looked left and right, seeking shelter and trying to decide what to do next. The light from the slowly sinking parachute flares sent sharp shadows waving back and forth amongst the rocks. Picturing in his mind how the area around the orderly room looked during the day, he remembered a small circle of stones where someone had placed a long empty ammo crate like a park bench, a place where he had sometimes seen soldiers sitting with a cup of coffee to watch the sunrise. Open only to the east, it would suffice as a small fort, at least for the time being. Gathering up his feet beneath him, he darted down the path in a low crouch, praying he wouldn't meet anyone coming the other way. The opening to the bench wasn't quite where he remembered, but he found it soon enough, and ducked into the alcove, his head constantly swiveling to scan the area around him. He scrambled over the wooden crate and scrunched down behind it, pointing his rifle menacingly at the opening in the rocks, halfway expecting a squad of Viet Cong to follow him in, guns ablaze.

When that didn't happen, he relaxed a little, and felt better than he had since before the attack. He was in a relatively protected position, and the helicopters showed that the outside world was at least aware of their situation on the mountain. Surely, he thought, that meant there would soon appear some reinforcements or relief. He imagined scores of Special Forces soldiers rope-lining down from hovering Hueys and driving the enemy back with their ferocious air assault. But he wasn't entirely sure they could do that at night, and would they even try it with the enemy firing back from the ground at the fragile choppers? But at least there was hope. He wondered where Kasperek and McDaniel were at that moment. He feared they were dead, but the appearance of the helicopters lifted his spirits enough that he could entertain the idea they were still alive and fighting back, somewhere on the Rock. He needed to find them, he decided, as soon as he could scrounge some more ammo.

Mathis snaked up the sloping side of a rock on the south side of the grotto until he could look over the top at the orderly room, now only a few yards away. The east end of the building was a shambles, the roof sloping down to the ground, but the middle and west end were still standing, albeit with gaping ragged holes in the walls and roof. Off to the right Mathis could see the old wooden cross atop a small hillock, glowing in the bright glare of the magnesium flares. "God help me," Mathis said out loud, not sure if he believed his prayer was heard or not.

There was movement at the door of the orderly room, and an American soldier was pushed out so hard he stumbled on the steps and sprawled on his face in the dirt. A Viet Cong soldier laughed viciously as he followed the American, stepping on the man's back. The communist wore the typical brown shorts and white T-shirt, and carried an AK-47. Over his shoulder he carried a canvas bag that appeared to be full of banana-shaped magazines. Another Viet Cong emerged, this one wearing black trousers and a black long-sleeved shirt. On his head was a dark-colored pith helmet, and in his arms was a bundle of cloth. His AK was slung over his shoulder.

The American started to rise, but the VC with the helmet barked "Stay down!" in heavily accented English, while the other one kicked the man in the side. Both of the VC looked up at the sky, trying to locate the two American helicopters. The man in shorts shielded his eyes with one hand, blocking out the glare from the flares, and then lifted his AK to his shoulder and fired off a burst almost straight up.

"Knock it off!" the man with the helmet ordered in the Vietnamese equivalent. "They cannot shoot at us." Mathis ducked his head as the man looked around sharply. He must be the officer in charge, Mathis told himself. He heard the Huey gunship make another pass, peppering the mountainside far below them. "See?" the officer assured the other man. "Now get him up."

Mathis eased his head up enough to see over the edge of the rock in time to see the soldier in shorts kick the prone American in the ass. "Get up!" the officer screamed in English. "Get up, you white bastard!" The American struggled to his feet, prodded by the barrel of the AK wielded by the man in shorts. Mathis now recognized him as the sergeant he had seen on duty in the orderly room earlier in the evening. His face was bloody, and he was hunched over like his stomach hurt. "Move!" the officer demanded. The two Viet Cong herded the American sergeant to the east, the one in shorts constantly poking him in the back with his gun. At first Mathis thought they were taking him as a prisoner to the chopper pad, but they stopped at the base of the flag pole just past the end of the building. The officer stepped in front of the American and pushed the bundle of cloth toward him. The American, confused, reached out and touched the bundle, gripping a small piece of it as if testing to see what it was. The officer released the bundle, and it unfurled down to their feet. Mathis could now see that it was a Viet Cong flag, the gold star at the center peeking through the folds of blue and red.

"Put up flag!" the officer commanded, pointing toward the flag pole.

The sergeant looked up at the flagpole, and then down at the flag dangling from his hand, acting a little dazed. "This flag?" he asked.

"Yes. Put up flag. Now!"

138

The sergeant used both hands to spread the flag out so he could see it better. He shook his head. "No," he said softly.

"Yes!" the officer yelled, and reached out to slap the American's face.

The sergeant turned his head, as if looking for help, but saw only the two Viet Cong. The officer pulled his AK from his shoulder and pointed it at the American. "Put up flag!" he screamed, spittle flying from his mouth. The sergeant's shoulders slumped in defeat, and he manipulated the flag until he found the grommets along one edge. He stepped to the flagpole, pulled the rope closer, and hooked the flag onto it. With reluctant hands he pulled on the other end of the rope and raised the flag to the top of the pole. There was a gathering breeze from the south, and the flag began flapping and standing out, not tidily, but well enough the symbolism was clear. The American took two steps back, his hands down at his side, his head tilted forward in shame.

Both of the Viet Cong were now grinning and looking up at the flag, proud of their accomplishment. Both threw a snappy salute and continued smiling. Then the officer spoke in his broken English again. "Salute flag, bastard!" The sergeant didn't bother to lift his head; he just shook it slowly from side to side.

"You futher-mucker, salute!" the officer shrieked. Mathis had to repress a chuckle at the Vietnamese man's miss-use of American profanity. The officer, however, was not amused, and knocked the American's forearm with the sight on his AK.

The sergeant raised his head and looked at the officer, still shaking his head. "No," he declared, squaring his shoulders.

"Salute or I kill you!" The Viet Cong officer was apoplectic, gripping his rifle tightly, his eyes wide with fury.

"No," the sergeant repeated. Then he raised his hand as if he was relenting, but instead shot the officer the finger, flashing the rude symbol directly in his face.

"Aaahh!" the officer shrieked, and pulled the trigger. The other Viet Cong dived out of the way as the AK erupted in a stream of bullets that ripped into the American's body, sending spurts of blood out his back and knocking him backwards until he collapsed in the dirt, his legs awkwardly sprawled beneath him. The Viet Cong officer walked over and put three more rounds into the sergeant's head. Mathis felt sick to his stomach. He had never seen such cold-blooded murder before, a vicious act without any justification. He wanted to strike back, wishing he had a full magazine for his M-16, or at least two rounds, anything to take revenge. But he didn't. All he could do was watch in horrified fascination. The man in shorts looked surprised and horrified as well. He just stood there looking at the fallen American.

"Let us go," the officer said calmly in Vietnamese, stepping around the body and heading back toward the chopper pad. The man in shorts shook his head wearily, and after a moment followed.

Mathis laid his head down on the rock, eyes closed, and tried to come to grips with the enormity of what he had just witnessed. He had never seen anyone murdered before, much less be shot at close range. Oh, sure, he had seen it in movies, but that was play acting. This had been real, and it shook him to his core. His whole body was numb with shock, and he had to remind himself to breathe. He had just been hit with a major dose of realism, and he didn't like it. And somehow, his strangling of the young boy a few minutes ago seemed entirely different, although he would have been hard pressed to explain why. On the other hand, the remorse that had been lurking in the back of his mind, the regret over that incident, was now fading, replaced by a righteous anger that somehow justified what he had done. All these conflicting emotions threatened to overwhelm him, and he groaned with frustration.

ELEVEN

Mathis lifted his head and scanned the areas around him. One of the flares from the loach was drifting off to the north and beginning to sputter out, making the long shadows sway and dance across the rocky terrain. Thankfully a new flare popped, giving Mathis a much better view of this part of the summit, and he saw little movement, but lots of destruction. There were still scattered shots from up around the Pagoda, and one explosion over somewhere near the reservoir, but here in front of the orderly room all was quiet. He decided to chance it. He gathered himself up and darted out of the alcove, down the path, and up to the entrance of the orderly room. He didn't go in, but instead squatted down beside the steps and put his head up near the wall, listening for any sounds from inside.

He heard a rustling sound, but soon identified it as paper on the bulletin board flapping in the breeze that blew through the partially destroyed building. Aware that enemy soldiers might come walking down the paths that met in front of the orderly room, he hesitated only a moment before climbing the steps and easing into the room, which was almost pitch black compared to the flare-lit outdoors. As his eyes adjusted to the dimness, he saw that the room was a shambles, the desks overturned and papers scattered everywhere. In the far corner a small fire smoldered. It appeared to be a pile of mail that had been set alight, but it wasn't burning well. Mathis maneuvered between the scattered furniture and stomped the fire out with his boot. He walked over to the switchboard, but it had been ripped apart and smashed, so there was no chance of calling for help, if that had even ever been possible.

"Ammo. First aid kit." He was whispering to himself, perhaps just to stave off the loneliness he felt. The company clerk's desk was lying on its side, the legs pointing horizontally toward what had been the back of the orderly room. The drawer handles were pointing up, with the drawers all closed except for one that was stuck half open. He figured that any first aid supplies or ammo would be in one of those drawers, but searching through them would be difficult. Dismissing the briefly-considered idea of trying to pull the desk back upright as too difficult and noisy, he propped his rifle against the side of the desk and pulled on the handle of the top right drawer. It slid up, but when it reached the built-in stop, Mathis heard most of the drawer's contents falling back inside. Jiggling the drawer back and forth, he finally freed it from the catch and pulled it all the way out, pencils and paper clips cascading into the vacant space where it had been, as well as bouncing off the desk and scattering on the floor. When he turned the drawer horizontal and propped it on the leg of the desk, all that was left inside was a spiral notebook.

"Shit!" Mathis reluctantly accepted the fact that gravity was against him, and he would have to pull out all the drawers and then dig around in the pile of contents that would inevitably accumulate inside the desk pedestal. With faint hope he felt around between the feet of the desk, but the pedestal had a metal bottom, blocking any access from that direction. Resigned to his fate, he pulled the rest of the drawers out and set them on the floor, checking each for anything that hadn't fallen out already. Then he leaned over the side and began digging around inside the pedestal, judging by feel what the contents were. The big bottom drawer had been filled with manila folder files, and they covered everything else. He pulled many of them out and threw them on the floor, then went back to probing blindly through the jumble of objects, none of which were useful to him.

Having found nothing he needed in the right pedestal, he did the same process on the other. Here he was more successful. When he removed the top drawer from that side, he found a flashlight that had stayed in the drawer. The batteries were weak, but at least he had a little light to work with. He quickly removed the other two drawers, which contained a variety of supplies and few files, and began digging through the mess with the flashlight to help. Sweeping random objects from side to side as the edge of the pedestal dug into his chest, he quickly spotted an M-16 magazine. Brass glinted from the opening of the magazine, and when he pulled it free he could tell by the weight that it was nearly full. He immediately stood up, reached for the barrel of his rifle, and quickly replaced the empty magazine with this new one. Releasing the bolt caused the immensely satisfying sound of a round being chambered. He was once again ready to fight.

He laid the rifle across the edges of the right pedestal where he could get to it quickly, and then resumed searching the contents of the left pedestal. There were no more magazines, and no first aid kit.

"Damn it!" he said, sitting down in the foot well of the desk and pulling his rifle down beside him. He was better off than before, but not by much. There was a small scratching sound from somewhere, and Mathis jerked his lead to the left, only to bang his head wound against the edge of the desk. The pain was excruciating, a jab of fire that radiated out through his entire body. "Ow! Shit! God-damn! Mother-fuck!" The curses flowed loudly and echoed in the room. He knew that was a mistake, but the initial jolt was so bad he couldn't control himself. Gripping his forehead tightly, he forced himself to calm down, groaning through gritted teeth. The throbbing eased a little, but he could feel new wetness running down his neck.

"Who's there?" an unknown voice called out, muffled but obviously American. Mathis stood up and looked around warily. The room was still vacant.

"Spec Five Mathis," he answered cautiously. "Who're you? And where?"

"Under the floor," the voice answered. "PFC Ross, and Spec Four Gunther."

"What are you doing there?"

"Hiding," a second voice said, presumably Gunther. "Are they gone?"

"Gone from right here, for now, but the camp's still crawling with them."

"So what are you doing?" Ross asked. Mathis found it strange to be talking to the floor, and knelt down to hear them better.

"I'm looking for ammo and a first aid kit. You guys got any?"

"No," Gunther said. "We were in bed when the gooks hit."

"We're in our underwear," Ross added.

"No weapons?" Mathis asked.

"We barely got out of the hooch alive," Ross protested, having perhaps detected the disdain in Mathis' question. "I was asleep, and then a mortar round hit the hooch."

"I think they stopped shooting mortars," Gunther said. "Is it safe to come out?"

Mathis shook his head. "If you don't have weapons, I wouldn't advise it. They're shooting anybody they find. I saw them execute the CQ. You're probably better off down there for now."

"Till when?"

Mathis shrugged, even though they couldn't see him. "Till morning, I guess. They can't land choppers here in the dark, with the gooks shooting at them."

"I thought I heard choppers," Gunther said.

"There a loach dropping parachute flares, and a gunship shooting at the side of the mountain, but they can't shoot up here without hitting us. But at least they know we're in trouble, so they'll be here at first light."

"What time is it now?" Ross asked with a trembling voice.

Mathis felt around for the flashlight, then flicked it on and shined it on his wrist. "Almost midnight," he told them.

"At least five more hours," Gunther said dejectedly.

"Are you going to stay with us?" Ross asked hopefully.

"Can't," Mathis told them. "I've got to find my buddies. We got separated. Look, you'll be okay under there. Just keep quiet." Mathis wasn't at all sure he was giving good advice, but didn't know what else to tell them. "I'll come find you in the morning, when we get relieved."

"But what if you get killed?" Ross whined.

Mathis was annoyed by the question, for a number of reasons. In particular, he didn't like being reminded of the possibility. "What if we all get killed?" he barked. "What if Martians invade tomorrow? There's no point in worrying about 'what ifs'. I gotta go." Before the two guys under the floor could reply, Mathis ran to the door and stuck his head out to look around. The coast seemed cleared, so he darted down the steps and over to the circle of rocks with the ammo-crate bench. Crouching inside the alcove, he turned to face the opening, his rifle held ready in case anyone followed him. Above him the loach dropped three flares in rapid succession, greatly increasing the brightness of the illumination, and at the same time Mathis heard the approaching rumble of an airplane, the kind with multiple propeller engines.

He searched the sky, but the glare of the flares blotted out the stars and made everything around the mountain pitch black. He could track the plane's course with his ears, however, and it was clearly coming in to circle the peak. Mathis wondered what kind of plane it was, and why was it out there. Maybe just someone taking a look to judge the situation? Or, better yet, a bunch of paratroopers. He dismissed that thought immediately; trying to parachute onto the small mountain peak occupied by the Viet Cong would be suicidal. He followed the sound of the plane, whose deep rumble made him think it was a very big aircraft, and tried to pick it out in the darkness. Suddenly a tremendously bright streak of red appeared, originating somewhere in the air and ending at the side of the mountain, followed quickly by a grinding roar. It was a Spooky! Mathis had seen them on the news. A giant lumbering cargo plane outfitted with a pair of Gatling guns firing bullets at the rate of 6000 rounds per minute out the side, the Spooky was a terrifying weapon that literally hosed down its targets with a stream of lead, the tracers coming so fast they appeared to be a solid beam of glowing red light. The sound the guns made was a harsh growl, the rounds firing far too quickly to pick out individual shots. It was the snarl of a giant angry tiger spitting a crimson torrent of death.

Mathis was astonished and amazed, marveling at the raw power of the futuristic display of firepower taken to the limit. The scarlet whip played over the side of the mountain, surely raining destruction on an area he couldn't actually see from his nest on the peak, and he was profoundly glad the enemy didn't possess an equivalent weapon capable of such horrifying devastation. When the hail of bullets suddenly ended, Mathis peered over the top of the rocks to judge the reaction of the Viet Cong. A shout drew his attention to the helicopter landing pad at the east end of the camp, where the flares hanging in the sky showed a group of enemy soldiers waving their arms in defiance and firing their rifles into the air as they shouted curses at the American aircraft. Mathis was disappointed in the response, but not totally surprised. The VC knew as well as he did that the Spooky couldn't fire at the camp itself; therefore, as long as they were within the camps boundaries, they were safe from any outside interference.

At this distance, and with the uneven and swaying light of the flares, it was hard for him to be sure what he was seeing down at the chopper pad, but it looked like several of the Viet Cong were lying on the ground. It took him a moment to figure out that these were wounded men, or perhaps dead ones. Either way, it gave him a deep sense of satisfaction. His religious upbringing had taught him to never take pleasure in the misfortune of others, but after the vicious execution he had just witnessed, such tenets had gone out the window. He wanted them all dead. They had violated his—HIS!— base camp, destroying buildings and killing his fellow Americans without provocation. As far as he knew, they might have even killed or wounded his best friends, and that was simply intolerable. The Viet Cong must pay for their arrogance.

The Spooky opened up with its miniguns again, this time on the north side of the mountain, spraying the mountain with radiant lead. As Mathis watched the moving jet of liquid fire, he saw green tracers rise from somewhere down the mountainside in retaliation. The Spooky stopped firing and zoomed away from the mountain, and Mathis could hear the aircraft receding into the distance. A minute later the roar of its big engines returned, from a different direction, and the plane began firing its guns at the place on the lower mountain side from which the Viet Cong had been firing at them only moments before. Whether they found their target or not Mathis couldn't tell, but there was no further anti-aircraft fire after that.

Mathis felt the need to do something, anything, but his mind was still fuzzy from the head wound. He gently touched the area around the wound, and found no new wetness, so he hoped that meant it had stopped bleeding. An explosion somewhere behind him made him duck down. It sounded like it came from the Pagoda. Cautiously he raised his head and peeked between a couple rocks at the building, which was only about thirty yards away. Dissipating smoke from the explosion was drifting away from the roof, but the building still seemed intact, and he heard occasional M-16 rifle shots coming from the far side. The Pagoda was still under siege, but holding firm for the time being. With all the antennas down and the power off, however, it was almost certainly unable to contact anyone by radio. And that thought reminded Mathis of something McDaniel had told him: Bunker Twenty was not only a defensive position, but it was also a commo bunker, with spare battery-powered radios. Near the reservoir and the cave, it would be a logical place for American soldiers to gather and defend. Maybe he should head over there.

From somewhere past the Ops building Mathis heard the distinctive "pomp" sound of an M-79 grenade launcher, and a second later a small detonation down near the chopper pad. Someone was firing on the Viet Cong gathering down there, and while the round had fallen too short to be a real danger, the soldiers had all ducked or sought shelter. A second grenade was fired, and this one landed far past the pad, blasting some bushes on the far side of the mountain. "He's got them bracketed," Mathis breathed approvingly. "Next one should be right on target." Just as a third round was fired, Mathis heard a shout and the flapping sound of sandals approaching. Crouching down behind the ammo crate bench, he saw a Viet Cong soldier with an AK run past his hiding place, obviously intent on silencing the M-79. Only then did it occur to Mathis that the American who was now being hunted might be his friend, John Kasperek. And that thought spurred him to action. Jumping over the ammo crate, he paused only a second at the entrance to the grotto to ensure no other VC were on the path, and then sprinted after the one he had just seen.

With the parachute flares overhead, the Ops building on fire to his left, and the burning billets down to his right, there was plenty of light, but it was a flickering, wavering illumination that sent confusing shadows dancing across the rugged landscape. Trying to watch his step on the uneven path while searching ahead for the Viet Cong soldier, he almost missed the fact that the man had stopped next to an outcropping and was bringing his AK up to his shoulder. Reacting instinctively, Mathis skidded to a halt and brought his own rifle up to fire off two quick shots at the other man, who was only some forty yards away. He saw a spark on the rock next to the enemy, one that caused the man to swing his rifle around looking for whoever was shooting at him. Mathis fired off another wild shot when the AK stopped its sweep and centered on him, before he dived to the ground as a burst of fire swept the air above him. His left hand and right elbow stung from breaking his fall, but he hurriedly brought his rifle to bear on the enemy from this prone unsupported position and snapped off three more shots. Simultaneously a new parachute flare popped above him and the Viet Cong disappeared from his sight.

Had he killed the man, or simply caused him to seek cover? It was a vital question, as it dictated what he would do next. He was lying in the middle of the dirt path, and he knew that was he was too exposed, despite his prone position. A quick glance left and right found a rounded stone poking up a few feet to his right, so he rolled like a log until he was behind it. The rotation had sent his head spinning again, and renewed the throbbing from his temple. Mathis squeezed his eyes shut for a minute, struggling to regain his equilibrium. He wasn't sure, but he might have even slipped into unconsciousness for a minute or two. When his dizziness subsided, he raised his head slowly to scan his surroundings. There was still no movement from where the Viet Cong had been standing before, but he couldn't see a body, either. Closer in, the particular configuration of the rocks looked familiar, more so than just from passing by here in the weeks prior to the attack. Finally he recognized this spot—it was where he had strangled the kid with the RPG launcher. Yet all evidence of that struggle had disappeared.

"I'd swear he was dead," Mathis whispered to himself. "He couldn't have just gotten up and walked away." He looked around again, thinking perhaps he was mistaken about the location, but it still looked like the same place as the deadly encounter. After a few seconds of confusion, it occurred to him that maybe someone had carried the boy's body away. He had heard that the Viet Cong always tried to recover their fallen and remove them from the battlefield. Yes, he told himself, that must be what happened. Meanwhile, what about the other gook, the one that was just shooting at him? Mathis raised his head enough to look over the round rock in front of him, and he saw nothing suspicious, nor did anyone take a shot at him. Gathering his legs beneath him, Mathis rose to a crouch, his head swiveling as quickly his wound allowed, to scan in all directions.

The Spooky's engines droned overhead, punctuated occasionally by the ugly growl of the miniguns, and further up he could hear the pulsating roar of the helicopter dropping flares, but the explosions on the hilltop had stopped, and there was only occasional small arms fire. Slowly Mathis began creeping up the path past the Ops building, warily scanning the rocks for any movement that might indicate his foe was lying in wait. Somewhere behind him he heard a booming blast like a shotgun and at the same time a burst of AK fire, causing him to duck down to a kneeling position, fearing he had been discovered. No bullets came his way, fortunately, so he again stood up and eased forward, assuming the gunfire was a separate firefight going on somewhere near the orderly room. Finally he reached the spot on the path where he thought the enemy soldier had been, but at first he could see no sign of him. Then the swaying parachute flare reflected off a wet spot on a flat stone beside the path. Mathis moved closer and bent down to examine what seemed to be a small puddle of liquid. Unable to resist the impulse, he reached out with his left hand and touched the wet spot with the tip of his index finger, then brought the finger up close to his face to examine it. The stain was dark, and when he rubbed it with his thumb it felt mildly sticky. It was blood, he was certain.

Searching the ground with his eyes, he saw other splashes leading away toward the west, in the direction of the Pagoda. So he had at least wounded the guy. He felt some satisfaction in that fact, proud of his own marksmanship if nothing else. He decided to follow the blood trail and finish the guy off, but had taken only two steps when he heard a voice calling.

"Trinh, where are you?" It was said in Vietnamese, and came from behind him, sounding like someone coming up the same path Mathis had just traversed. Over the rocks Mathis could see at least two heads bobbing, approaching his location quickly. He had to make a decision immediately. He didn't know how many rounds he had left in his magazine, and he didn't know for sure how many VC soldiers were coming his way. Remembering the expression, "discretion is the better part of valor," Mathis chose to avoid any confrontation for now and get the hell out of there. Keeping low, and trying to run as quietly as he could, he bolted down the path to the north, toward the mortar pit. At least there he could find cover.

TWELVE

The mortar pit was deserted, but the Viet Cong had obviously been there. The mortar had been torn apart and its components scattered, and the crates of ammo had been opened and dumped on the ground. A canvas pouch the size of a dictionary lay on the mortar tube; Mathis guessed it was a satchel charge that had failed to detonate. That, or perhaps it had been left as a booby trap. Regardless, he wasn't going near it, concluding that the pit was not a safe location in which to hide out, even for a minute. The sound of the Spooky had changed very subtly, and Mathis turned his head and listened intently. From the sounds he deduced that a second Spooky had arrived on the scene, and it joined the first in hosing down the mountainside with its rain of fire. The stark white light from the flares contrasted with the deep shadows here on the peak, giving the scene a nightmarish touch of sharp angles and threatening crevasses. When Mathis looked up toward one of the drifting flares he noticed the halo that surrounded it, and at the same time he noticed the moist coolness of the air on his face. There definitely was a haze in the air, something that usually presaged a heavier fog or even rain. Mathis wasn't sure if that was a good thing or a bad thing.

Mathis heard voices, and they were the distinctive cadences of Vietnamese. They seemed to be coming from the west, so he scurried over to that side of the mortar pit and flattened himself on the sandbags of the sloping side, his head right at the rim. A few yards away three Viet Cong soldiers came into view, traveling from right to left. One of the soldiers was hobbling, his arm thrown around the shoulders of another man for support, while the third man, with a back pack, followed behind carrying two AK-47s. "Hurry," the third man said in Vietnamese. "We must join the others."

151

"We will make it in time," the man supporting the wounded one said.

"The airplanes worry me," the third man said, looking up at the sky.

"Why? They will not shoot up here."

"But when we go back down, then they can shoot at us."

"You worry too much. Stop. There is a body here."

From where he was hiding, Mathis could not see what they were talking about, but he saw them halt and stare down at something beside the trail.

"American," the second man said with disdain.

"I have a grenade," the third man suggested.

"Good idea," the second man said. The third man laid his rifles down and shrugged out of the back pack straps. Reaching into the pack, he pulled out a small object and bent down out of Mathis' sight.

When the third man stood up and pulled the backpack on again, he said, "That will be a nice surprise for them." Picking up the two AKs, he followed as the other two continued on down the path, soon passing out of Mathis' field of vision.

Mathis realized they had just booby-trapped the American soldier's body with a grenade. While that was a sneaky and heinous act, it told him that they weren't coming back here, and their conversation led him to believe they were going to leave the mountain top entirely, and fairly soon. Or, at least, some of them were. Meanwhile, Mathis was alone in a mortar pit filled with high explosives and a satchel charge that might go off at any moment. He had to find some other refuge.

To the southwest the Ops building continued to burn, the flames highlighting the side of the Pagoda. There was no more gunfire from that direction, but he had no way of knowing whether that meant the Pagoda occupants had driven off their attackers, or if they had succumbed. To his south were the burning generator shed, the collapsed officers' hooch, and the demolished orderly room;

beyond those buildings were a few Americans holed up in Bunker Eight or sheltering in the rocks outside the wire. To his southeast were the burning billets and mess hall. Through the smoke and flames rising above this conflagration he caught glimpses of the distant helicopter landing pad, which seemed to now be crowded with men, some standing, some sitting, and some prone. Closer in, to his northeast, the Special Forces billets was a mass of flame, and from inside he could hear occasional snaps as small arms ammo popped off in the heat.

He then realized that there seemed to be no other gunfire occurring on the peak. The drone of the two Spookies was incessant, and every few seconds one would rip the air with its miniguns, but down here on the ground it was largely silent. It was hard to accept, but he knew that what little resistance the Americans had offered against the Viet Cong had now vanished. The American forces on Nui Ba Den were either dead or gone to ground. And here he was, alone in a dangerous location, armed with maybe half a magazine of ammo. A wave of despair washed over him. He wondered what the enemy had planned for the near future. Were they now consolidating their gains, regrouping to begin searching out the remaining survivors? Or were they preparing an ambush for the dawn, when the Americans would mount a rescue operation by helicopter? He could just imagine the slaughter as the enemy shot down approaching choppers, knowing the attackers would be reluctant to shoot back for fear of hitting their own men still hiding in the camp, or worse, being held hostage.

The only hope in such a situation would be to have all the camp survivors in one protected area, isolated from the battle, and in radio communication with the assault. And that thought brought Mathis back to the idea of seeking out Bunker Twenty. It contained battery-powered radios that could direct the fire of an American air assault. And the cave would provide a shelter for the remaining soldiers on the peak. If the Viet Cong had not successfully taken that bunker and the cave, then that is where Mathis needed to go.

Mathis stood up and looked around to get his bearings. When he faced north, with the blazing Special Forces hooch to his right front, Bunker One should be just beyond and slightly to the left, and

153

Bunker Twenty was therefore somewhere to the right, just the other side of the reservoir. The reservoir was out of sight, blocked by the flames of the SF hooch and the water purification shed. The cave, he remembered, was between Bunker One and Bunker Twenty, slightly down the hill from them. He would have to skirt past the SF hooch toward Bunker One, and then curve around the reservoir to Bunker Twenty. And hope he was right in thinking the Viet Cong were no longer in this area.

Climbing out of the mortar pit, Mathis shielded the right side of his face from the burning building so he could see better. The parachute flares seemed to be throwing less light than before, and the path in front of him looked fuzzy. Only then did he notice that the air was beginning to swirl with visible moisture. A fog was rolling in. He needed to find the other Americans, and quickly.

He spotted the rectangular roof of Bunker One through the gathering mist, but saw no movement nor heard any sounds from inside. Veering right around the SF hooch, he became engulfed in the acrid smoke of its fire, the prevailing wind pushing it to the north. He began coughing, and the reaction caused his head to ache again, while he narrowed his eyes to reduce the stinging of the smoke. When he emerged from the smoky plume he found himself on the rim of the reservoir, reflections of the flares glinting off the dark pool at the bottom of the circular crater. He paused to breathe in the clean and increasingly moist air, blinking rapidly as he looked around to plan his next move. One of the Spookies circling the mountain opened up with its miniguns again, the crimson beam of bullets raking the mountainside somewhere below the peak. An answering stream of green tracers arced up from a different part of the mountain, reaching up toward the invisible cargo plane with rounds that were obviously much larger than the 7.62mm the Spooky was firing. "Twenty-millimeter," Mathis guessed out loud, following the rising barrage as it began exploding in small bursts that peppered the night sky. The fire from the miniguns ceased abruptly and the sound of the plane's engines changed dramatically as it veered away from the mountain.

Mathis hoped the Air Force guys had gotten away unscathed. He resumed his trip to Bunker Twenty, but belatedly realized he

154

made an attractive target standing on the rim of the reservoir, backlit by the burning buildings. He dropped down into a crouch and continued edging toward the bunker, whose roof he could now just barely see. When he was close enough, he knelt behind a rock and called out softly but insistently. "Hey! Is anybody in the bunker?" He had considered first calling out in Vietnamese, in case the gooks had captured the bunker, but was afraid that would simply confuse the situation.

At first there was no answer, although he heard a scuffling sound. He worried that the VC were in the bunker, and he had lost his last chance at shelter. Then a suspicious voice replied.

"Who's there?"

"Mathis," he told them, keeping his voice low enough that hopefully only the guy in the bunker could hear it. He detected a whispered discussion inside.

"Mathis? We don't know any Mathis."

"I'm ASA. I work in the Pagoda. John Kasperek knows me, and Sergeant McDaniel."

More whispered discussion. These guys were really spooked, Mathis thought. "Okay, so you're the guy with red hair?" This question caught Mathis completely off guard. None of the ASA guys were redheads. Then he guessed this was another test to prove he wasn't a Viet Cong with excellent English language skills.

"No, my hair's brown. None of us have red hair." Mathis was glad he hadn't tried to use his Vietnamese on them.

"Anyone with you?"

"No, I'm by myself. Can I come down there?"

"Okay, but take it slow."

Mathis crept down the path toward the door in the side of the bunker, which appeared to be larger than most. The barrel of an M-16 poked out of the half-open door, aimed directly at him. Mathis held his own rifle out to his right side, his left hand open and slightly raised. He paused a couple feet from the door, until the M-16 disappeared and the door was pushed open all the way.

155

"Come on in, quick," someone ordered. Mathis scurried forward and ducked inside. The bunker was crowded and dark, with only a weak flashlight that was pointed at the top of a PRC-25 radio as someone manipulated the dials. The guy at the radio had a handset pressed to his ear and was making hushed calls into the mouthpiece.

"Is this everybody?" Mathis asked quietly, afraid to hear the answer. There couldn't be more than eight or ten soldiers crowded into the small bunker.

"Fuck if we know," somebody answered caustically.

"There's more guys down at the cave," someone else offered.

"Maybe twenty," a third voice said doubtfully. "Don't know about the rest of the camp."

"There's a few guys hiding over at Bunker Eight," Mathis told them. "Last time I was there, there were still some guys holding out in the Pagoda."

"Fucking gooks!" another voice cursed angrily.

"Anybody seen John Kasperek or Two-dan McDaniel?" Mathis was almost pleading.

No one answered for a moment. "Don't think so," a voice finally said.

"McDaniel might be down at the cave," someone said. "I know there's a couple SF guys there."

Through the open gun port Mathis caught a glimpse of red minigun tracers as a Spooky made another pass, presumably seeking out the source of the anti-aircraft fire. There was now a definite halo around the scarlet stream, softening the glow.

"I think I'll go down to the cave," Mathis announced. "Hey, you guys got any spare M-16 ammo?"

"We've barely got enough for us," a voice said somewhat defiantly.

"They might have some in the cave," a different voice said, sounding a little apologetic.

156

"Okay. What's the best way to get there from here?"

"Go down from the door about ten feet, then hang a left at the little ledge. You can't miss it."

The guy with the radio jerked his head up and said excitedly, "I've got someone! Go tell the first sergeant."

"Yeah!" someone said enthusiastically. "Finally. Uh, Mathis, when you go to the cave, tell the first sergeant to come up here, okay?"

"Roger," Mathis said and pushed the door open to leave. "Anything else?"

"Just go, man."

After the hot and stuffy confines of the bunker, the cool night air felt remarkably pleasant. A single parachute flare floated down through the gathering mist, and the drone of the Spookies ebbed and flowed around him. The only other sound was the crackling of the fires on the other side of the reservoir. The relative silence was ominous; the Viet Cong had apparently achieved all their goals, as there were no more buildings to blow up, and no one left to shoot at. Conceivably they would now initiate a mop-up operation, seeking out the remaining Americans in their various hiding places. Mathis again considered the possibility of trying to make his way all the way down the mountain and out onto the safety of the plain, but the problems seemed almost insurmountable. Negotiating the steep slope in the dark, avoiding trails, hiding from patrolling VC, all would be incredibly difficult, and if he didn't get killed or captured, he would likely fall off a cliff or break a leg. He had no canteen, and that fact made him suddenly aware of just how thirsty he was right now. No, escaping from the mountain just wasn't practical.

Fighting a gathering despair, Mathis edged down a path below the bunker until he found the narrow ledge, then turned toward the dark overhang a few meters away. Remembering how jumpy the men in the bunker had been, he half-stepped forward and held his body in an as un-threatening posture as he could manage.

"American coming in," he announced in a quiet tone. There was no answer, but as he edged onto a wider shelf of stone, he saw a man's head peek around a rock, his eyes glistening.

"Go ahead," the man said with a nod.

The cave was in fact just a deep grotto under an overhang, going back only short distance into the side of the mountain. Steeped in shadow, Mathis could make very little out visually, but he could sense the presence of many men. There were painful groans from the back of the cave, and somewhere closer was a pitiable weak whimper.

"First Sergeant?" Mathis called out, just loud enough to be heard.

"Yeah," Robinson's distinctive voice answered him. Mathis turned toward the man, who was still invisible. His single word response had been laced with weariness.

"The guys in the bunker need you. I think they've established comms with someone."

"Finally!" Robinson said with suddenly renewed hope. Other men in the cave echoed his enthusiasm with grunts and whistles. "Thanks," the first sergeant said, clapping Mathis on the shoulder as he brushed past him to exit the cave.

"Bill? Is that you?" Mathis heard McDaniel calling to him from deeper inside the cave.

"Two-dan?" Mathis was incredibly glad and relieved to hear from his friend. He stared into the Stygian darkness trying to find McDaniel, only to have his friend grab his bicep and shake him boisterously.

"Where the fuck you been?" McDaniel asked.

"Oh, just taking a midnight stroll around the camp. You know, getting some fresh air."

"Jesus, I thought you were dead. After that RPG, we called out, but you didn't answer."

"Well, I got hit in the head, knocked me out for a minute. Is John here?"

McDaniel didn't answer immediately. "Uh, I was hoping he was with you. We got separated while we were looking for you. So you didn't see him?"

"Shit, no." Mathis felt his initial ebullience at meeting up with McDaniel fade away as quickly as it had come. He had pinned so much hope on finding both his friends here at the cave, only to have his desire only half fulfilled.

"You got hit in the head?" McDaniel asked with concern. "How bad?"

Mathis shrugged in the darkness. "I'm still vertical, so it can't be too bad."

"Let me see," McDaniel said, and clicked on a flashlight, using his fingers to block most of the beam. He played the weak light on Mathis' face, and Mathis turned his head so McDaniel could see the wound on his left temple.

"Holy shit! Man, you must have bled like a stuck pig." Mathis reached up with his left hand and gently stroked his neck, feeling the flakes of dried blood.

"Guess so," Mathis admitted.

"You sure you're okay?"

"Kind of dizzy," Mathis allowed.

"Yeah, but that's normal for you," McDaniel joked. He tugged on Mathis' arm. "Come on back here, let's get you cleaned up and take a closer look at that wound."

McDaniel played the flashlight beam around the floor of the cave so Mathis could find his way through the crowd of men sitting or lying in the dirt. There seemed to be at least twenty guys, many dressed only in boxer shorts, others with just fatigue pants and unlaced boots. Only a couple were in full uniform, and none held weapons. The brief glimpses Mathis got of their faces showed deep despondency and a fatalistic resignation. "Here. Sit down." McDaniel pulled Mathis down next to the wall of the cave, near a

159

canvas bag and a canteen. Kneeling beside him, McDaniel opened the canteen and began pouring a thin trickle of water down the side of Mathis' head as he examined the wound with the flashlight.

"We don't have a medic?" Mathis asked when McDaniel set the canteen down to rummage through the canvas bag.

"Not here in the cave. Doc Kilgore was the only one up here, and no one's seen him since the attack. I guess I'll just have to do."

Mathis knew that the Green Berets got far more first aid training than regular soldiers, so he was confident in McDaniel's ability. But he wondered what sort of medical supplies were available, and what McDaniel could do if the injury was more serious than he was trained for.

McDaniel found a white gauze pad and wetted it with the canteen. "This might sting a little," he warned as he reached up to gently pat Mathis' temple.

"Yeow!" Mathis yelped. It was a sharp burning pain that electrified his body. He squeezed his eyes shut and balled his left fist while squeezing the hand grip of his rifle with all his might. "Easy! Easy!"

"Pussy," McDaniel admonished him with a chuckle. "Doesn't look too bad. Might be some brain damage, but how would you know? You're already brain damaged."

"Thanks," Mathis said sourly. He felt McDaniel continue to pat around the wound, then wipe at the blood that had run down his neck. Next McDaniel got another gauze pad and placed it over the wound.

"Hold this for a second," McDaniel told him. Mathis obeyed, gently pressing the pad to his head while McDaniel unwound a little from a roll of gauze tape. After a few wraps around Mathis' head, McDaniel tied off the strip and began putting the leftovers away. "There you go," he told Mathis. "Good as new."

The pain of cleaning and bandaging the wound began to subside, and Mathis leaned back against the side of the cave and tried to relax, having been tense for what seemed like hours. The entrance to the cave was bright, in sharp contrast to the interior, the moonlight and parachute flares making the increasing moisture in the air glow like a blank movie screen. Then a human figure passed through, and First Sergeant Robinson's voice called out. "Where's the guy who just came in?"

"Back here, Top," McDaniel answered. "I was just patching him up."

Robinson strode to join them, skillfully dodging the other men on the floor despite the total darkness.

"What's your name?" he demanded.

"Mathis, William," Mathis answered. "Spec five. ASA."

"So where have you been, since the attack?"

"I was in Bunker Five, but McDaniel, Kasperek, and me came out and shot at the gooks on the chopper pad. Then we got separated."

"Did you see anybody else?"

"I saw the Korean guy shooting at them with his M-60, and I talked to some guys at Bunker Eight."

"Bunker Eight?" Robinson showed some real interest. "What were they doing?"

"Mostly just hiding. The gooks had damaged the building, and they were out of ammo."

"Hmm. Probably all they can do."

"Oh, and I saw the gooks execute the CQ when he wouldn't salute their flag."

"What?" McDaniel blurted with consternation.

"Yeah, they made him raise their flag and then told him to salute. When he gave them the finger, they shot him."

"God damn motherfuckers," Robinson grumbled. "See anything else?"

"I talked to a couple guys hiding under the orderly room, and I saw the gooks booby-trap an American body. And it looked like they were regrouping down at the chopper pad."

161

"That's all we fuckin' need." Robinson paused. "We've got comms through Red Horse Retrans. They'll keep the Spookies and the LFT up as long as they can, but they can't send us any relief until morning. So we've just got to hold out until then." With that the first sergeant stood up and hurried back out of the cave.

THIRTEEN

Mathis took a long drink of water from the canteen McDaniel had handed him.

"We were lucky," McDaniel told him. "Some guys had just filled a bunch of jerry cans at the water purification hut, and a couple survived when the gooks blew it up. So we've got water, at least."

"How about ammo? I've only got half a magazine left."

"I'll see if I can scrounge some up for you. There was some in the commo bunker, but they've been passing it out to anyone who needs it."

"We've got to go find John," Mathis announced flatly. He felt surprisingly revived by this short break from danger. His wound had been treated, he had slaked his thirst, and there was a promise of more ammunition. Now that his own immediate needs were taken care of, his concerns turned to his friend who was still out there on the Rock, exposed and alone. He hoped. He avoided thinking about the possibility that Kasperek was dead.

McDaniel took a breath, and Mathis could sense that he was about to protest, but then the Green Beret sighed. "Yeah, we do," he agreed, albeit without enthusiasm. "It's going to be a bitch, though."

"I know," Mathis said. "But we can't just leave him out there."

"He might be, uh," McDaniel began, and then paused before he continued. "He might be in one of the other bunkers, holed up until morning." Mathis knew what McDaniel had started to say, and appreciated that he had changed his mind. They both knew the possibilities, but it was better to ignore the worst ones.

"Yeah, or he could be wandering around looking for us." That thought had just come to Mathis, and it gave him even more motivation to go back out. It made it seem that he and McDaniel had somehow abandoned Kasperek, and it was their duty to find and rescue him.

"Wait here," McDaniel said. "I'll go get some ammo and tell Top what we're doing." He got up and hurried out of the cave. Mathis stretched his muscles, which had begun to cramp up from sitting on the floor, and took another drink of water. He wondered what time it was. It had to be long after midnight.

* * *

"Top wasn't happy about this," McDaniel told him as they knelt on the rim of the reservoir. Across the crater they could see the line of fires that represented what had been the billets, the club, and the mess hall, stretching across the middle of the camp toward the tumbled-down orderly room. Through the increasing fog they could just make out the Viet Cong flag hanging loosely from the flagpole. Off to their right the Ops building flames had died down, but still reflected off the side of the Pagoda. Past the wreckage of the officers' hooch the generator shed still burned brightly, the diesel fuel stored there feeding the flames.

"Why not?" Mathis asked distractedly.

"We're taking needed manpower and ammunition away from the main force," McDaniel explained pedantically, imitating the first sergeant's voice. "Which is true, but I convinced him we were going to be scouts, checking out the situation and bringing in other stragglers."

"Whatever works. Is he in charge? I mean, aren't there any officers around?"

"Haven't seen any so far."

To their left the east end of the camp was mostly dark, lit only by the parachute flares still drifting down from above. One of the far bunkers smoldered, wisps of smoke mixing with the fog. Mathis could see figures moving on the helicopter landing pad.

164

"Taking their wounded and dead back down the hill," McDaniel commented. Mathis saw that he was right. Limp bodies were being dragged or carried from the concrete pad and down the ravine to their left, disappearing between the bunkers and through the broken perimeter.

"Think they're all leaving?" Mathis asked hopefully.

"Maybe," McDaniel answered. "Or just clearing the decks for the next phase."

Mathis noticed a change in the ambient sounds on the peak. The rolling rumble of the big cargo planes seemed to be diminishing. "The Spookies are leaving," he said.

McDaniel tilted his head to listen. "Sounds like it. Maybe going back to refuel and reload. Not that they can really help us up here."

"This fog's not helping," Mathis added. The air was thick with tiny droplets of water, suffusing the glare from the flares and softening the outlines of distant objects.

"Yeah, we better get moving, before it gets any worse. Which way you want to go?"

"Let's head up toward our bunker," Mathis suggested. "He might have gone back there."

McDaniel nodded and moved out smartly, aiming for the gap between Bunker One and the smoldering remains of the SF hooch. Mathis followed close behind, his head swiveling as he searched for any potential threats or signs of his friend.

From over on his right Mathis saw a brief flash and the unmistakable crack of a rifle. He and McDaniel both dived to the ground, and Mathis skinned his left palm as he reached out to break his fall.

"That was an M-16," McDaniel complained quietly. "Probably from that bunker."

"They must think we're gooks," Mathis said. "Should we yell at them?"

"We do that, and every gook in the area will come running over. Naw, let's just crawl until we get out of their line of sight."

Mathis saw the wisdom in that suggestion, since they were backlit by the glowing embers of the ops building, and followed McDaniel on his hands and knees as they scooted to a place where rocks shielded them from the itchy trigger fingers of the guys in the bunker.

"That could be a problem," McDaniel commented. They had found shelter in an outcropping and sat down to regroup. Mathis rubbed the dirt and blood off his left hand onto his pants leg.

"Hadn't thought of that," Mathis admitted, feeling a touch of defeat. "And for all we know, it could have been gooks in that bunker, using one of our M-16s."

"Not likely," McDaniel said, "but yeah, it's possible."

"So what do we do?"

"Play it by ear, I guess. Come up on the bunkers real slow, take cover, and call out as quietly as possible."

Mathis shrugged. It was as good a plan as any at this point. "Well, we know Bunker One is occupied. Shall we try Bunker Two?"

"Might as well," McDaniel said, "can't dance."

"Yep," Mathis said, finishing the worn catch-phrase: "too deep to dig, too wet to plow."

Together they rose into hunched-over positions and picked their way through the rocks toward Bunker Two. When they got close, they could see it was just a pile of lumber and sand bags, even in the wavering light of the flare and the increasingly dense fog. McDaniel patted the air as he crouched down lower, and Mathis knelt behind one of the larger rocks.

"Anybody there?" McDaniel whispered.

"We're GIs," Mathis added, speaking a little louder in case whoever might be there didn't hear McDaniel. There was no reply. The only sound was the whop-whop sound of the flare helicopter way overhead and the muffled crackle of dying flames from the distant buildings.

"Come on, guys," McDaniel pleaded, "let us know if you're there. We're looking for survivors." Silence.

"No one there," Mathis suggested glumly.

"So, on to the next," McDaniel told him, rising to his feet. Mathis followed him along the shoulder of the mountain toward the next bunker. It, too, was a shambles, and there was no answer to their calls.

"This is where that one group of gooks slipped in through the wire," McDaniel noted. "Makes sense they would destroy those bunkers."

Stealthily they continued their patrol, stopping when they reached the rocks just above Bunker Four.

"We're Americans," Mathis called out this time. "Anybody alive in there?"

Surprisingly, he heard a weak groan.

"Hey," McDaniel whispered urgently, "are you okay? Can we come in?"

It sounded like "Uh-huh," but it might have just been a strangled grunt. Worried it might be Kasperek, Mathis ignored McDaniel's cautioning gestures and scrambled down to the side door of the bunker, which seemed to be intact. The door was partially open, so Mathis pulled it the rest of the way, revealing a pitch black interior. He felt McDaniel come down and stand close beside him, his rifle pointed at the opening. McDaniel nudged his shoulder and handed him a flashlight. His right hand curled tightly around the pistol grip of his rifle to keep it pointed ahead of him, Mathis clicked on the flashlight for just an instant, so he could get a glimpse of the interior. Blinking to clear his night vision after the short blast of light, he analyzed what he had just seen. Over at the gun port a fifty-cal machine gun pointed uselessly skyward. At the back of the bunker were two cots, one of which was empty. The other held a nearly naked man lying on his side, his knees drawn up and his

167

hands clutching his stomach. Mathis was both tremendously relieved and somewhat disappointed to see that it wasn't Kasperek.

Mathis stepped all the way into the bunker, making room for McDaniel to follow, and then turned the flashlight back on, pointing it at the roof of the bunker to dissipate the light. McDaniel rushed over to the cot and knelt down beside it, leaning his rifle against one end. "How bad are you hurt?" he asked gently.

"Don't know," the young man answered shakily. "Shot in the stomach."

"Let me look," McDaniel told him, pushing him onto his back and drawing his hands away from his bloody torso. The guy wore only his boxer shorts, and they were soaked with blood. There was still a rivulet of fresh blood running down from a hole in his abdomen, left of center, just below his rib cage. Mathis wasn't a medic, but he could tell this was serious.

"Doesn't look too bad," McDaniel said encouragingly, but Mathis knew he was lying for the wounded man's sake. McDaniel reached into one of the cargo pockets of his pants and pulled out a field dressing package. Ripping the plastic open, he withdrew the pad, unwound the straps, and placed it carefully on the hole. With remarkably tender hands he slid one strap under the man's body and brought it around to tie off with the other. "We'll get the medics here with a stretcher as soon as it gets light," he promised. The young man nodded, but Mathis couldn't tell if he really believed it, or was just willing to pretend he did.

"What's your name?" Mathis asked.

"Cochran," the young man managed to say.

"You seen any other guys," Mathis asked him.

"Hiding in the rocks, I think," Cochran gasped. When McDaniel was done, the wounded man rolled back onto his side and moaned. "Water?" he asked.

Mathis looked around the scattered junk in the bunker and found a canteen. When he picked it up, he could tell that it held on a small amount, but figured that was probably for the best. He remembered something about not giving water to a wounded man,

168

for some reason. Nonetheless, he handed the canteen to Cochran, who took it and held it to his chest like a child clutching a teddy bear.

"We'll send someone for you," McDaniel promised again. "Just hang in there. We're going to go look for the other guys."

Cochran nodded, squeezing his eyes shut and grimacing in pain.

"Come on," McDaniel whispered to Mathis, and turned for the door. Mathis clicked off the flashlight and followed, handing the plastic cylinder to his friend once they were outside. They climbed back up to the path that circled the camp just inside the bunkers and stopped to get their bearings.

"Think he'll make it?" Mathis asked quietly enough that Cochran couldn't hear.

"Doubt it," McDaniel said, shaking his head slowly. "No exit wound. The bullet could be anywhere."

"Fuck."

"My sentiments exactly."

Depressed by the situation, Mathis followed McDaniel as they crept toward the next bunker, number Five, where Mathis and Kasperek had been when it all started. Mathis had great hopes that Kasperek had eventually ended up there after they had become separated; it seemed the logical place to go.

Here at the far west end of the camp, Mathis hoped the gooks had bypassed this bunker as non-essential to their strategy, and as they approached, they saw it was apparently untouched. They stopped at the top of the path that led down to the bunker entrance, and Mathis called out.

"Anybody there? John, you there?"

"Who is it?" a frightened voice answered. Whispering and alarmed, the speaker's voice was too distorted for Mathis to identify, but he was pretty sure it wasn't Kasperek.

"McDaniel and Mathis," McDaniel replied for both of them

"Oh, thank God!" Mathis now recognized the sound of Yoder's voice. They heard scuffling and then the door to the bunker swung open. "Come on in."

"Man, I'm glad to see you guys," Yoder said once they were all inside the bunker. "I thought maybe I was the only one left alive."

"Have you seen John?" Mathis asked him. "Kasperek?"

Yoder shook his head. "Not since you guys left the bunker together. When I ran out of fifty-cal ammo, I went looking for you. Where'd you go?"

"All over the place," Mathis told him dismissively. "We came back looking for you, but you were gone."

"I wasn't gone but a few minutes. We must have just missed each other."

"You seen any gooks lately," McDaniel asked.

"When I left the bunker, I saw three of them running around, so I came back. Man, I nearly pissed my pants. So they're still around?"

"Far as we know," Mathis told him. "Last we saw, they were down at the chopper pad, removing their dead and wounded. We're not sure what they're going to do next."

"And no one's coming to help us?"

"Can't," McDaniel explained. "Spookies and gunships are all they can send until daylight. And that's still a ways away."

"So what do we do?"

"Not much," Mathis said. "We're just looking for John, and checking out the rest of the camp. A bunch of guys are at the cave and the commo bunker. The first sergeant's in charge."

"Can I go with you guys, then?" Yoder was begging, obviously fearful of being left alone again.

"Yeah," McDaniel said, "the more the merrier. You got any ammo for your sixteen?"

Yoder bent down and retrieved his M-16 from a cot. He patted the magazine. "I just got this one magazine, but it's full."

When they stepped outside, Mathis noticed how the fog was getting thicker, and doing so pretty rapidly. The moisture in the air was condensing on his face and on his rifle, making the weapon somewhat slippery to hold on to. The light from the parachute flares was substantially diffused, and the swirl of fog around them reminded him of old horror movies set on English moors. They climbed up to the perimeter path and stopped.

"Next bunker?" McDaniel asked.

"Maybe we ought to check the Pagoda," Mathis suggested. "He might have gone there."

"They were getting hit pretty hard earlier," McDaniel reminded him.

"It's quiet over there now," Yoder offered.

"Worth a shot, I guess," McDaniel acknowledged. He led them through the rocks to the southwest corner of the stone building, and all three of them pressed their backs against the exterior wall. Above them was the slit window of the ASA SCIF.

"Sergeant Johnson," Mathis called out tilting his head back. "You still in there?"

"Who's that?" a worried voice replied from inside.

"Bill Mathis and a couple other guys. You all right in there?"

"For now," Johnson answered, his cigarette-blurred voice distinctive. "Can we come out now?"

"Don't know," Mathis told him. "There's still some gooks down by the chopper pad. We don't know what they're going to do next."

"Shit. I want to get out of here."

"So the gooks never got inside the building?"

171

"Nope. We've been talking to the guys in the main room. A couple are wounded, but they held the VC off. Meanwhile we've been trying to do our destruction protocol."

Mathis knew that the equipment and paper inside the SCIF was all highly classified, and there were strict rules about destroying it if there was any danger the enemy could get to it. Johnson and Farley had begun the process earlier, when Mathis, Kasperek, and McDaniel had come by near the beginning of the attack. Once the power went out, the shredder was no longer operational, and with the two men locked inside the small room, using the thermite grenade taped to the top of the file cabinet was out of the question.

"We got the equipment pretty well smashed," Farley's voice floated out the window. "But the tapes and documents are still sitting here."

"Okay," Mathis said, "once we know it's safe, we'll get the burn barrel going out here. It shouldn't take too long to destroy that stuff."

"Meanwhile," McDaniel interjected, "just stay in there. You're pretty safe there."

"Roger that," Johnson replied.

"Have you heard from John Kasperek?" Mathis asked.

"Not since you came by before."

"Could he be in the main room?"

"Don't think so," Johnson told him. "No one's come in or gone out since the shit hit the fan."

"Okay," Mathis said dejectedly. "We'll keep looking. Keep your heads down."

Mathis felt drops of cold water hitting the back of his head. The fog was condensing on the roof and starting to run off. Or was it more than that? He held out his left hand, and felt occasional drops of rain splatter on it. Above them the latest parachute flare died out, plunging them into darkness, and no replacement flare sprung into life.

"Chopper's leaving," McDaniel noted. Mathis could hear the helicopter's roar diminishing as the aircraft departed.

"Maybe another one will come and replace him," Yoder suggested hopefully.

"Not if it's raining," McDaniel said. "I think we're on our own now."

It was a light, gentle rain, but they were soon soaked. The rain clouds hid the moon and stars, and Mathis' vision was now limited to dark shapes and shadows. Just when you think it can't get any worse, he thought, it does.

FOURTEEN

The three young men stumbled through the dark, their way lit only by the sputtering flames of the ops building and generator shed, and those fires were dying quickly in the rain. Moving slowly as they stepped carefully around the rocks that littered the sides of the paths, they skirted around the back of the Pagoda, past the collapsed officers' hooch, and circled wide around the generator shed to avoid being silhouetted by its remaining blaze. By mutual agreement they had decided to go to Bunker Eight, where Mathis had found some survivors earlier. Mathis hoped that Kasperek had joined those guys as they sheltered in place.

As they approached the bunker, Mathis could just barely discern the cross on the big rock to their left. It still stood proudly, and he hoped that it was somehow a symbol of faith in the future and ultimate redemption, but feared it simply marked the graves of so many men, possibly including John Kasperek. They stopped just above the roof of the misshapen bunker and McDaniel announced them in a hoarse whisper: "Hey, guys, we're Americans. You still in there?"

A high-pitched voice behind them answered, "No shoot!" Mathis swung around violently and raised his rifle, his finger tightening on the trigger. Out of the mist and rain a small figure approached, dressed in a white shirt and black trousers. He had his hands high in the air, and took small tentative steps. "It's one of the KPs," Yoder said. Mathis had quickly reached the same conclusion. The Vietnamese men who worked in the mess hall and club were mostly ignored by the Americans, and Mathis had forgotten they were on the Rock and just as threatened by the Viet Cong attack as the Americans.

"Who are you?" Mathis asked in Vietnamese.

"I am Thao. I work in kitchen."

"Where were you?" McDaniel asked, also in Vietnamese.

"We hide when VC attack. Are VC gone now?"

"We do not know," Mathis said. "Have you seen other Americans?"

"Yes, and many are dead. A civilian man is over there somewhere, and he is still alive." Thao motioned vaguely in the direction of the officers' hooch. Mathis guessed he was talking about Weller, the NSA rep.

Yoder spoke up, in English, asking, "Should we take him with us?"

McDaniel shook his head and spoke again in Vietnamese. "Go back to your hiding place and wait until dawn. That is the safest thing to do." Despite the darkness and rain, Mathis could detect the look of disappointment on the man's face, but he agreed with McDaniel. Having the Vietnamese along would endanger them all. Thao nodded and slipped away.

McDaniel turned back to the bunker and called out, a little louder this time, "Anybody in there?" There was no answer.

"They probably heard you guys talking Vietnamese," Yoder said. Mathis suspected Yoder was right. The sound of Vietnamese would have convinced the guys in the bunker, if they were still there, that the men outside were VC provocateurs.

"I think we need to go back to the cave," McDaniel announced authoritatively.

"But what about John?" Mathis protested, knowing in his heart that McDaniel was right.

"You can't see shit now," McDaniel told him. "Everyone's hiding, afraid the gooks will come back. We're just wasting our time. It'll be light in a few hours, and then we can find him."

"Okay," Mathis said. "You guys go back, and I'll keep looking."

"Bill!" McDaniel scolded. "That's just plain stupid. You won't find him in the dark, and probably get your ass shot off looking, either by the gooks or by our own guys." Mathis understood the logic, and realized his chances were virtually nil, but he felt compelled to find his friend.

"He's probably holed up somewhere, and he'll come out when it's safe," Yoder added. "You got to stay with us."

Mathis weighed all the pros and cons, and finally reached the conclusion that his companions were correct. Getting himself shot wouldn't help Kasperek.

"All right," he finally conceded. "But let's keep looking on the way to the cave."

"Sure," McDaniel agreed. "Hell, he might already be there ahead of us."

Mathis felt a slight surge of hope at that thought. It was possible. John knew of the cave, and might have been making his way there while Mathis was out looking for him. There were only so many places to go on the Rock, and that cave was one of the most promising.

With McDaniel leading, the three men headed north across the camp, staying just to the west of the line of destroyed billets and other buildings. The flickering flames from some of those buildings, as well as from the ops building to their left, provided barely enough light to guide them along the twisting rocky path. Mathis marveled at the destruction. Every building in the camp, it appeared, had either been blown up or burned down. The rain soaked his hair and ran down his face into his eyes, and he kept brushing the water away to clear his vision. He visually searched every dark nook and cranny between the rocks and the rubble of fallen buildings, hoping to see John, but also making sure there were no Viet Cong lurking in the shadows. Across the jumble of the broken billets he tried to make out what was happening at the helicopter pad, but the swirling fog and constant rain obscured his vision so much he could only see a wide dark area that might or might not contain movement.

They made their way slowly, striving to pick out landmarks in the moisture-laden darkness and watching their steps to avoid hidden obstacles on the rough terrain. Soon Mathis realized they had passed the last ruined building and a gaping dark hole in the ground dropped away on his right. It took a second for Mathis to recognize the reservoir. McDaniel held one hand up to signal they were halting.

"Americans coming in," McDaniel called out in a voice just loud enough to be heard over the pattering of the rain on the rocks.

"Identify yourself," a disembodied voice replied.

"Sergeant McDaniel, Spec 5 Mathis, and PFC Yoder."

"Okay. Come on ahead. Take it easy."

They edged forward and started down the path to the cave. The guard who had stopped them revealed himself as he held his rifle vaguely pointed in their direction until he was convinced they were who they said they were.

"Top in the cave?" McDaniel asked the man.

"Last I knew," the guy replied, lowering his M-16. "What's happening out there?"

"Fuck if we know," McDaniel told him.

""The whole camp is blown to shit," Yoder piped up. "Man, you ought to see it."

"I'll wait," the guard said as he ducked back down to his hiding place.

Inside the cave Mathis welcomed the relative dryness the cave's roof provided. While McDaniel sought out the first sergeant to report, Mathis moved around the crowded floor of the cave, asking each man if he had seen Kasperek. No one had seen him, but Mathis did find Albertson and Davies, two of the other ASA guys who worked in the SCIF. He reassured them that the SCIF was so far secure and the Sergeant Johnson and Farley were okay. Moving on, he caught up to Yoder, who had joined up with a couple of his buddies and was excitedly—and exaggeratedly—telling them about his adventures during the night. When no one else knew anything useful about Kasperek, Mathis found the place at the back of the cave where McDaniel had treated his head wound and sat down, resting his head on his crossed arms atop his drawn-up knees.

177

Instead of welcoming the relative safety and comfort afforded by the cave, Mathis was blanketed with despair and depression. His friend—possibly the best friend he had ever had—was still out there somewhere, and Mathis didn't know if he was dead or alive, or maybe seriously wounded. The camp was decimated by the enemy attack, there was no chance of rescue until dawn, and the Viet Cong might be massing for yet another assault to finish off what few Americans remained. It was hard to imagine how the situation could be any worse, but such scenarios did flit through his mind.

Someone plopped down beside him. "Tired?" McDaniel asked compassionately. Mathis raised his head.

"Yeah. No. Yeah. I don't know. Everything is so fucked up. No one's seen John."

"He'll turn up in the morning," McDaniel assured him.

"Yeah, but how?" Mathis wanted to believe Kasperek was hiding in the camp or the rocks somewhere, but a nagging voice in the back of his mind kept reminding him of the CQ who had been executed at the flag pole.

"Well, we can't do shit about it right now, so quit worrying about it."

"What'd Top say?" Mathis asked him, wanting to change the subject.

"Not much," McDaniel said. "We've still got just one radio working, and can only reach one retrans. Supposedly my SF guys are loading up their choppers and will be here as soon as it's light."

"They bringing reinforcements?"

"I assume so. They better. I could use some hot chow, too."

Until McDaniel mentioned it, Mathis hadn't realized how hungry he was. It somehow felt like a betrayal of John to think about food, but his growling stomach ignored such concerns. "I'd settle for C-rations," Mathis replied. "Are there any here?"

"Not that I know of. Any that were up here on the Rock were stored in the mess hall, and that burned down."

"So now we just sit and wait?"

"Afraid so." McDaniel took a drink from his canteen, and then passed it over to Mathis. Mathis gulped down several swallows before handing it back.

"Why don't you catch some Z's, Bill," McDaniel suggested, almost paternally.

"What are you going to do?"

"Me and Top and some other NCOs need to plan what we'll do if the gooks attack again, and what we'll do in the morning. You just stay here and rest."

"Okay," Mathis replied weakly. "And Dan?" McDaniel had started to get up, but he paused and turned to listen to Mathis. "Thanks." Mathis knew it wasn't enough, but it was all he could manage.

"No sweat," McDaniel responded warmly, then rose and walked away.

Mathis crossed his arms over his knees again and let his head sag against them, only to jerk back when a sharp stab of pain reminded him the left side of his head had been wounded. Cursing his own stupidity, he turned his head the other way and gently rested it on his forearm. It was far from ideal, but the floor of the cave was littered with small sharp rocks and he didn't want to lay down on them. He also didn't want to surrender to a deep sleep, for fear he might not react quickly enough if anything happened.

Forcing his tense muscles to relax, Mathis strove to clear his head and not think at all, but his mind wouldn't cooperate. The events of the evening swirled through his thoughts, bouncing around like pinballs, out of sequence and devoid of context. Images of John and Two-dan flashed by, along with scenes inside the SCIF, in the billets, and in the bunker. It was all a jumbled mess, with dark undertones of danger and despair. He tried not to think about the scene at the flagpole, but to no avail. He couldn't stop replaying that horrific moment when the young sergeant was blasted by the VC officer's AK. The man's defiant gesture was both admirable and stupid, for it had gotten him killed. Would he have been spared if he had actually saluted the enemy flag? Mathis doubted it, but who could say for certain? Mathis wondered what he himself would have done in that situation, and then shied away from the answer. He decided to just be glad he hadn't had to make that choice.

He wondered what had become of the Korean, Park, who had so bravely taken on the invading VC with his illicit M-60 machine gun. Mathis hoped the man survived. He also hoped that Park, even if he had died in the process, had taken many of the enemy down as well. And that reminded Mathis of his own body count. He had killed that young man with the RPG launcher with his bare hands. Due to his religious upbringing, Mathis knew he should feel tremendous guilt over the taking of another person's life, no matter what the circumstances, and he was ashamed that he didn't. He didn't regret the Vietnamese's death, which had been unavoidable anyway, and in a way he was inwardly a little proud of the act. He had proven, to himself at least, that he was a real man, not a pussy. He was the Jimmy Stewart character, the peaceful man who shot Liberty Valance because it was the right thing to do. Yes, it was a shame the young man's life ended so soon, but he shouldn't have been on the mountain in the first place. The Viet Cong soldier had chosen to attack the Americans, and had paid the price.

Mathis kept rationalizing until he was convinced, in the front of his mind, that he had done the right thing in the eyes of the Lord, and he had no reason to punish himself. A tickle of reflection at the back of his mind suggested there was more to the situation than he had acknowledged, but he pushed that thought away, knowing nonetheless that it would return at some inconvenient time in the future. In the prevailing spirit of avoidance, he focused his thoughts on McDaniel, who had been such a rock throughout this ordeal. Mathis' admiration of the man had grown tremendously this night. He had been consistently calm, competent, and courageous, and Mathis wished deeply that he himself could be half the man that Two-dan was. Here, he thought, was a man to emulate, unlike his father, who had been so caught up in his petty squabbles with the Church that he had no time for Bill. Mathis realized that had been one of the things missing in his life up until now—a hero, a mentor, a person to inspire his life and be a model for what he wanted to become. For years he had convinced himself he was his own man, setting his own course for the future, independent and beholden to no one, but tonight had proven how hollow that conviction was. Now, at last, he knew what sort of man he wanted to be, and believed he could achieve that goal.

Mathis fell into an uneasy sleep, briefly waking ever few minutes but nodding off again immediately. Vivid dreams roiled his brain, to be forgotten instantly each time he awoke, other than leaving a vague sense of unease behind. Then one dream took on a life of its own, coherent and realistic, and Mathis' chest swelled with emotion. It was daylight on the Rock, and Mathis strolled across the rocky path with glib indifference, admiring the sweeping views of the surrounding plains. All the buildings were undamaged and fresh, as if newly constructed, and the sun shone brightly down from a cloudless sky, yet the temperature was mild and pleasant. A figure appeared in the distance, approaching along the same path as Mathis was walking. As the man approached, Mathis recognized his friend John, and they smiled at each other. "You're safe!" Mathis called to him when he was still a hundred feet away. John nodded, but another man appeared on the path, far behind John, waving his arms in the air frantically. It was McDaniel, shouting some sort of warning.

Suddenly a ring of Viet Cong soldiers rose up from hiding places in the rocks and surrounded Kasperek, pointing their AK-47s at him and shouting in French so that Mathis couldn't understand them. John froze and answered them in French, and that made dream sense because John was from Canada. Whatever he said didn't appease them, however, and all the soldiers released the safeties on their rifles and raised them to their shoulders. "No!" Mathis screamed, an M-60 machine gun suddenly appearing in his hands, but he couldn't fire for fear of hitting John. "Stop them!" he yelled at McDaniel, but the Green Beret had no weapon at all. Mathis could see their fingers tightening on their triggers, and knew his friend's imminent death was inevitable. Unwilling to witness such a horrifying scene, and suddenly realizing it was dream, Mathis forced himself awake with a gasp, the image still burned in his brain. He shook his head violently to clear it, and then noticed that

181

he could see the outlines of the cave opening and silhouettes moving across it. Dawn was near.

FIFTEEN

Mathis felt a stirring beside him, and looked over to his right, where he could just barely make out McDaniel sitting there.

"About time you woke up, sleepyhead," McDaniel chided him gently.

"Is it really morning?" Mathis asked groggily.

"Close enough for Army work. How's your head?"

Mathis reached up and gently touched the damp bandage, and felt only a dull pain. He wondered if the wetness was due to blood, or just residual water from the rain. "Not bad," he told his friend, referring to his wound. "Is it still raining?"

"Negative," McDaniel said. "Quit about an hour ago. Looks like it's going to be another glorious morning in the Army."

"Aren't you tired?" Mathis asked seriously. "Have you gotten any sleep at all?"

Mathis sensed McDaniel's shrug. "I dozed a bit here and there. Us Green Beret's don't need any sleep, you know."

"Yeah, I know," Mathis said cynically. "That's why you've got that big red S tattooed on your chest."

"What can I say?"

Mathis rolled his eyes and stretched out his legs, attempting to ease the various aches and pains that plagued his body. "So what's the plan, Stan?"

"Dan," McDaniel scolded him. "It's Dan, not Stan. You ASA pukes just can't get anything right, can you?" Mathis elbowed him. "Hey, watch it. If you're not careful, I'll use all my ninja kung fu shit on you."

183

"Sir, yes, sir!" Mathis responded with false heartiness. "Beg your pardon, sir! Kiss my ass, sir!" They both began laughing, shaking off the tension that had gripped them since the previous evening.

"Hey, knock it off!" someone grumbled from nearby in the dark. Mathis stifled his laughter.

"Sir, yes, sir," McDaniel replied in a quieter but no less mocking tone, and that set both of them to snorting and snuffling as they tried to laugh with their mouths closed. Mathis had no idea why this was so funny, and the circumstances certainly didn't warrant any laughter, but he nonetheless enjoyed the relief it brought.

"All right, gentlemen, listen up," the first sergeant's booming voice echoed through the cave. Mathis saw the short wiry figure at the cave entrance, backlit by the grey sky behind him, his fists on his hips. "Everyone awake now?" Like all the others, Mathis knew it was a rhetorical question, so no one spoke up.

"Get your gear together and get ready to move out. Once it's full daylight, the medevac choppers will be coming in, so I need all you wounded guys to get ready to assemble down at the chopper pad, once it's secured. We still don't know what the gooks are going to do, so be ready for anything. Men, it's going to be a long fucking day, so get your shit together." And just like that he was gone, presumably back up to the commo bunker.

"Inspirational," McDaniel commented mildly.

"At least he's got a plan."

"Yeah, I know," McDaniel apologized. "We worked it out last night. What about you? Do you want to be medevacked?"

"Naw, I'm fine for now. I've got a really good doctor, you know. He's got a big red S and everything."

"Are you talking bad about my ass again?" McDaniel challenged. They both chuckled. Mathis found the canteen, opened the lid, and took a long swallow of the tepid chlorinated water. Then he splashed some on his face before handing the canteen to McDaniel. While McDaniel did the same hasty ablutions, Mathis retied his boots. Picking up his M-16, he brushed dirt from it and checked the action by dropping the magazine, ejecting the round from the chamber into his lap, and working the charging handle back and forth a couple times. Satisfied, he pushed the ejected cartridge back into the magazine, slapped the magazine into the well, and released the bolt. He made sure it was on SAFE and then used the stock to push himself up into a standing position. The night sky visible through the cave opening was noticeably lighter now.

"Do you think he's still alive?" Mathis asked somberly as McDaniel came to stand beside him.

"Well, sure, probably," McDaniel answered with dubious sincerity. "He knew—knows—how to take care of himself."

The first sergeant reappeared at the entrance, and this time Mathis could make out some of his features. "Sergeant McDaniel, you ready?" he called out.

"Roger that, Top," McDaniel answered.

"Okay, every able-bodied man with a loaded weapon will go with McDaniel to sweep the camp for any remaining gooks. Non-wounded without weapons will follow behind to locate any more wounded out there and help them down to the chopper pad. You wounded guys in here help each other down to the pad. I'll be setting up down there with the radio to guide the choppers in. Any questions?"

"When are the choppers getting here?" someone asked weakly.

"On their way. Anything else?" No further questions were voiced. "Sergeant McDaniel," the first sergeant said, turning it over to him.

"All you guys with weapons, meet me up behind the commo bunker." McDaniel paused, and no one moved. "Now!" he ordered, and Mathis heard more than saw the reaction. McDaniel strode forcefully toward the cave entrance, and Mathis hurried to keep up. They scrambled up the path and found an open area just behind the commo bunker, where McDaniel immediately took up a kneeling position facing the east, his rifle held ready. Taking a cue, Mathis knelt down a little to the right of McDaniel. Behind them other men stumbled up to area and after a brief moment to assess the situation, took up similar positions until there was a defensive ring facing outward.

The sky to the east was showing definite signs of the approaching dawn. The horizon there was a lighter charcoal gray, and no stars could be seen in that direction. There were plenty of stars overhead and to the south, which meant there were no clouds or any chance of rain. The shape of the mountaintop was becoming evident in the diminishing darkness, and Mathis could see rectangular shapes off to his right, the remnants of the billets and other buildings in the center of the camp. Apparently the rain had doused any remaining fires, and it was still too dark to assess the damage, but Mathis could tell it was definitely extensive. To his left Mathis could just make out the rectangular concrete landing pad, which appeared to be empty. Beyond it the mountain dropped away, and he saw scattered twinkling lights far out on the level landscape of Tay Ninh Province. He supposed they represented rice farmers rising early to go tend their crops, and marveled at the seeming peacefulness in the middle of a vicious war.

"Okay," McDaniel said sternly, turning around to face the other men, "How many we got?" Nodding at each man in turn, he silently counted his patrol. "Eleven, including me," he announced with some disappointment. "First thing we gotta do is secure the helipad. We do that by checking all the bunkers at this end of the camp to make sure there aren't any gooks hiding in them. Now, remember, there may be some of our guys in the bunkers, so be careful you don't get shot by friendly fire."

"How do we do that?" one of the men asked.

"Announce yourselves," McDaniel explained, "but do it from cover, in case you draw fire. You find any GIs, have 'em come out. If they've got weapons, they'll join up with us. If not, send them to Top." He paused to allow any other questions, and when there were none, he continued.

"We'll split into two groups for now. You five," he nodded at the men directly to his right, which included Yoder, Mathis now noticed, "and me, we'll cross over to Bunker Thirteen and start

186

circling around counter-clockwise. Spec 5 Mathis here," he reached out and touched Mathis' shoulder, "will take you four clockwise, starting with Nineteen. We'll meet up somewhere around Fifteen or Sixteen. Got it?"

Mathis felt a surge of pride that he had been placed in charge of a team. Although he doubted his own abilities, McDaniel's vote of confidence gave him the mental strength to seize the opportunity. "Let's go," he said to the four men on his left, rising to his feet. Remarkably, they followed his command without question. Even more amazing was the fact that one of the men wore sergeant stripes, but had meekly acceded to Mathis' authority. While McDaniel led his men south across the camp, Mathis crept cautiously down the path toward Bunker Nineteen, only fifty or sixty feet away. As he got closer, he began to perceive the destruction. The corrugated tin roof tilted downhill, and broken lumber poked out from beneath it. Mathis made hand gestures to the guys behind him, having them spread out and take cover in the rocks. He himself knelt down behind an outcropping.

"Don't shoot, guys," he called out, "we're Americans. Anybody in there?" Silence. "Are you there?" Still no response. "I'm coming in, don't shoot." Mathis moved forward, found the path down to the entrance, and edged down until he could see in. The door was hanging askew by a single hinge, and through the opening Mathis could only see a jumble of wooden beams. It was still too dark to really see inside, but the clutter he could see seemed to preclude anyone being there, at least anyone alive. But just to be sure, Mathis called out again. "Anyone there?" As before, there was only silence. Shaking his head, Mathis climbed back up to the perimeter path, where his four men came out of the rocks to meet him. "Nothing," he told them. "On to the next."

It was still not light enough to see well, but the path between Nineteen and Eighteen seemed to have had a lot of cross traffic, and was littered with spent shell casings, papers, and rags. Furrows in the dirt indicated something—perhaps several things—had been dragged between the chopper pad and the ravine that ran down from the top here. To Mathis, this confirmed the theory that the VC had first penetrated the perimeter in this area, and apparently departed the same way.

Bunker Eighteen was a shambles as well, and had been apparently hit by an RPG or grenade, as the tin roof was peeled back and curled. Mathis announced himself and called out repeatedly, but heard nothing. The wall where the door had been was totally missing, and the grey light of approaching dawn penetrated further here than in the previous bunker. Mathis saw the corner of a cot and one leg of a machine gun tripod. And a bare human foot.

"I need some help," he called out to the men waiting above. "There's somebody in here." Two of his team scrambled down the path and joined him, although neither appeared enthusiastic about it. He pointed out the foot to them, and both recoiled in horror. "I'm going to try and pull him out," he told them, handing one of them his rifle. "You guys make sure this thing doesn't fall down on top of me."

While Mathis edged into the broken mess, the other two reached out to grasp some of the tilted beams and hopefully keep them from falling farther. Mathis ducked under a two-by-four that stretched crookedly across the room and knelt down to grasp the bare ankle he had seen. The skin was cool and there was no reaction to his touch. He tugged on it, but it moved only a fraction of an inch. A blanket hanging from a couple nails blocked his vision of the rest of the man, the dark wool gathered just below the man's knee. Mathis lifted the blanket and after two tries managed to stuff it out of the way. Now he could see the entire form, and he fought back the urge to retch.

The man was dressed only in boxer shorts, and his left leg was tucked awkwardly up under his hips. His arms lay at his side, and his bare chest was sprinkled with small cuts and holes. His face was gone. Where it had been was now just a dark depression littered with white bone fragments and gelatinous globs Mathis didn't want to identify. There was no doubt the man was dead. Mathis backed away as fast as he could, stood and grabbed his rifle from the guy hold up the roof, and then scrambled back up to the path. The two who had been helping him scuttled after him. "What is it?" one of them asked anxiously, perhaps fearing an explosive booby-trap.

188

Mathis took a deep breath. "A dead guy. We'll collect him later."

Continuing on, they approached Bunker Seventeen, at the east end of the peak. Although it showed signs of damage, it was still largely intact. Mathis sent two of his men—he didn't know any of them by name—on ahead to watch the far side of the bunker.

"Anybody in the bunker?" he called out. He was now speaking in a normal conversational volume. "We're Americans. It's time to come out now."

As before, there was no answer.

"Coming in," Mathis warned, and climbed down to the door, which remained closed but unlatched. Reaching across, he grabbed the handle and jerked the door open while falling back against the wall, out of the line of fire from inside, should there be someone in there. Nothing happened, so he peeked around the door frame into the darkened interior. The open gun port allowed just enough of the gray morning light in to show the bunker was empty.

"Is it safe?" someone asked quietly. Mathis at first thought it was one of his team, until he realized the question came from somewhere down the hill. He backed away from the bunker door and peered down at the rocks and shrubs scattered across the slope. A man's head appeared above a rock, and a hand tentatively waved.

"So far," Mathis replied. "Come on up." The man stood up, revealing himself to be a muscular black man with no shirt. He reached down to help another man up, a small white guy with glasses, wearing a shirt far too large for him. The two men began climbing up toward Mathis, who now saw that the white kid had only white underpants and green wool socks on underneath the uniform shirt, which he apparently had borrowed from the black man.

"Jackson? Is that you?" One of Mathis' patrol members greeted the black man as he reached Mathis' position.

"Yeah, who's that?" Jackson responded, looking up at the shadowy figures above the bunker.

189

"Dorchester," the man responded. Mathis made a mental note of the name.

"Hey, Dork, good to see you, man." Jackson grinned and pushed past Mathis to the top of the path. The white kid, looking bedraggled and ashamed, stopped and waited with Mathis, his head hanging down.

"Can I go in and look for my pants and boots?" he asked meekly.

"Knock yourself out," Mathis told him, striving to keep his tone neutral. "We'll wait up top." The kid ducked inside, and Mathis went up to join the others. Jackson was telling his story, and the others were trying to tell theirs at the same time, all five jabbering away excitedly about the terrifying events of the previous night.

"At ease!" Mathis barked, surprising himself with his command voice. "We've still got a job to do. Jackson, do you know if there's anybody else out there in the rocks?"

"No, Sergeant," Jackson replied respectfully, responding to Mathis' authoritative tone more than any rank insignia on his sleeve. "We didn't see nobody but gooks."

"Where are your weapons?"

"Mine's back at the billets," he asserted with an attempt at defiance. "Don't know about Tally's." The white guy, who Mathis assumed was Tally, climbed up and stood beside Jackson, handing the black guy his uniform shirt. Tally was now fully dressed, although his boots were only haphazardly tied.

"Thanks, Mike," Tally told Jackson.

"No sweat, man," Jackson answered, his gruffness not fully disguising the tenderness in his voice as he shrugged on the shirt.

"The VC must have taken my gun," Tally told Mathis apologetically.

Mathis' field of vision was now expanding rapidly. He looked across the deserted helicopter landing pad and saw a gaggle of men emerging from the area near the reservoir. Leading them was a short

190

wiry figure that was instantly recognizable. "Okay," he told Jackson and Tally, "you two go see the first sergeant over there. I'm sure he's got something for you to do."

Tally nodded rapidly and followed Jackson as the two men walked away, following the perimeter path around the pad.

"We've still got another bunker," Mathis told his waiting team. "Let's go check it out."

Mathis arrived at Bunker Sixteen at the same time as McDaniel and his team arrived from the south. Together they cleared the bunker, finding one man dead and another seriously wounded.

"I'll go have Top send someone over for these two," McDaniel told Mathis. "You find anyone?"

"There were two guys hiding out in the rocks. I already sent them to the first sergeant. There's a Kilo in Bunker Eighteen."

"Roger that. I'll let Top know." McDaniel paused and looked around appraisingly. "No gooks so far. That's a good thing. Fuckers are probably back in their caves, sleeping it off."

"I sure hope so," Mathis wished fervently.

McDaniel walked away to report to the first sergeant, and Mathis watched as the other men milled around and talked quietly, three of them lighting up cigarettes. Mathis knew they should be taking up defensive positions and watching for another attack, but his gut told him there wouldn't be one. Besides, he wasn't really in charge; he was a Specialist Fifth Class, not a sergeant, and as such he had no inherent authority. Still, it had been oddly gratifying when the other men had deferred to him and let him make decisions for them. Maybe he was a leader and just didn't know it. With that in mind, he spoke up in a tone that mixed suggestion with command. "Let's, uh, let's spread out a little and keep an eye out for gooks. They might still be out there, you know." Mathis moved closer to the down slope and lifted his rifle into a port arms position. Taking the hint, the other men wandered apart slightly and tried to look attentive.

* * *

191

"Listen up," McDaniel said when he returned. "The first sergeant's having some guys clear off the chopper pad and secure it for the dust-offs. He's also separating the wounded so the most serious go first. He wants us to finish sweeping the Rock for gooks and start accounting for people.. Let's move out." McDaniel led the others briskly down the path past the bunkers his team had just cleared, headed toward Bunker Twelve. Mathis fell in behind McDaniel, both relieved and disappointed that he was no longer in charge. Twelve was totally demolished, so they quickly moved on to Eleven, from which they could look down the line of devastation that marked where the billets and mess hall had been. McDaniel sent Yoder and two others down to inspect the bunker, while he and Mathis gazed speculatively at what had been the main garrison area.

"There's nothing left standing," Mathis commented dejectedly.

"The buildings weren't that great to begin with," McDaniel noted. "Won't be that hard to rebuild."

"Should we go check them out?"

McDaniel pursed his lips and squinted his eyes. He looked around at the upper end of the camp, where the Pagoda sat draped in broken antenna cables and masts. "Let's do that last," he said finally. "We need to get the Pagoda secure and operational. We'll all be sleeping in tents for a while anyway."

"Yeah," Mathis agreed, "my guys need to get a burn barrel going right away, before the gooks come back."

"Sarge!" Yoder yelled from the bunker. "We got someone."

"A gook?" McDaniel shouted back, gripping his rifle with both hands.

"Naw, a couple GIs," Yoder replied. Talking downhill, Yoder said in a gentler voice, "Come on guys, it's okay." McDaniel and Mathis, followed by the rest of the patrol, went over to the path leading down to the bunker and crowded around as two bedraggled soldiers climbed up from the rocks and shrub far below, pulling themselves up the steep slope by grabbing branches and rock outcroppings. When they reached the bunker, Yoder and his buddies boosted them the rest of the way up. Both were thin and short—one had bright red hair with bits of leaves stuck in it, and the other looked Hispanic. Mathis noticed that the redhead was limping badly.

When they reached the top, Mathis was surprised to discover that there was now enough ambient light for him to read their name tapes. The redhead's name was Callaway, the other was Rodriguez. "Is it over?" Callaway asked tremulously, his eyes darting left to right.

"For now," McDaniel said. "How bad is your leg?"

"I think he broke his ankle," Rodriguez told them, holding Callaway up by his arm.

"Take him down to the chopper pad for medevac," McDaniel instructed Rodriguez. "Then help Top get shit organized."

"Yes, Sergeant," Rodriguez answered obediently. He seemed just a little dazed by the previous night's events. He pulled Callaway's arm over his own shoulder and guided him down the path toward the east end of the camp. The rest of the men stood around, awaiting orders. Mathis kept glancing over at the nearby orderly room, and the Viet Cong flag still flying above it.

"Mathis and I are going to check out the orderly room," McDaniel announced. "The rest of you guys go on to Ten and Nine, see if there's anyone else hiding in the rocks." At first the men just looked around, unsure how to proceed without leadership, but finally Yoder spoke up. "Come on, guys. No big deal." With that Yoder strode off toward the next bunker, and the rest meekly followed.

McDaniel looked over at Mathis and raised his eyebrows. Mathis smiled and shrugged. Together they wended their way through some rocks toward what had been the orderly room. Because of the uneven terrain, the building had been erected on pilings, and the floor appeared to be intact. The rest of the building's framing was broken and twisted, with tilted plywood walls holding up swaths of ripped canvas. Filing cabinets were knocked over on their backs. The desk Mathis had rifled still lay on its side, the drawers scattered around it. The other desk and the tables were littered with debris.

193

"What a mess," Mathis commented.

"Hope it doesn't screw up my pay," McDaniel countered. That hadn't even occurred to Mathis, and now it worried him. Everyone knew that if your pay paperwork got messed up, it could take months to get it straightened out. They stopped a few feet away to assess the situation. They were approaching the orderly room from the back, where the flooring was higher due to the slope of the ground, and were trying to decide whether to go around to the front or try to climb up and work their way through the debris.

"Who's out there?" a voice demanded from somewhere beneath the floor.

"Americans," McDaniel answered. "You can come out now."

Mathis just now remembered talking to someone hiding under the floor of the orderly room when he had searched it, and watched three men crawl out and stand up in front of them, brushing dirt from their uniforms. He assumed the two enlisted men were the guys he had spoken with; what were their names? The third man was Lieutenant Gretchen, whom Mathis had met yesterday evening, an event that now seemed like ancient history.

"Morning, sir," McDaniel greeted the young officer.

"What's going on, Sergeant?" Gretchen asked. "Is the camp secure?"

"We're checking now, sir. So far, so good."

Gretchen kept straightening and brushing at his uniform.

"Where's Captain Ashbrook? I need to report to him." Gretchen ran one hand through his hair to smooth it out.

"Haven't seen him. You're the first officer we've come across."

"Me?" Gretchen seemed taken aback by this information. "So, who's in charge?"

"First Sergeant."

"He's down at the chopper pad," Mathis interjected. "Getting ready for the dust-offs."

"We have comms with Division?" Gretchen asked.

"Yes, sir," McDaniel answered. "A single prick twenty-five, but that's good enough."

Mathis looked over at the other two guys who had been under the orderly room with the lieutenant. Their nametapes refreshed his memory: PFC Ross and SP4 Gunther. "You guys okay?" he asked. They nodded. "See. I told you I'd be back." Mathis instantly regretted the self-serving comment, but what was done was done. He spoke to Lieutenant Gretchen. "Were you down there all night, too, sir?"

"Most of it," Gretchen answered. "I guess that was you these two spoke to before I arrived. A terrible thing. We were lucky the VC didn't find us."

"It was bad all over," McDaniel pointed out. "Lots of casualties. But at least they didn't get into the Pagoda."

"And they're all gone, now?"

"Looks like it. No one's seen any gooks since just after midnight. Doesn't mean they won't come back, though."

"We need to find Captain Ashbrook," Gretchen said.

"Where would he be?" Mathis asked politely. He figured that if Ashbrook hadn't been seen, he was probably dead.

"He was at the officers' quarters just before the attack," Gretchen said. "Let's go over there."

"We've got to do something else first, sir," Mathis told him, and pointed at the red, blue, and gold flag hanging limply at the top of the flagpole. Gretchen had to step farther away from the building to see it.

"Understood," Gretchen said, nodding to Mathis to lead the way.

"I'll meet you at the officers' hooch," McDaniel told Mathis, tilting his head toward the group of men led by Yoder, who were now approaching Bunker Eight. Mathis nodded in understanding, and led Gretchen and the two enlisted men around the east end of the orderly room to the small circular area around the flag pole.

"Oh, shit!" Gunther yelped when he noticed the CQ's battered and bloody body. "Who's that?"

"The CQ," Mathis told them, all three of them now staring at the body and stepping back. "The gooks made him run the flag up, and then shot him when he wouldn't salute."

"Motherfuckers!"

"Exactly," Mathis said, untying the rope and bringing down the flag. He unfastened it from the rope and dropped it on the ground.

"What are you going to do with it?" Ross asked. There was an acquisitive look in his eye.

"We'll turn it over to Division," Lieutenant Gretchen said. "Specialist Gunther, please secure it."

"I got it," Ross said, rushing forward to scoop it up and stuff it under his shirt.

Mathis was sure Division would never see that flag, but he didn't really care. If Ross wanted a souvenir, that was okay with him. He certainly didn't want it.

Let's go," Gretchen said, striding away toward the officers' hooch.

SIXTEEN

Sunrise was now only minutes away. Although the plains around the mountain were still shrouded in coal-mine blackness, aside from a few tiny sparks of light, the camp at the peak was slowly resolving into definable shapes, none of them appealing. On his left Mathis could now see the remains of the generator shed. There was a large blob of blackened metal at the center, surrounded by kindling from which thin wisps of smoke still rose. As they climbed the gentle slope up to the officers' hooch, he looked back and saw the cross on the rock, now clearly outlined against the sky. Again, he wondered what, if anything, it signified. Resurrection? Salvation? Or simply a memorial to the fallen?

Voices erupted from beyond the cross, but they were cheerful, joyful shouts of greeting and welcome. Apparently McDaniel's group had found a group of survivors, probably the ones Mathis had encountered last night near Bunker Eight. Ahead of Mathis, Lieutenant Gretchen had suddenly run and dropped to his knees next to a man lying on the ground in front the pile of wood that had been the officers' hooch. Mathis stood behind him as Gretchen gently pulled at the man's shoulder and rolled him over onto his back, revealing the ripped front of his uniform shirt, now crusted with dirt and dried blood.

"It's Captain Ashbrook," Gretchen said grimly. Mathis could see that for himself. The company commander stared lifelessly at the disappearing stars overhead. His .45 automatic pistol lay at his side.

Scuffling sounds came from the remains of the hooch, and Mathis spun to face them, bringing his rifle to his shoulder. He could hear boards being moved against each other, and grunts and groans. Gretchen grabbed Ashbrook's pistol and jumped up to stand beside Mathis, while Ross and Gunther hid behind them. Finally a board next to the intact steps was pushed aside, and a human head poked out, his eyes gleaming through the shadows. Seeing the rifle pointed at him, the man cringed and cried, "Don't shoot! It's me." Mathis recognized the voice of Carson Weller, the NSA rep.

Mathis lowered the rifle. "Come on out, Mr. Weller."

"Thank God!" Weller proclaimed, crawling out from underneath the floor of the building and pulling himself to his feet. While he brushed dirt from his plaid shirt and black slacks, another head appeared in the hole under the hooch. "It's okay," Weller said to the guy, waving him forward. Weller turned to Mathis and Gretchen. "It's three of the KPs," he explained. And sure enough, three Vietnamese men dressed in white shirts and black slacks emerged to crowd together behind Weller, as if seeking his protection.

"Anyone else in there?" Gretchen asked.

"No," Weller said, shaking his head. "Just us." He looked over at Captain Ashbrook's body. "I was afraid of that. When we heard the first explosions, he ran out and didn't come back. I heard shots, but wasn't sure what happened. Then this hut exploded, and I found myself under the floor somehow. These three showed up a little later. At first I thought they were Viet Cong, but when I heard them talking about what was happening, I knew they weren't."

"What about Captain Starr?" Gretchen asked. "Where is he?" Starr was the company XO.

Weller shook his head. "He went out just before the attack started. I think he was going to the operations center. I haven't seen him since."

Everyone looked over toward the Ops building, but it was just a smoldering ruin. If he had been there when it was attacked, there was virtually no chance he survived.

"He might be at the Pagoda," Mathis suggested, with an ulterior motive. He was hoping that Kasperek had sought shelter there, and wanted to get up there as soon as possible to check.

"You're right," Gretchen said, and took off in that direction, with Mathis and the others close behind.

"Did they get into the SCIF?" Weller asked Mathis quietly, as if it needed to be kept confidential.

"Don't think so," Mathis told him. "As of a few hours ago, anyway."

"That's good. So they had time to go through the destruction protocol."

"Once the power went out, they couldn't use the shredder," Mathis said, "so we'll need to get a burn barrel going. But I'm pretty sure they smashed all the equipment."

Before Weller could continue, the men came around the corner of the Pagoda and approached the door. As they gathered in front of the Pagoda, McDaniel and three other soldiers joined them.

"Found a dead gook," McDaniel announced. "Over in the rocks."

"So how many does that make?" Gretchen asked.

"He's the first I know of," McDaniel answered with a shrug. "They hauled away the rest, I imagine."

"No doubt," Gretchen agreed. He turned to the door of the Pagoda. "Is there anybody in there?" he shouted. "It's Lieutenant Gretchen. You can come out now." Mathis could hear surprised voices inside, and the sound of furniture being moved away from the door.

"Just a minute, sir," someone yelled from inside.

"I found a Manchu sergeant at Eight," McDaniel told Mathis—and indirectly Gretchen. "He's taking the rest of the guys around to check out the other bunkers."

"Thank you, Sergeant," Gretchen said distractedly, watching the door of the Pagoda. Finally the door jiggled and swung open slowly. One man stumbled out and took a deep breath of the cool morning air. Other men filed out and milled around, obviously glad to once again be outside that stuffy stone building. "Is Captain Starr in there?" Gretchen asked.

"Who?" one man mumbled.

"No, sir," another answered. "Haven't seen him since yesterday."

"How about John Kasperek?" Mathis asked anxiously.

"Huh-uh," a couple men answered. "Just us."

Weller pushed past the last man exiting the building and rushed inside to check on the SCIF. Mathis followed him in, wrinkling his nose at the smell. Those men had been cooped up in the Pagoda all night, and now it stank of sweat, fear, and urine. Weller pounded on the metal door to the SCIF, shouting, "Sergeant Johnson, open up, it's me, Mr. Weller." A few metallic clunks later the door was unlocked and opened a few inches so Johnson could peer out and verify who was there. Mathis was relieved. At least the classified documents and equipment had remained secure, because he was now convinced that the SCIF had been the primary objective of the communist attack in the first place. Johnson opened the door wider and allowed Weller to enter. In the still-dim light Mathis could see that the room was a disaster area of broken equipment and piles of documents and books.

"Hey, guys," someone said behind him, and Mathis turned to see Kelso and little McIntosh, the two remaining members of the ASA crew.

"Time for trick change?" Kelso asked facetiously.

"It's all hands on deck, now," Mathis told him seriously. "Why don't you two get a burn barrel set up outside. We've got a lot of classified trash to deal with."

"It's all over now, isn't it?" Kelso asked. "Won't we need that stuff today?"

"They smashed all the equipment," Mathis explained. "So we can't operate, and the Rock still isn't totally secure. The gooks could come back at any time."

"Really?" McIntosh squeaked. "They might come back?" Mathis thought about describing the reality of the situation to McIntosh, but decided he didn't have enough time to convince the hopelessly naïve young man.

"Just get the burn barrel going," he told them.

"What are you going to do?" Kelso asked suspiciously.

"I'm still looking for someone, and guarding the camp." Mathis lifted his rifle up to emphasize the point, with an unspoken

200

accusation about their lack of arms. Grumbling under his breath, Kelso pulled McIntosh outside.

When Mathis emerged, he found McDaniel waiting for him. "We still need to check out the billet area," McDaniel told him. Mathis nodded, watching as Kelso and McIntosh found the rusty fifty-gallon drum on its side and set it up so it could be used to burn tapes and documents.

The barracks area was a shambles. The mess hall at the south end had burned to the ground, as had the Special Forces hooch at the north end. In between, the billets hooches and club had either been blown up or burned, the paths littered with shattered wood, scraps of canvas, and assorted personal belongings. At Mathis' insistence, he and McDaniel first went to the hooch Mathis had shared with Kasperek. Yoder had tagged along, preferring not to go with Lieutenant Gretchen to the chopper pad.

The roof was gone from the hooch, and the walls were shattered, pushed outward by an internal explosion. Wooden beams lay in every direction, with splinters and nails poking out dangerously. Mathis started to pick his way through the mess, and then stopped when he heard a familiar sound. McDaniel heard it too.

"Choppers," McDaniel observed, tilting his head back to scan the sky. Only a couple stars could still be seen; the rest of the sky was indigo, brightening to a medium blue in the east, where Mathis thought he detected a transparent ray of light rising from beyond the horizon. The staccato roar of at least two or three helicopters could be heard, growing in volume as they approached from the west.

"Thank God," Mathis breathed with deeply felt relief. For hours he had been suppressing the despair and helplessness that being trapped on the mountain top brought, knowing there was no escape and no relief possible. Now, at last, they were reconnecting with the outside world, with the rest of the Army and the security that massive organization could bring. More than anything, he wanted to get in one of those choppers and fly away, to go somewhere safe, to go anywhere but here. Twisting around, he searched for any sign of the helicopters, and finally saw a flickering

201

of the blades. He took a deep breath and continued feeling his way forward through the debris of his former billet.

The floor of the billet was still relatively intact, and once he was on it he began shoving aside the broken beams to make his way over to where his and Kasperek's bunks had been. His own wooden cot was right where he had left it, although two of the legs were broken and it tilted sharply on one side. His foot locker was untouched. Kasperek's metal bunk looked almost pristine, the dark green Army blanket pulled tight over the thin mattress, but it was covered with small pieces of wood and ashes. Kasperek's foot locker, however, was completely wrecked, its contents spilling out over the floor. The eight-track player was shattered, batteries gone, and his tapes were scattered under the bunk. The Who, Jefferson Airplane, The Doors, Blue Cheer, the labels soaked and wrinkled. Mathis knew from experience with the ASA recordings that the tapes were ruined, unsalvageable. What a waste. "John will be pissed," he told McDaniel, surveying the damage.

"They can be replaced," McDaniel noted. What he didn't say, and Mathis was grateful for that fact, was that Kasperek couldn't be replaced, and so far they hadn't found him.

"Here they come," Yoder announced, pointing to the southwest. Mathis and McDaniel turned and watched as three helicopters came in high above the mountain and circled around them counter-clockwise. The sky was brightening quickly now, and Mathis could see there were two Hueys and a Cobra flying in line.

"Smoke," McDaniel said, and Mathis turned to see that a smoke grenade had been popped down at the chopper pad, the yellow billows rising slowly in the abnormally still air. On the second go-round, one of the Hueys peeled off and came in to land on the chopper pad, its downdraft spraying the smoke sideways as it made a hasty landing. Immediately men on the ground began loading wounded men in the chopper, First Sergeant Robinson gesturing and yelling to be heard over the roar of the helicopter.

Suddenly there was an explosion just past the southern edge of the chopper pad, rocks and dirt spewing up in the air.

"What the fuck?" Yoder yelped.

"Mortar," McDaniel said, jerking his head around, looking for the source.

"Somewhere below," Mathis suggested. After briefly ducking for cover, the men at the pad resumed loading wounded, and when the last one for this trip was aboard, they hurriedly backed away as the chopper spooled up and began to lift off. Another explosion rocked the area, this time at the northeast corner of the pad. The dustoff tilted as it quickly gained altitude and zoomed away from the mountain, while the men on the ground went flat, seeking cover. As soon as the medevac was clear, Mathis saw the Cobra come roaring in toward the north side of the mountain and fire a cluster of rockets that blasted the rocks and trees somewhere below the summit. Zooming around in a tight circle, the Cobra made another pass, firing the minigun in its chin turret. More explosions occurred, but this time they were out of sight, halfway down the mountain, a rapid ragged string of blasts that caused the Cobra to veer away and gain altitude.

"Secondaries," McDaniel said. "He got their ammo supply."

"Yeah!" Yoder hollered jubilantly. "Serves those fuckers right."

As the remaining Huey and the Cobra continued to circle overhead, Mathis noticed more soldiers appearing in the area. Dirty, bedraggled, and somewhat befuddled, they were literally crawling out of the woodwork. Some had on their uniforms, some were only partially dressed, none had weapons. They had been hiding under the floors of the shattered buildings, or in bunkers, or behind the rocks, and the sound of the choppers had finally convinced them they could come out.

"If you're wounded," Mathis yelled at them, "go on down to the chopper pad."

"And if you're not," McDaniel added, "help those that are, and report to the first sergeant."

"Anyone seen John Kasperek?" Mathis asked loudly. A couple guys shrugged or shook their heads, but no one responded positively. They just trudged wearily in groups of two or three toward the landing site.

"Let's keep looking," McDaniel told him encouragingly. The three of them climbed over the debris and off the floor of the billet, dodging around the remains of the buildings while they searched the rest of the area. The second Huey came in to collect more of the badly wounded, but there were no more mortar rounds coming in.

"There's somebody here," Yoder called out, pointing down behind a fallen wall. McDaniel and Mathis rushed over, and could see one boot and part of a man's torso, the rest covered by plywood and canvas. Quickly they cleared away the obstructions, only to find that the man's torso was no longer attached to his legs, a bloody ragged gap between the two sections.

"Who is it?" Mathis asked with trepidation.

Reluctantly Yoder leaned down and pulled at the man's shoulder until his face came out of the dirt. "I think it's one of the cooks," Yoder said, letting the man back down gently. A wave of relief washed over Mathis, to be quickly replaced by shame that he was glad that the dead man wasn't someone he knew.

"Oh, fuck, look at this," McDaniel said with a grimace, nodding his head toward the ground a few feet away. Mathis stepped over closer to see what the sergeant was talking about, and felt a lurch in his stomach when it came into view. It was another body, dressed in the white shirt and black slacks of the Vietnamese KPs, but his clothes were slashed to bloody rags. Sprawled on his back, the man had been repeatedly sliced by some kind of knife or bayonet. His slacks had been pulled down and his genitals were missing. Then Mathis noticed that the man's ears had also been sliced off.

"Isn't that the KP pusher?" Yoder asked, his voice tinged with revulsion.

Despite the blood and initial bloating, his face did look familiar. It apparently was the Vietnamese man who told the other KPs what to do, and had never been gentle in his approach.

"Wonder who did it?" McDaniel asked. "Might have been the VC, but might have been the other KPs, too. They sure hated him, and this might have been a good opportunity to get back at him."

204

Yoder knelt down and reached for the man's trousers, apparently intending to pull them up and hide some of the damage, but Mathis blurted out, "Don't touch him!"

Yoder jerked back like he had touched a hot stove. "Why?"

"He's booby-trapped," Mathis told them, and pointed to a curved piece of metal jutting out from under the dead man's armpit. "That's an RPG round under him."

"Shit! You're right!" Yoder backed away.

"I saw them doing that last night, to another body," Mathis explained to Yoder, having already told McDaniel about it.

Suddenly Mathis felt a slight heat on his back, and long shadows appeared in front of him. He spun around to see the rim of the sun just peeking over the eastern horizon. Dawn at last. At the landing pad another Huey had just set down, and men were hurriedly unloading boxes from it. Several soldiers in full battle gear jumped down as well. They all wore green berets.

"About time my guys showed up," McDaniel said approvingly.

SEVENTEEN

Having finished a cursory search of the billet area, and having been joined by the other soldiers who had been sweeping the camp, who in turn reported no sightings of the enemy, Mathis and McDaniel made their way over to the west end of the landing pad, where Lieutenant Gretchen and First Sergeant Robinson were conferring with two of the special forces men who had just arrived.

"You EOD?" McDaniel asked the two men, interrupting the conversation. EOD, Mathis knew, stood for Explosive Ordnance Disposal. Gretchen looked a little annoyed, but apparently recognized McDaniel's authority. One of the men nodded.

"So what do we got?" the man asked. Mathis saw that the man's name was Scallini.

"The gooks booby-trapped some of the bodies with grenades and RPGs," McDaniel told him. "Not sure how they're rigged. There's a Vietnamese KP up by the mess hall with an RPG round under him, and Mathis here saw them plant a grenade under a GI's body up the hill."

Scallini nodded. "Yeah, they do that sometimes. We'll deal with it." He turned to Gretchen. "Sir, don't let anybody move the bodies until we've checked them out, okay?"

"I'll pass the word, sir," Robinson said, and walked away. Meanwhile a large group of walking wounded had gathered near the north edge of the landing pad, awaiting the next medevac. Two Green Berets who had come in on the previous helicopter had set up a small aid station at a cluster of rocks and were applying bandages and antiseptic before sending the wounded over toward the pad. It looked to be at least thirty guys waiting there, all sporting bandages on various parts of their bodies. They had been milling around aimlessly, but suddenly they all looked up and let out a collective cheer. Another Huey, with a big red cross on the nose, was coming in for a landing. The chopper swooped in, hovered for a couple seconds, and then settled down on its skids, its rotors slowing only slightly. The two medics inside jumped out and prepared to load the wounded men, but they were met by a mad rush.

Anxious to get off the mountain, terrified by the events of the previous night, the wounded men abandoned all discipline and order and surged toward the chopper in a pushing, shoving cluster, elbowing each other out of the way to be the first on board. The two medics spread their arms and tried to block them, but to no avail. It was madness, a mob rushing for tickets at a concert or a sale at Sears, with some men stumbling to their knees and others pulling at the men ahead of them to prevent them from getting on ahead of them.

First Sergeant Robinson ran over, screaming at the men to knock it off, and Mathis and McDaniel rushed forward to help him. Yelling and using their rifles like staves they pushed the men back from the chopper, knocking some on their asses. Mathis had to actually point his rifle at one big young man who glared at him with wild eyes, hollering, "I'm going, and you can't stop me!" Before Mathis could decide what to do, McDaniel appeared and punched the man in the stomach, causing him to bend over so McDaniel could shove him backwards.

"Everybody out!" Robinson hollered at the men who had managed to secure a place on the chopper. "No one leaves until I say so." Some meekly, and some sullenly, the men slowly dismounted and rejoined the crowd at the edge of the landing pad. "Now fall in!" the first sergeant ordered, and grudgingly the men formed two ragged lines.

"How many can you take in this load?" Robinson asked one of the chopper medics.

"Twelve," the man answered briskly.

Robinson went over to the left end of the formation and counted off six men in the front row, and six men in the second row. "You men get in the chopper. In an orderly fashion!" The men walked or limped over to the chopper and climbed on board as the medics directed them to their seats. As soon as they were all on board, one of the medics gestured to the pilot and the chopper immediately rose and zoomed off.

Robinson addressed the rest of the men in the formation, his anger evident. "If something like that happens again, I'll court-martial the lot of you! Do you understand me?"

"Yes, First Sergeant," a couple mumbled, and the rest nodded their heads.

"Fall out, but don't go anywhere." The formation broke up, and the men again began milling around. Robinson went over to talk to the medics, and Mathis assumed he was asking them to triage the walking wounded and prioritize their evacuation.

Mathis had been searching the faces of all the wounded, and none were Kasperek. Over on the south side of the landing pad two bodies had been laid out, and as he watched, two men brought another body over and lay it beside the first two. Filled with dread, Mathis crossed the empty concrete pad and approached the bodies, seeking to identify them. McDaniel came up and put his hand on Mathis' shoulder. They stared down at the lifeless forms, their blank eyes staring at the vivid blue sky. He recognized one of the men from the club, but couldn't remember his name. The other two looked vaguely familiar, but they weren't Kasperek.

"This sucks," McDaniel commented.

"Shouldn't they be covered?" Mathis asked. He had never been near bodies before, and didn't know the Army protocol, but somehow it just didn't seem right to leave them out like this.

"Yeah," McDaniel told him.

Mathis spun around and marched over to Lieutenant Gretchen, who was scanning the sky for the next medevac. "Sir," Mathis said, coming to a halt in front of him. "We need to cover up the bodies."

Gretchen looked confused for a moment. Mathis nodded in the direction of the makeshift morgue.

"Yes, of course," Gretchen said. He looked around. "Uh, what with?"

One of the Green Beret medics had walked up and caught part of the conversation. "We brought in a case of poncho liners," he announced. "That would work. They're over here somewhere." He walked over to a stack of boxes and began sorting through them.

"Yes," Gretchen said, "we need to do that. Sergeant," he said to McDaniel, who had come up behind Mathis, "can you get a detail to take care of that?"

"Roger that, sir," McDaniel answered. He stepped away and waved at Yoder, who was sitting on a rock with a couple other guys, smoking cigarettes. "Bring your buddies," he yelled. "Got a job for you."

While Yoder and his two buddies wearily—and warily—ambled over to see what McDaniel wanted, Mathis was surprised to see the Korean generator mechanic, Park, approaching from the direction of the orderly room, carrying a limp soldier in his arms. "Dead?" Park called out as he got closer. Mathis pointed to line of bodies beside the landing pad. Park nodded and carried the man over, gently laying him down and straightening his limbs.

"Who is it?" Mathis and Lieutenant Gretchen asked simultaneously. It didn't look like Kasperek, but he wanted to be sure.

"Captain Starr," Park said, standing up. He gazed down at the body for a moment, slowly shaking his head, and then turned and headed back up toward the Pagoda. "More," he said simply.

Yoder and his friends reluctantly took the stack of poncho liners McDaniel handed them and went over to the line of dead men. After a brief discussion among themselves, they began spreading out the camouflage liners over the bodies, tucking them under to hold them tight.

"Captain Ashbrook and now Captain Starr," Lieutenant Gretchen said mournfully.

"Guess that makes you OIC, sir," Mathis told him. The young lieutenant looked crestfallen, suddenly pressed into the role of Officer In Charge of an entire camp. He took a deep breath and raised his head, apparently accepting his new role as his duty.

First Sergeant Robinson walked up with a questioning look on his face when he noticed Gretchen's face.

"Captain Starr's dead, too," Gretchen informed him.

"Yes, sir," Robinson acknowledged. "Next dust-off is on its way."

"Make sure it's more orderly than last time, Top."

"Will do, sir."

"Mathis and I are going to go look for more wounded," McDaniel said, signaling to Mathis.

"Good idea," Gretchen said without conviction. The lieutenant looked over at the line of bodies being sealed in camouflage nylon fabric and shook his head again. Mathis could guess at what was going through the lieutenant's head. He was the man left in charge, the man who would have to answer all the questions about what happened. Someone would have to be held responsible, and it most likely would be him, even though he was only a visitor on site at the time. Shit rolls downhill, and as the only remaining officer, he would be the main recipient. Mathis didn't envy him.

Mathis left the lieutenant there to ponder his fate and joined McDaniel as he trudged up the center of the camp toward the Pagoda. The sun, just barely above the horizon now, warmed their backs and threw long shadows ahead of them. By a mutual unspoken decision they spread out and swept around the rocks and debris in a zig-zag pattern, searching all the nooks and crannies. As they approached the ruins of the housing area, Mathis found a dead Viet Cong soldier crumpled in a depression, his AK-47 beside him, the wooden stock of which was shattered.

"Another dead VC," Mathis called out to McDaniel in a bored tone.

"Good," was McDaniel's only response.

They slowed as they went through the blasted and burned ruins of the billets and mess hall, taking time to pull aside boards and corrugated tin to look underneath.

210

"Found another body," McDaniel announced quietly. "Soul brother." Mathis knew the additional information was to reassure him that it wasn't Kasperek. He appreciated the kindness.

"Booby-trapped?" Mathis asked. McDaniel bent down to inspect the body, then stood up and shook his head.

Mathis heard something and looked to his right, where he saw a bare-chested soldier rooting through a foot locker while his buddy looked on. The guy on his knees pulled out a clean uniform shirt and stood up to put it on.

"Hey, guys," Mathis called to them. Both turned toward Mathis with questioning looks. "There's one of our guys over there by Sergeant McDaniel. He didn't make it. Can you two please carry him down to the chopper pad for evacuation?"

The guy with a clean shirt nodded and finished buttoning up, but the other guy frowned as if he was about to protest.

"We'd really appreciate it," McDaniel said, his menacing tone belying the polite words. The frowning man paused, and then grudgingly nodded as well. Mathis and McDaniel waited until the two men had made their way to the body and began lifting it out of the rubble before resuming their search. All around the camp men were active, some wandering aimlessly, others moving with a purpose, carrying equipment or weapons. Mathis saw Park sitting on Bunker Twelve, facing outwards, his beloved M-60 machine gun on his lap. Some of the other bunkers also had armed men on or near them, providing at least a semblance of security.

"Fire in the hole!" someone yelled over near the reservoir, and Mathis automatically crouched down. A moment later a small explosion ripped the still morning air, and a small puff of smoke rose to glow in the horizontal sunlight. The EOD guys had apparently just taken care of one of the booby-traps. The sky was getting crowded with helicopters, as a medevac Huey dodged around two small loaches undoubtedly carrying senior officers, while a Cobra circled farther out, ready to swoop in and disrupt any new ground attack. Ignoring them, Mathis pushed on, wending his way through the destroyed buildings and around the rocks, still searching for his friend. A thick column of white smoke rose from the far side of the

Pagoda, evidence that the ASA burn barrel was now in full operation.

Mathis reached one of the main north-south paths that crossed the camp, and realized it was the one on which he had strangled that young Viet Cong. There was no longer any evidence of the struggle that he could see, but it reminded him of the little alcove in the rocks where he had hidden while observing the terrible execution at the orderly room. Crossing in front of McDaniel, who had not yet reached the path, Mathis hurried along until he found the narrow opening in the rocks, which looked much more obvious now in the daylight. He accidentally kicked a shell casing lying on the ground, sending it tinkling into the rocks, and noticed how many of the brass shells littered the ground here. He hadn't noticed them last night, but in the dark and the danger, that wasn't surprising. And the entire camp was littered with spent brass, so it wasn't unusual.

He peered around the rocks and looked into the small grotto. The ammo crate bench was still there, but the hinged lid was up, leaning back against the rocks behind it. The wooden ammo crate was over six feet long, and about two feet high and two feet wide; Mathis assumed it had once housed air-to-ground rockets like the Cobras carried, although why it would be up here on the Rock was a mystery.

McDaniel had come up behind him. "Blood," McDaniel observed, touching some brown splotches on the rocks with one finger, observing his finger tip, and then wiping it on his pants. Mathis noticed that the near side of the box and the lid had several splintered holes, such as would have been made by bullets. He also noticed a black object protruding from behind the end of the crate, one that had distinctive ridges—a combat boot.

"There's someone behind the bench," Mathis said quietly, dread forming in the pit of his stomach. Stepping slowly forward into the alcove, Mathis leaned his rifle against a rock and reached for the upraised lid. He took a deep breath, and then pulled the lid forward and gently closed it so he could see behind it. As he feared, there was a body behind the bench, a man in an Army uniform lying on his side, perfectly still. In his left hand was an M-79 canister round, and halfway beneath him was the grenade launcher, open at

212

the breech. Mathis sank to his knees, staring at the man's torso, afraid to look at his face.

"Is it. . .?" McDaniel asked, staying a couple feet back.

Mathis forced himself to shift his gaze to the head of the body. The man's face was turned downward, his nose in the dirt, and brown specks of dried blood splattered his ear and neck. Although he could only see part of the man's face, he knew instantly who it was. All he could do in response to McDaniel's question was nod once. He placed both hands palm down on the lid of the crate and let his head sink lower and lower.

"Shit!" McDaniel cursed. He took two steps forward and leaned over to look at the body. "Looks like he went out fighting."

"That's small consolation," Mathis mumbled while many emotions washed over him—anger, sadness, disappointment, grief. An overwhelming lethargy engulfed him, and he gradually twisted around and sat down in the dirt, his legs stretched out in front of him, his back supported by the ammo crate. He folded his hands in his lap and stared down at the play of sunlight on the front of his uniform. His mind was a twirling jumble of thoughts and feelings.

"Bill?" McDaniel said, kneeling down beside him. "You okay?"

Mathis nodded, unable to speak.

"We need to take him down to the chopper pad."

Mathis didn't move. He could barely breathe, and the thought of carrying John's body was way too much to bear right now.

"We'll need a stretcher or something," McDaniel said nervously. "I'll go find one. Okay?"

Mathis gave a barely perceptible shrug.

"I'll be right back," McDaniel promised, and leapt to his feet. In an instant he was gone, leaving Mathis alone in the sunny circle of stones. Alone with something that had once been his friend, his best friend ever. Mathis closed his eyes against the glaring sun, but welcomed the searing heat on his face, as if it was well-deserved punishment for some unknown misdeed.

The music began. It was only in his head, but it was crystal clear and reverberated among the stones, the mournful organ and achingly beautiful guitar ringing like a dirge as The Doors played in his mind. Mathis sang along with Jim Morrison: "This is the end. My only friend, the end." And then he sobbed; one huge gulping sob that racked his body and made him clench his fists. He pounded the dirt on either side of his legs and moaned, as hot tears ran down his cheeks. He tried to stifle them, ashamed at his weakness, but he couldn't. He gritted his teeth to muffle the groans rising from his chest, and squeezed his eyes shut, but nothing could stop the flow of tears that ran down his chin and dropped onto his chest. The only solace he could find was in the knowledge that no one saw him in this state, no one could see how pathetic and emotional he was. He was a man, by God, but he wasn't acting like one. Men don't cry, especially warriors. That thought gave him a fleeting lift, as he realized he now was indeed a warrior, but that brought to mind his killing the young Viet Cong on the path, and the execution of the sergeant at the flag pole. The futility of those deaths, compounded by John Kasperek's death, sent him into new paroxysms of grief, and he sat there shaking as sobs racked his body.

EIGHTEEN

By the time McDaniel returned, Mathis had regained at least some of his composure. He had wiped his face dry and taken several deep breaths until he could stand up and look into the sun. He narrowed his eyes to block the strongest rays, but could still feel the heat and see the helicopters flittering around like overgrown insects. McDaniel had brought Yoder with him, and the young PFC was awkwardly carrying a broken cot under one arm, and a folded poncho liner in the other. From the position of the broken legs, Mathis recognized it as his own cot, brought from the devastated billets. He also saw the look of shock pass over Yoder's face when he saw Mathis, and Mathis realized his own face must still look awful, with his eyes red and his face streaked, all wrapped in an expression of extreme sorrow. Yoder quickly recovered and blurt out a falsely cheerful greeting.

"This is all we could find," McDaniel said apologetically, nodding at the cot.

Mathis shrugged in resignation. "Whatever works," he said, embarrassed by the squeaky tone of his voice.

Yoder crowded into the alcove and set the cot down parallel to the ammo crate, resetting it a couple times in a futile attempt to make it sit level.

"Just hold it there," McDaniel told him. "We'll get John." He leaned his rifle against the rock next to Mathis', and stepped over to the end of the crate. He surveyed the situation for a moment, then reached down and grabbed the crate on both sides. Nodding toward Mathis, he said, "Let's pull the crate out of the way first."

Still somewhat in a daze, and not wanting to look at Kasperek's body, Mathis moved to the other end and gazed steadily

215

at the top of the wooden box as he tugged to pull it away from the back wall. The crate was heavier than it looked, but together they were able to scoot it in the dirt almost a foot, until there were only a few inches of gap between it and the cot. Steeling himself, Mathis side-stepped around the end of the crate and squatted down to put his hands under Kasperek's shoulders, while McDaniel straightened Kasperek's legs and reached under his knees.

"On the count of three," McDaniel said quietly, and waited until Mathis looked up and locked eyes with him. Mathis felt the strength that McDaniel was sending him with his gaze and took another deep breath. He nodded that he was ready. McDaniel counted, "One, two, three!" and together they lifted Kasperek's body up and swung it across the ammo crate onto the cot, while Yoder struggled to keep the cot level. McDaniel straightened the body's legs, and Mathis gently folded Kasperek's arms across his chest. Mathis then stretched one of his legs over the crate so he could reach down and retrieve the M-79. Holding it in two hands, he swung the barrel closed on the stock with a sharp click, and then pulled his leg back. He held it out to Yoder, who was still holding the cot upright. McDaniel took over for him, grasping the ends of the cot, so Yoder could take the weapon. Mathis reached down and retrieved his and McDaniel's rifles and passed them to Yoder as well. Yoder juggled the three weapons as he pointed to the poncho liners he had set down on a nearby outcropping. Mathis silently picked up the liners, shook them both free, and laid them across Kasperek's body. McDaniel tucked one around the legs, and Mathis pushed the sides of the other under Kasperek's shoulders.

Mathis suspected that McDaniel had brought Yoder along to help carry the cot, and relieve Mathis of that additional burden, but he wasn't going to allow that. Kasperek had been his friend, and he would take care of him as long as possible. When he looked at McDaniel, his blond hair ruffled and his expression solemn, the Green Beret gave him a return look of understanding and got a better grip on the ends of the cot. Mathis nodded and moved to the head of the cot, his back to Kasperek, and bent over at the waist so he could put his hands around the near end of the wooden cot. While McDaniel's end still had the wooden cross-piece attached, Mathis' end did not. He gripped the doweled ends of the side-supports and lifted until he was standing upright. By the shifting weight, he sensed that McDaniel had his end up as well. Shuffling sideways as Yoder backed out of the grotto ahead of him, Mathis swung the cot around until it was pointed out the entrance and began walking forward, trusting that McDaniel would follow.

With Yoder leading the way, the three-man funeral procession followed the paths down toward the landing pad, at which another medevac chopper had just set down. *I'm too young to be a pall-bearer,* Mathis thought. *And John's too young to be dead.* He felt the pain behind his eyes swell, and sniffled as his nose began to run. With his lips pressed tightly together, he forced down the welling emotions and concentrated on putting one foot in front of the other without tripping or stumbling. It just wouldn't do for him to drop John's body now.

Mathis stood in a daze, seeing and hearing all the things going on around him, but somehow feeling apart, uninvolved. After respectfully laying John's body down along with the many others at the landing pad, he had backed away a few steps and simply observed the growing line of shrouded figures with a detached sense of wonder and unexplained guilt. He hadn't counted them, but there were clearly more than twenty men lying there motionless, a terrible toll.

McDaniel and Yoder had left him there to grieve in his own way. Yoder had been sent to retrieve yet another body that had been found near the billets, and McDaniel was conferring with Lieutenant Gretchen, First Sergeant Robinson, and some Green Beret major that had arrived on one of the helicopters. Mathis looked back down at the row of corpses, and felt a brief surge of panic when he couldn't immediately identify which one was Kasperek. All had their faces and upper torsos covered, rendering them anonymous in death. Then he realized that Kasperek's body was one of the few whose legs were also covered, and was relieved that he could pinpoint his friend's resting place. *I'm being morbid,* he told himself. *What's done is done. I need to move on.* It was easy to say, far less easy to do. He shook his head violently to clear the fog from his brain. From the corner of his eye he saw the diminishing plume of smoke above the Pagoda, and realized he was shirking his duty to the ASA. Those were his people, the ones with whom he shared a shoulder patch, a security clearance, and tons of secrets. It was time to rejoin them.

Adjusting the grip on his rifle, Mathis did a sharp left face and began marching across the camp, up the hill to the Pagoda with its spider web of broken antennas and cables on the roof. He ignored the other men he passed, some of whom were eating C-rations that had apparently been brought in on one of the choppers. Some of the men even had bottles of whiskey that they shared, although Mathis had no idea where those had come from.

When he rounded the southwest corner of the Pagoda, he saw Weller and most of the other ASA crew standing around the burn barrel at a distance, watching the flames and smoke rise in the still air. The barrel itself was glowing a deep red, and ragged holes near the bottom had their own plumes of smoke emanating from within. Thirty feet away Sergeant Johnson sat on a rock overlooking the plain below, coughing and wheezing.

"There you are," Weller said when Mathis joined the group, a slight note of accusation in his tone.

Mathis did a quick mental head count of the men around him, ignoring Weller's implied criticism. "Where's Albertson?" he asked.

McIntosh, the skinny little black kid, said, "He got wounded. I think they took him to Tay Ninh."

"I talked to him in the cave. He didn't say anything about being wounded."

"It wasn't bad," Weller said authoritatively. "Just his arm."

"What about you?" Davies asked, staring at Mathis' head. Mathis had forgotten about his head wound, and realized how the bloody bandage must look.

"No big deal." Mathis jerked his head toward Johnson, who was hacking up phlegm and spitting. "What happened to him?"

"Smoke," Weller said succinctly.

Kelso expanded on that with a note of derision: "To get the fire going good, he dropped that thermite grenade in the barrel. It burned REAL good then." The filing cabinet had had a thermite grenade taped to the top, to allow instant destruction if the SCIF had been invaded. The canister-shaped grenade was an incendiary that burned so hot it would melt through metal. Using it to start a paper fire was like using a sledgehammer to kill a mosquito. Mathis could just imagine the burst of flame that would have resulted, and was surprised that Johnson had even survived.

"What about the equipment?" he asked, looking toward the high window of the SCIF.

"It's all smashed," Farley said proudly, hoisting up the hammer he had used to do it.

"So we'll have to start from scratch to rebuild, huh?"

Weller glared at him. "Rebuild? No, definitely not. This place isn't safe."

"Maybe now they'll reinforce the garrison, build a better a perimeter," Mathis suggested. "We're in the middle of a war. Things like this happen. We were getting good intel here."

Weller scoffed. "We have other sources. It's just not worth it."

Mathis shrugged. It wasn't his decision to make, and it wasn't Weller's either. The great god DIRNSA, as the director of NSA was jokingly referred to, would proclaim the future of the site, and all his underlings would obey. After all that had happened in the last twelve hours, Mathis no longer really cared one way or another. He certainly didn't relish the idea of remaining here on the Rock, with its unpleasant memories and equally unpleasant living conditions, but he regretted the failures, both of the camp's defenses, and the intercept site's intelligence gathering. He wanted to be part of a success for once.

Soldiers were hustling in and out the door to the Pagoda, some carrying cables and poles, as they worked to get the radio relay station again operational. A couple guys were on the roof, propping up the antennas and stringing support wires and coax cables. It occurred to Mathis that Kasperek would have been one of them, had he survived. Everyone looked up when they heard the approach of another helicopter, one whose rotors had a different beat to them. Mathis saw the banana-shaped Chinook lumbering through the air, its twin rotors reduced to blurs, the small jet engines on the sides blasting the air behind it. Mathis wondered if it was coming for the bodies, and decided that it probably was. He turned and walked away from the men around the burn barrel.

"Where are you going?" Weller demanded.

"I'll be back," Mathis told them over his shoulder.

By the time he reached the landing pad, the delivery-truck-sized Chinook was on the ground, its rear ramp lowered so men could unload it. Soldiers rushed in past the hot jet exhaust and grabbed boxes and crates, struggling to carry them back out and pile them a few yards away. First Sergeant Robinson stood at the bottom of the ramp, waving his arms as he shouted directions. As soon as the last crate was offloaded, the helicopter crew chief shouted something to Robinson while pointing at the front of the cargo bay. Robinson signaled for all the men to come back inside, and a moment later they began trickling out, each man carrying several lightweight litters. The men carried the litters over to the rows of bodies and stacked them nearby. Mathis saw what the plan was, and ran over to Lieutenant Gretchen, who was watching the action without appearing to understand it.

"Can you watch my rifle, sir?" Mathis asked, dropping it on the ground at the lieutenant's feet. "We've got to load the bodies." Without waiting for an answer, Mathis gestured to some other men who had come down to watch. "Come on," he ordered them, "let's get 'em loaded."

Accepting that Mathis was somehow in charge, the other men followed him at a run over to the grim make-shift morgue. Mathis directed them to pair up and load the bodies on the litters, and then carry them inside the Chinook, where he assumed the crew chief would show them how to load them. The men who had unloaded the Chinook joined them, and soon the first couple bodies were being

220

lifted and carried inside. Mathis and a guy he didn't know rolled a body onto a litter and lifted it up. This time Mathis was at the back of the litter, and they quickly carried the heavy burden over to the Chinook, dodging the roaring hot exhaust and climbing up inside. They had to wait while another body ahead of them was loaded, and then the crew chief showed them how to lift the litter onto a rack mounted on the side of the chopper and strap the body down.

Back outside a line of stretcher-bearers was forming, and Mathis walked over to the steadily diminishing rows of shrouded bodies, observing with satisfaction that the process was going relatively smoothly.

"Need some help?" Mathis turned to find McDaniel beside him, smiling grimly.

Mathis nodded. "Let's get John next," he said.

"Lead the way," McDaniel responded with a sweeping gesture.

"Get a litter," Mathis instructed him, since McDaniel was closer to the stack than he was. While McDaniel picked up the canvas and aluminum stretcher, Mathis walked over and stood at the feet of Kasperek's corpse. There were still bodies on either side, so they wouldn't be able to set the litter down alongside. When McDaniel arrived, Mathis told him to lay it down a few feet away. Stepping carefully between the bodies, Mathis took a position at Kasperek's head. "I'll get his shoulders, you get his feet," he told McDaniel, and then squatted down to reach under the poncho liner. McDaniel squatted at the feet and wrapped his arms around the knees. Mathis nodded he was ready, and together they lifted the stiffening form and shuffled over to the litter, gently laying it down and re-tucking the poncho liner.

Turning and backing up the litter, Mathis crouched down, gripped the handles, and after looking back to see if McDaniel was ready, he stood up slowly. With the weight pulling at his arms, Mathis stepped out, guiding the litter toward the end of the queue. "You okay back there?" he asked McDaniel over his shoulder.

"Sir, yes, sir!" McDaniel answered with a sympathetically mocking tone. It made Mathis realize he had been ordering McDaniel around, even though the Green Beret outranked him.

Remarkably, he wasn't embarrassed about it; it just seemed like the right thing to do under the circumstances. Maybe he had some leadership skills after all.

When it was their turn, Mathis and McDaniel carried the litter into the helicopter's cavernous cargo bay and lifted it onto the rack indicated by the crew chief. Mathis took extra care to strap down Kasperek's body so it wouldn't fall off the stretcher during flight. Then he and McDaniel hurried back out to make room for the next pair of loaders. Mathis led the way back toward the make-shift morgue, only to discover that all the bodies had already been prepped for the flight, the somber line of stretcher-bearers shuffling slowly forward to the open maw of the Chinook.

Mathis and McDaniel retrieved their rifles and then joined Lieutenant Gretchen, First Sergeant Robinson, and the Green Beret major as they solemnly watched the parade of fallen soldiers disappear into the chopper. After the last body had been loaded and the two stretcher bearers had exited, the crew chief came to the open ramp with raised eyebrows and open hands, asking with gestures if there was anything else. The major shook his head and gave him two thumbs up gestures, signaling they could take off. The crew chief plugged his headset into a port and began talking to the pilot while he pulled a lever to begin raising the ramp. The whistling roar of the jet engines began to gradually increase in pitch, and the rotors spooled up to a higher speed.

Acting solely on instinct, Mathis came to attention and lowered the butt of his rifle to the ground with his left hand, in an "order arms" position next to his foot. Then he slowly raised his right hand to his forehead in a heartfelt and respectful salute. From the corner of his eye he saw that McDaniel and the others, noticing his gesture, quickly followed suit. In moments everyone gathered around the chopper pad was standing and saluting as the Chinook's ramp clanked shut and the chopper began rising from the ground. The big aircraft lumbered into the sky, and Mathis held his salute, turning slightly to follow the flight path. Tears were running down his cheeks, but he no longer cared how that looked.

All he could think about were the good times he had had with John—the music, the conversation, the camaraderie. He had known

John for only a couple months, but that had been long enough to develop a closer relationship than he had even had before. And now it was over. He felt grief, he felt loneliness, and he felt guilt that he had survived. And he mentally chastised himself for concentrating on how Kasperek's demise was affecting him. He thought about how Kasperek's family would be affected, and that image made the tears flow even more freely.

The Chinook crossed in front of the sun, banking right and sweeping around the mountain toward Tay Ninh. Mathis brought his right hand sharply down to his side, and through his tears he saw that the rest of the men did the same, having been waiting for him to do so first. Now he was a little embarrassed, not by his crying, but by the fact that everyone else had followed his lead. He cleared his throat a couple times, surreptitiously wiped his eyes with his sleeves, and picked up his rifle. He took a deep breath and walked a few steps away to compose himself. A minute later McDaniel joined him.

"You okay, Bill?" he asked with genuine concern.

"Yeah," Mathis answered with a sigh. "Could be better, but . . ."

"Yeah, I know," McDaniel commiserated. "You hungry? My guys brought up some C-rations. The major brought some liquor, too, if you're interested."

Mathis didn't really feel hungry, but it had been a long time since he had eaten anything, and he was beginning to feel a little weak and shaky. "I guess I could eat something. As long as it's not that damn spaghetti and meatballs." McDaniel chuckled at this lame attempt at humor. "No booze for me, but did they bring any Cokes?"

"I'll check. They'll be warm."

"I'll deal with it." Mathis was grateful that McDaniel was distracting him from more morbid thoughts about Kasperek. He found a convenient rock to sit down on while McDaniel went over to a pile of boxes to get their meals.

223

"All they had was RC," McDaniel apologized when he returned, handing two cans of the cola to Mathis. "But I snagged a beanie-weenie C for you." He retrieved the cardboard box from under his arm and passed it to Mathis, who set it down while he opened one of the soda cans with the church key he carried in his pocket. He raised the can to his lips, tilted his head back, and let the warm burning carbonated sugar wash over his tongue and down his throat. It wasn't Coke, but it was good enough. McDaniel found a nearby rock to sit on and pulled a small bottle of Jim Beam out of his cargo pocket. With an anticipatory smile, he opened the bottle and took a swig. Coughing, he laughed and declared, "Oh, man, that's good." Mathis finished off his first soda and opened the other one, but sat it down to start on his food.

Baked by the sun, hatless, they sat there and scarfed down their food, their conversation limited to well-worn jokes about C-rations and duty in Viet Nam. They avoided any talk about what had happened the night before, or their mutual friend. Around them the other survivors performed various tasks lethargically, stumbling around and in some cases just falling asleep on the ground. One of the Green Beret medics came over and insisted on changing the bandage on Mathis' head. He applied antiseptic to the wound and covered it with a fresh bandage, and then took down Mathis' name, serial number, and unit in a little notebook.

McDaniel was called away by the major, and Mathis just sat in the sun, letting his head droop and dozing off for a few seconds at a time. He knew he should be doing something productive, but his body was imploding with exhaustion, and it was all he could manage to stay sitting up and not stretch out in the moist dirt at his feet. Propping an elbow on his knee, he rested his chin in a cupped hand and struggled to stay awake, with limited success. He would slip into a deep sleep, only to be jerked awake when his chin slipped off his hand. The sun beat down on the top of his head, and his butt hurt like hell from sitting on a rock for so long, but he kept resting his head on his hand and dozing off, for how long he didn't know.

He awoke again when he heard the sound of more helicopters, and watched as a line of Hueys swooped down and dropped off squads of heavily armed soldiers in full battle gear. He could see they wore the lightning-blazed taro leaf patch of the 25th Infantry Division on their shoulders, so they must be one of the division's infantry companies, sent to reinforce the camp. "Closing the barn door after the horse got out," he mumbled to himself. He watched with only mild interest as a couple officers and several NCOs efficiently directed the men into positions all around the camp.

"Specialist Mathis," voice said behind him. "There you are." It was Carson Weller, scurrying up to confront him. Mathis looked up at the civilian, but didn't stand. "I just got through to headquarters," Weller said proudly. "We have comms again. They're going to come evacuate us this afternoon."

"Us?" Mathis asked, unsure who all was included.

"All of you ASA-ers and me. They've decided this place is too dangerous for us."

"They've brought in reinforcements," Mathis pointed out, nodding at the infantrymen who were rebuilding defensive positions.

"Doesn't matter. The decision was made at the top. We're leaving."

Mathis shrugged. He was still too tired to care.

"There's still some equipment left that we'll need to take with us," Weller continued. "Can you get the men organized and have them bring it down here to the landing pad?"

"What about Sergeant Johnson?"

"He's, uh, he's still not feeling well. That smoke really got to him."

Mathis thought about asking why Weller didn't have Albertson or Davies take over, since both men were technically his superiors by date of rank, but already knew the answer. Both men were excellent technicians, intelligent and competent in their jobs, but neither was a leader. And while Mathis had never considered himself a leader, he had come to realize today that perhaps he had the makings of one. With a deep sigh he pushed himself erect, his butt numb and his legs wobbly from inaction. "Let's go," he told Weller wearily.

EPILOGUE

The Honolulu airport was teeming with people, all anxious to be somewhere else, either out in the Hawaiian sunshine, or on a plane bound for their next destination. Like Bill Mathis, many of the people in the terminal were in uniform—Army, Navy, Air Force, Marine, some flying overseas, some headed back to the States. Mathis was one of the latter. All the airport chairs were taken, so he leaned against a wall near one of the restrooms, his duffel bag at his feet, and watched the mass of humanity flow by him in both directions. Occasionally an attractive young woman would catch his attention, especially if she was dressed in light tropical clothing. He had over three hours to kill until his next flight started boarding: too soon to leave the terminal and see the sights, but not soon enough to satisfy his desire to get home again as soon as possible. It had been two years since he had been in the States—or on the mainland, he corrected himself—and he was genuinely homesick.

Three soldiers passed in front of him, all PFCs, and all with worried looks on their faces. Their ill-fitting dress greens had no medals, and their haircuts were fresh and short. No doubt they were just out of training and headed to Nam. Mathis pitied them, but was also glad it was them and not him. He had only been in Viet Nam for four months, but that had been plenty, and he had no desire to go back. After the Nui Ba Den disaster, he had returned to the Japan field station and served the rest of his overseas tour there, transcribing tapes and living in a nice clean barracks. Now, finally, a year after that terrible night on the rock, he was on his way back to the World, back to the land of round-eyed women, air-conditioning, fast cars, and more than one channel on TV. He stared out the big windows across the concourse as another big jet taxied away and prepared to take off. The noise of the terminal washed over him like a warm shower, pleasing him with its innocuous normalcy.

"Wake up, soldier!" a familiar voice barked in his ear. Mathis jerked his head around to find Daniel McDaniel dropping his duffel bag next to his, his face split in a wide grin. He wore his green beret proudly, his blond hair close-cropped beneath it, and his blue eyes shone with welcome. He had slung his greens jacket over his shoulder, held with his left forefinger, leaving only the thin tan shirt and narrow black tie to cover his well-muscled torso. He held his hand out, and Mathis shook it forcefully, surprised and extremely glad to see his old friend.

"Two-dan! How the hell are you?"

"Not bad, Bill. How about you?"

"Couldn't be better," Mathis told him, finally letting go of his hand. "What are you doing here?"

"Headed back to the land of the little people," McDaniel told him. "You?"

"I'm going back to the World. You're going back to Nam? Where have you been?"

"California, on leave. I re-upped for Nam, so they gave me two weeks. Going to the Highlands this time."

"You re-upped for Nam? Are you fucking crazy?" Mathis shook his head in amazement. McDaniel just shrugged.

"That's where the action is." McDaniel pointed to Mathis' sleeve. "Whoa, look at that. You made E-6." His rank insignia now had two gold rockers over the eagle, marking him as a Specialist Sixth Class. Mathis nodded and tried to look humble.

"Yeah. You stay in long enough, and it happens."

"I know what you mean," McDaniel said, and swung his jacket around so Mathis could see the Sergeant First Class stripes.

"Hey, congratulations," Mathis said sincerely. "You're moving up in the world."

"Yep, now I can buy hard liquor at the NCO club." Both men chuckled. It was a long-standing gripe among the enlisted men in the Army that only senior NCOs could buy liquor; junior NCOs and enlisted were limited to beer and wine. The rule was irrelevant to Mathis, but he had always questioned the logic behind it.

"Purple Heart, huh?" McDaniel asked, nodding toward the medals on Mathis' chest.

"Yeah, I guess that green beanie medic on the Rock put my name in for it. I may be the only ASA guy to have one."

"Well, you deserve something for that night. So where you been since then?"

Both paused to watch a pretty girl walk by. When she was out of sight, Mathis answered the question. "They sent me back to Japan, and I've been there ever since. Did you stay on the Rock?"

"Afraid so." McDaniel rubbed the side of his face. "At least for six more months. Then they moved me to an outpost near Saigon to train the ARVNs."

"Were there any more attacks up there?"

McDaniel shook his head. "Not really. Twenty-Fifth beefed up the security, built better bunkers, brought in more infantry. The gooks probed a few times, but never got in the wire. Last I heard, they were going to install these big arc-lamps all around the perimeter."

"What's that saying?" Mathis offered. "The generals are always preparing to fight the previous war?"

McDaniel chuckled. "Ain't that the truth. So, are you staying in?"

Mathis nodded glumly. "Looks like it. They offered me big bucks to re-up, and promised me a good assignment. And it came through. I'm going to Ft. Meade."

McDaniel looked at him strangely. "Isn't that where, you know. . . ?"

"Yep. No Such Agency."

"And you'll be working there?" McDaniel's eyebrows rose in admiration.

229

"Looks like it. In air-conditioned comfort, no less. A lot better than on the Rock, for sure."

"I guess so. Far out, man. Good for you."

They stopped talking for a minute to observe the passing parade. Finally McDaniel asked, "How was Japan? I've never been there."

"Not bad," Mathis told him. We were kind of away from things, so we weren't like going into town every night or anything. But we were allowed out on passes, and the people there were mostly pretty nice to us. Didn't care for the food, myself, but the women were nice to look at."

"How nice?" McDaniel asked, raising one eyebrow.

Mathis pursed his lips and nodded a couple times. "Very nice." He looked at McDaniel knowingly, or at least he hoped he looked knowing. In reality he had not really gotten to know any of the local women, other than the ones who helped out on base with cooking and cleaning. He had flirted with one of the cleaning girls, but it had been harmless and went nowhere. Still, he had surprised himself with his ability to engage in even such simple and innocent conversations with a female, something that would have been painfully difficult when he was in high school.

"The only women I'm going to see for a while are little Hmong girls whose daddies have M-16s," McDaniel said ruefully. "Don't want to mess with them."

"Nope," Mathis agreed. "Might get it shot off, and then what would you do?"

They both watched two young women in hippie garb approach the women's restroom. They had on ankle-length tie-dyed dressed of thin cotton, and were obviously not wearing bras. One girl's brown hair hung to her waist, and the other's blond hair was wound around her head in a complicated braid. Neither had make-up, and neither one needed it. Mathis couldn't help staring, and saw that McDaniel was also captivated. The brunette glanced over at them and her look of disdain was almost palpable. "Baby-killers!" she hissed at them, just before she and her friend ducked into the restroom.

"What the fuck?" Mathis breathed in astonishment.

"Get used to it," McDaniel advised. "They've been listening to that Donovan song, "The Universal Soldier," and now the war is all our fault."

"Shit!" Mathis scoffed. "I didn't vote for him."

"Which one?"

"Any of them. They're all to blame."

An announcement was made over the terminal's PA system, one of a constant stream of announcements that Mathis had only half been listening to, but this one caught McDaniel's attention. "That's my flight," he said, reaching down to grab his duffel bag. "Take it easy, Bill." Throwing his jacket over his shoulder again, he turned to go.

"You, too, Two-dan," Mathis said, wishing he had more time to talk. Mathis raised his hand in a brief wave, and McDaniel nodded in return. Then he was gone.

Mathis leaned back against the wall. It had been great seeing McDaniel again, but the meeting had been too short, and had brought back too many bad memories. Mathis suddenly felt extremely tired, and he sat down on his duffel bag, pulling his feet in to avoid tripping one of the many people crossing in front of him. His mind roiled with the memories of that long terrible night on Nui Ba Den. Images of explosions and burning buildings flashed before his eyes, and his hands twitched as he remembered strangling that young VC. Once more he relived that horrifying execution of the sergeant at the flagpole, and the heart-rending moment he had found John Kasperek's body. It was the worst experience of his life, yet he knew that it had been transformative as well. He had learned so much about himself, and it had changed his outlook on life and the way he interacted with people. In a weird sort of way, he was glad he had been there, but he never, ever, wanted to go back and do it again.

The people in the waiting area across from him began standing up and shuffling toward the gate. Apparently his flight was getting ready to board, although he hadn't heard any announcement. Creakily he stood up and grabbed his duffel bag, and then began dodging the people coming from left and right so he could go get in line with the others. It was time to move on.

Made in the USA
Coppell, TX
18 March 2022

75168370R00142